remembering her racing heartbeat, the shy touch of her fingers on his neck.

Lust. Pure, simple lust. It was no more than that, he reminded himself as he put his confused wife at arm's length. "Truly it would be easy to take you right now, lady, but unfortunately I have more pressing engagements elsewhere."

Ghislaine's cheeks fired with humiliation and confusion.

"You are nothing but a scheming, stinking brute with no regard for anything but your own ambitions." Her true feelings were written on her face as she turned her back to him and attempted to get some control over her shaking body.

He closed his eyes,
remembering the feel of her.

ELIZABETH
HENSHALL
BETRAYED
HEARTS

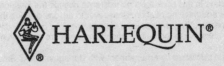

HARLEQUIN®

TORONTO • NEW YORK • LONDON
AMSTERDAM • PARIS • SYDNEY • HAMBURG
STOCKHOLM • ATHENS • TOKYO • MILAN • MADRID
PRAGUE • WARSAW • BUDAPEST • AUCKLAND

ISBN 0-373-30315-7

BETRAYED HEARTS

First North American Publication 1998

Copyright © 1996 by Elizabeth Henshall

Printed in U.S.A.

ELIZABETH HENSHALL

is married with two young sons and lives in Cheshire, England. Following a degree in French and German, she had a variety of jobs before deciding to give up office life. A year in Germany teaching English convinced her that this was certainly more exhausting! She now teaches French and German at a local secondary school and finds her life is indeed very busy. Fascinated in particular by local history, Elizabeth enjoys writing and researching with wine at hand.

Chapter One

The thin rope binding her wrists cut into her as Ghislaine struggled desperately to get free. The destrier beneath her snorted with what sounded alarmingly like disgust, and she hoped that the huge war-horse would not take her doomed movements amiss.

"If you do not have the wits to stay still, wench, then you will find my temper far less amenable than the horse's," growled her captor.

Ghislaine narrowed her eyes in fury and would have answered that threat with the contempt it deserved, but unfortunately her mouth had been gagged with a foul rag that smelled as if it had come from the midden.

Her guard's fingers pressed painfully into her arms as he pulled her back against his chest. The rivets of his protective leather hauberk gouged through her clothing. She was left with no option other than to remain where she was. If she tried to sit up without touching him, she risked being trapped tightly by two very muscular thighs. Opting for the lesser evil and pain Ghislaine sank reluctantly back against her foe.

The covering over her head was stifling and she

wondered honestly just how much longer she could endure being trussed up like a sack of grain, pummelled about on a horse and ripped to shreds by twine, without being sick. It seemed like hours since she had breathed fresh air.

The heartbeat of the man behind her thudded loudly in her ear and she whispered a desperate appeal to heaven to arrange for it to stop. Nothing terrible or messy, she suggested quickly. Just to have it stop. Father Thomas had warned her on many occasions of the dangers of malicious prayers but Ghislaine was convinced that, just once, God might grant her this small wish. After all, she had done nothing to deserve such treatment.

Well, she amended hastily, at least she had not deserved to be kidnapped by a bunch of marauding outlaws. Her crime was merely to have ventured further than she should from her manor. And, of course, had she heeded Edwin's warning in the first place, she would not be in this predicament at all.

The morning had been crisp and dry, promising to be the most clement day they had seen this February. Ghislaine, fed up with being inside the manor after a long, wet winter, had saddled her horse and set off, bow in hand, to see if she could shoot some game. The long-suffering Edwin had reluctantly followed his headstrong mistress, warning her repeatedly that outlaws had been spotted in the forest nearby.

She had, of course chosen to ignore him. Since she was hunting the Earl of Chester's game to give to the villagers, God, she was sure, would not interfere. After all, it had not been the villagers who had caused the murrain that had devastated the cattle herds. No one else, least of all the Earl, would provide them with other food.

It had not been until she reached the border that divided her land from the Earl's that Ghislaine had begun to feel uneasy. Even then, she had not heeded her own instincts. Disaster had struck whilst she had been patiently stalking a deer. Just as she had been about to loose an arrow, a large hand had clamped over her mouth and dragged her back towards the cover of the trees.

Instinctively she had bitten hard and kicked backwards, causing her assailant to curse loudly before yanking her up into the air and throwing something dark over her head. Within seconds her wrists and mouth had been bound and she had been dumped unceremoniously into the saddle of a large horse. Her captor had issued a few gruff orders and, since then, had barely uttered a word.

At first she had remained paralysed with fear, not daring to move in case she incurred the wrath of the man behind her. When she had realised that she was not going to die immediately, Ghislaine had come to the conclusion that she was being taken for some other purpose.

It was common enough in such a lawless county for young heiresses to be held captive and married for their lands, although Ghislaine found it hard to believe in her case. Aye, she had lands and a manor, but they were small compared to most. Nor did she look much like the lady of the manor. Mostly Ghislaine resembled one of the peasants, and her captor would have to be very shrewd to have known who she was.

It was a moment before she realised that the horse

had at last come to a halt. None too gently, Ghislaine
was pulled down from the saddle and set on her feet.
Her eyes blinked rapidly when the covering was
yanked from her head.

"If you have any desire to survive the hour, girl,
you will not utter a word," a deep voice growled in
her ear. Swirling round unsteadily, Ghislaine stared at
the man who towered above her. He was tall, very tall,
and swathed in a filthy cloak and stained leather hauberk. His thick black hair hung around his shoulders
and cold, ice-blue eyes impaled her. Danger seeped
from the very depths of his black soul, and in an instant, Ghislaine knew that he was capable of murder.

Satisfied that his captive would not move, he pulled
away the gag along with several clumps of her long
hair. Her shriek of pain brought his hand over her
mouth and she was pulled roughly into his chest once
more.

"Hell's teeth, girl," he hissed furiously. "Do you
want to die?"

Ghislaine toyed with the idea of biting his hand
again but decided against it when she caught sight of
the knife close to her throat. When she finally shook
her head, he sent her sprawling to the ground.

Indignantly, Ghislaine rose as gracefully as her
mud-covered cloak would allow and fixed him with a
look of burning hatred.

"Have you always possessed such natural charm,"
she spat, her dark eyes flashing, "or are you merely
practising on me?" Tossing her wild, red-gold hair
over her shoulder, Ghislaine lifted her chin defiantly
and waited for the death blow. If he was going to kill
her, she would prefer it to be quick.

His eyes blazed, but instead of hurling the knife at her as she had expected, he turned to a blond-haired man standing a few yards away. "Are you sure it's her?" he ground out, the muscles in his jaw rigid with control.

When the blond man nodded, her captor rounded on her once more.

"So, Lady de Launay, you do not value your life overmuch?"

He knew her name so it was clear that this had been planned. Closing her eyes in fear, Ghislaine could not even begin to think why he had taken her.

"Oh, but I fear you have made a mistake," she began, her eyes widening. "I am Lady de Launay's maid. Effie."

His eyes narrowed as he assessed her appearance. "Effie is small, plump, blonde and," he added with grim conviction, "pretty. You are none of those."

The words were a deliberate attempt to upset her, but Ghislaine fixed him with a smile. "I am sure that…"

He advanced on her and grabbed her chin between his fingers interrupting her explanation most effectively.

"And I am sure that unless you co-operate, lady, your handsome companion over there will be meeting his maker earlier than he expected."

Ghislaine swivelled her eyes in the direction he nodded to and caught sight of Edwin, his long, thin frame bound and trussed between several armed men. Her eyes returned to her assailant. Pulling her chin from his fingers, Ghislaine glared at him. "Very well," she replied flatly. "What do you want?"

"I want you to behave like a lady, if that is possible." His stinging sarcasm caused her to raise no more than an auburn brow in response. "We travel on to Chester and my men and I wish to enter the city as unobtrusively as possible."

None of this made sense. "Why?" she demanded curiously.

"Because I have a desire to speak with the Earl of Chester, and by bringing him one of his wards I believe it may help him to view my cause in a more positive light."

So, she was to be a hostage. "And if I do not co-operate, you will kill Edwin," she concluded.

The dark-haired outlaw stared at her for a moment before nodding. "I hope you remember that, Lady de Launay," he warned ominously before turning back to the small army of men waiting some yards away.

Despite her brave words, Ghislaine was terrified. Edwin's life depended on her co-operation, but she was not at all sure that the Earl of Chester would look favourably on anyone using her as a hostage. Her tendency to poach his game had angered him greatly, and were it not for the fact that her father had been one of his most loyal and trustworthy vassals, Ghislaine did not doubt for a moment that she would have been confined to the abbey months ago.

Trapping her bottom lip between her teeth, she looked over at Edwin. Her father was no longer alive and their fate now depended on a greedy man who had never bothered to hide his dislike of her.

They reached the pink sandstone walls of Chester late in the afternoon and Ghislaine heaved a sigh tinged with relief and apprehension. Having had several hours to debate the matter, she fervently hoped that the Earl of Chester would save her from this ordeal, but remained uncertain. Nagging doubts crowded her mind. He was her guardian, despite their mutual dislike, but he was not averse to conniving with base outlaws if it meant filling his purse.

Her captor and his blond companion left the others with Edwin in the castle bailey, and accompanied her silently to the great hall. They stopped outside the heavy wooden door, and she barely had time to shake the dust from her dishevelled tunic before it was heaved open. The soft strumming of a lute and raucous laughter melted away as they entered the long, narrow hall which was lit by wall torches and a myriad hissing wax candles.

A huge fire blazed at the far end of the hall and around it clustered five or six of the Earl's favoured barons and some women Ghislaine had never seen before. From the tone of the laughter and the way the women were dressed Ghislaine suspected they were not ladies. The Earl was well-known for his lechery.

The sheer opulence of the place never failed to reduce Ghislaine to awestruck silence. Shadows caught in the candlelight danced on the crimson and gold wall-hangings, lending the room an air of other-worldliness that was far removed from her daily life. It also stank like the midden and Ghislaine held her breath as the stench hit her for the first time.

Anxious to put an end to this frightening ordeal, Ghislaine picked her way carefully through the filthy floor rushes towards the far end of the hall where the Earl was slouched in a large wooden chair, his huge

bulk instantly recognisable. Indolently he scratched
the ears of a hound sprawled at his feet.

Silence echoed around the tapestry-hung walls as
Ghislaine and her two companions faced her guardian.
His barons and their consorts whispered quietly and
listened whilst she awaited her fate in the suffocating
gloom.

The bleary blue eyes of Hugh d'Avranches, Earl of
Chester, slid over the three newcomers and then returned once more to the tempting dishes awaiting his
pleasure. His puffy white fingers trailed across two
platters before his full lips twitched in almost salacious
anticipation of the succulent viands.

To the Welsh, Hugh d'Avranches was Hugh the Fat,
and to his own, he was Hugh Lupus, the wolf, but
none underestimated the shrewd cunning that had set
him above all others in the Conqueror's affections. He
was King William's favourite nephew and the most
powerful man in the north of England. Decisive, underhand and very brutal in his dealings with his vassals, the Earl wore the mantle of his success with arrogance. The county of Cheshire was firmly in his grip
and he was determined to wring as many silver marks
from the population as he could.

His appetite temporarily sated, Hugh dipped his fingers delicately in the scented hand-bowl and carefully
wiped them with almost ritualistic obsession. Waving
the food from view, he returned with a sigh to the task
in hand.

"So, de Courcy, to what honour do I owe this
visit?"

To Ghislaine's amazement, the question was addressed to her scowling captor in most familiar terms.

How on earth did the Earl of Chester know this stinking outlaw? It did occur to her, however, that Hugh Lupus was staring at them with little sign of pleasure.

"I have come to request protection under your law of advowry." The low, rich voice was almost a growl and used none of the fine words usually reserved for the Earl.

The Earl appeared to ignore the slight as he heaved himself to his feet before the men, his thumbs hooked into his jewelled belt. A smirk hovered on his grease-spattered lips.

"To what do I owe this happy occurrence?"

De Courcy just scowled more deeply. His smaller companion, however, returned the smile and bowed gracefully, his blond curls falling forward onto his handsome face. "My name is Arnaud d'Everard, my lord. De Courcy is here to request an audience with you."

Hugh d'Avranches surveyed them silently for a moment before merely nodding his assent.

D'Everard continued. "De Courcy has been unjustly accused of a crime and wishes to reside in Cheshire under your protection until he is able to clear his name. As he has been of help to you in the past, he naturally hoped you would be willing to return the favour." The blond man's voice was soft and confident and he was clearly no base-born outlaw.

She looked nervously up at the tall man by her side, her brow wrinkling in disgust. The Earl was indeed famous for harbouring all manner of criminals within the county under the auspices of advowry. For a fee, Hugh d'Avranches was always willing to provide a safe haven in one of Cheshire's great forests for out-

laws from other counties fleeing the consequences of
their wrongdoing. His coffers might be full of silver
marks, but the forests were crawling with dangerous
outlaws.

Not even the King's men would attempt to cross the
county borders to follow a criminal without having the
King's seal first, and William was reluctant to interfere
in the Earl's domain. No one was safe to ride abroad
these days. It was suspected that her father and Peter
Staveley had been attacked and killed a few months
earlier by one such notorious band. Understandably,
the Earl appeared reluctant to deal with criminals effectively since his treasure chests groaned with the
fruits of such practices. Any criticism of his regime
was dealt with harshly.

Ghislaine's mouth was as dry as dust and she gratefully picked up a goblet of wine offered to her by the
page at the Earl's bidding. Her stomach, ever unaware
of the sensitive situation, began to make loud gurgling
noises. Her cheeks fired in embarrassment but, if anyone heard, nothing was said.

"And what is this crime?" Hugh d'Avranches'
voice held little of his customary boredom.

De Courcy's scowl deepened if that was possible.
"The murder of a noble woman. One Margaret Staveley."

The harsh gruff voice echoed in Ghislaine's ears.
Margaret was dead and the man accused of her murder
was standing beside her.

Ghislaine stared at de Courcy in silence, horror and
disbelief echoing in her mind. The healthy glow from
her freckled face paled as she watched her friend's
murderer demanding help from Hugh d'Avranches. No

trace of remorse had softened his dark, stubbly face. She must have made some small noise, for once again, Ghislaine found those glittering eyes spear her for no more than a few seconds before returning to stare at the Earl.

"Margaret Staveley was the widow of Peter. She lived to the east of the Macclesfield Hundred, if I have the right of it?" The Earl's voice was slow and speculative "What business had you in that area?"

De Courcy's expression had not changed. "I had recently purchased a manor about half a day's ride from Staveley." The tone was weary and his irritation at the questioning was apparent to all.

"I had no knowledge of this," replied the Earl in such a way as to convince Ghislaine that he had indeed been privy to this fact. De Courcy's snort of disbelief earned him no more than a raised eyebrow from his questioner. Whoever this man was, thought Ghislaine, he had to be of some consequence, for Hugh d'Avranches was not normally so equable when faced with such appalling manners. He had shifted position slightly so that his arms were folded across his broad chest, and his strong legs planted wide apart. When he lifted his head a little, Ghislaine could see his blue eyes narrowed in anger.

The smaller man at de Courcy's side, clearly sensing his companion's unease, stepped into the breach.

"He purchased the manor last year from Bigot de Loges. My friend's services have been much in demand and he had a desire to settle. He took up residence a few weeks after Yuletide and my lord and I went to pay the lady a...courtesy visit a few days ago. When we left, she was in good health.

"However, it would seem that the lady and her people were killed in an unprovoked attack not long after our departure and we stand accused of her murder. No witnesses survived," he added quietly. "The lady's brother, Henry Dettingham, is demanding our execution. Dettingham managed to seize my lord's manor in our absence and has sworn revenge."

Light dawned in Ghislaine's mind. De Courcy was a mercenary. Cold seeped through her body. Margaret had been butchered by a mercenary. She scanned the harsh planes of his dark face, but found no trace of softness there. He would show no mercy to a woman, she was sure. What manner of man would kill someone as gentle and sweet as Margaret?

A vision of the pretty Margaret came to her mind. She had been married to Ghislaine's brother, Richard, for little more than a year. Whilst Richard was involved with the campaigns against the Welsh, Ghislaine and Margaret had struck up an unlikely friendship. Margaret was gentle and sweet, and often shocked at Ghislaine's tomboyish adventures with Edwin. But she had been loyal to her new family and had provided Ghislaine with the female companionship she needed.

The shock of Richard's death had forged an even closer friendship. Small and slender, her ash blonde hair and honest blue eyes had attracted many young suitors. That she had chosen a quiet, steady widower of middling years had surprised several of her friends except for Ghislaine. Peter Staveley had been a close companion of her father's and she had known him to be a gentle, wise and essentially lonely man who needed a young wife and family on whom to bestow his hidden well of affection and his wealth. And now they were both dead.

"And your men?" questioned the Earl, a thoughtful look on his face. Ghislaine was reminded of a hawk hovering over its prey. A very fat hawk.

"Twenty survived the subsequent attack by her brother on my manor and await my sign." De Courcy's toneless voice sent shivers down her back.

The Earl inhaled deeply through his nose and pushed back his silver-blond hair. "Pray explain the need for a sign, de Courcy." The blue eyes had narrowed as they scanned the back of the hall before returning to the men before him.

Before her captor could answer, Ghislaine turned to him. Propelled by fury and perhaps a surfeit of wine, she determined to find out about Margaret. "Why?" she demanded hoarsely. "Why did you kill her?"

All eyes in the hall turned now to her. Behind her, some of the women gasped at her effrontery. Women did not interfere in men's business. She could feel the whole hall hold its collective breath as they waited for the axe to fall.

Guy de Courcy turned once more to his hostage. Her dark eyes spat anger and condemnation, her whole body demanding that he respond to her question. Despite his tiredness and irritation, he had to admit to a small amount of admiration for the girl. Few men dared what she had.

"I committed no crime," he replied simply, his blue eyes boring into her.

His words only fuelled her ire. "Then why are you here?"

He gave her a hard, soul-searching stare. "My busi-

ness is with the Earl of Chester." His cold words hung
in the air between them until destroyed by the coarse
laughter of Hugh d'Avranches.

"Aye. You have the right of it," he growled. "I
had not recognised you, my Lady de Launay." His
cold eyes raked her dishevelled, dirty clothes and tangled hair. "I had thought that you might have been
one of de Courcy's camp followers."

Such sarcasm only fired Ghislaine's cheeks and
caused her chin to lift a little. From the corner of her
eye, she saw Guy de Courcy's jaw tighten in anger.
"But since de Courcy seems to have the measure of
you it brings to mind your purpose here." Although
he was staring at Ghislaine, the words were clearly
addressed to the mercenary.

"Lady de Launay is here to…persuade you to provide us with your protection."

A slow smile formed on Hugh d'Avranches' generous lips. "And what benefits would I receive in return for my protection?"

De Courcy frowned. "I have my usual skills at your
disposal for the forty days."

"I believe your skills to be most unusual," came
the Earl's reply. "But I regret that forty days of
knight's service is perhaps not quite what I had in
mind."

De Courcy's dark head shot up, but Arnaud
d'Everard's arm stayed him. "And what do you have
in mind, my lord?"

The other man's softer, more co-operative tone
seemed to please the Earl. "The wars with the Welsh
have drained many of my normal resources of late. I
find that sixty days' service may be more acceptable.

In addition to one hundred marks of silver, should I accept.''

Hugh d'Avranches and Guy de Courcy eyed each other with dislike, tempered with something akin to respect. It would pay neither to underestimate the other.

De Courcy's brusque nod indicated his acceptance of the terms. ''I have a demand of my own.'' The words were received in silence.

''If I and my men are to provide sixty days' service in full combat, it will be necessary to accommodate us in better surroundings than Macclesfield forest. We need somewhere to live and train, preferably in a quiet area with few neighbours. The de Launay manor of Chapmonswiche is suitable for our needs. The one hundred marks will be forthcoming for as long as your full protection is required. When I clear my name, I shall quit the de Launay manor and return to my own.''

Hugh drew a deep breath as he pondered this latest demand. Ghislaine felt herself turn rigid. He could not turn her home over to this criminal.

''Which brings me back to Lady de Launay.'' Hugh's eyes slid once more over Ghislaine with barely concealed scorn. ''What role does she play in this?''

''She ensures your goodwill, my Lord. I am sure that you have no desire to see her come to harm.'' The blond eyebrows raised in question.

The Earl looked unimpressed by this latest threat. ''And if I do not agree to protect you from the King's men or Dettingham?''

''My men are scattered throughout the city awaiting

my signal should you decide against me, then they will set fire to key buildings.''

She was sure it was a lie, but the hand gripping her arm gave it a painful squeeze. Ghislaine did not need to be reminded about Edwin.

The Earl drew a deep breath as he pondered this proposition. His fingers stroked at his stubbly jowls. ''Let me think on the matter whilst you share bread and wine.'' He beckoned to the servants who hurried to do his bidding. There were no laggards in the castle of Chester.

Guy de Courcy, satisfied that the Earl would accede to his request in the end, relaxed his scowl and the grip on Ghislaine's arm. When they mounted the dais, Ghislaine found herself seated in between her captors. Was she now to sit by the man who had killed her friend and exchange pleasantries?

''Is it your custom to butcher innocent women?'' she began, a fire blazing within. She would not let Margaret die without a fight. Not for one moment did she believe his story of innocence. After all, only guilty men run.

The two eyed each other with intense dislike. Her words, de Courcy found, had destroyed any appetite he might have had. Taking a deep draught of the soft red wine, he glared at her with his customary frown. This was not the moment for a shrewish red-haired wench to start questioning him. Her dark eyes were smouldering with loathing.

''I take it, then, that as your father is no longer alive you did batter him to death with your tongue? My sympathies lie entirely with him.''

The sheer audacity of the man was breathtaking and

left her, for once, speechless. Ghislaine opened her mouth and then closed it quickly, realising what he was about.

"Your pretty speeches, sir, together with that natural charm you possess, will ensure your success in the court here. You will no doubt find yourself most at home." The silence about her should have been clear warning that she really was overstepping the mark, but Ghislaine could only think of Margaret.

"Murderers, thieves and outlaws inhabit the land in great numbers. I am sure that you will find a suitable stone to crawl under."

A large, tanned hand raked the black locks before slamming down onto the table. "Unless you are keen to join your father, wench, I suggest you hold your tongue."

Guy's head was throbbing and he was in dire need of sleep. Most girls usually cowered away from his scowls in terror. Why this one had to choose now to assault him with her tongue was beyond his reasoning. It was becoming clear to him that the dampness that abounded in this part of the country addled a body's wits. He took another gulp of the wine. At least that was palatable.

Help came from an unexpected source. "You must forgive the Lady de Launay, sir. She is clearly overset by the news of Margaret Staveley's death." A thin, grey-haired woman sitting to the far side of Hugh leaned forward to address him.

De Courcy's eyes glanced sideways, noting the curl of Ghislaine's lips at these words and gulped another goblet of wine down. His curt nod was the only indication that he had actually heard her.

"Perhaps," the woman continued smoothly, "if you were to explain the circumstances, it would be easier for us to understand?"

De Courcy suddenly jerked his head towards the unknown woman and stared at her. Ghislaine could not help feeling that her captor knew this woman, although he gave no clear sign of doing so. "I need explain myself to no woman," he growled, giving her a look of such distaste that even Ghislaine felt herself recoil.

The woman inclined her head in acceptance of his outburst, but did not seem at all surprised or even upset by the words. Ghislaine glared at him in outrage.

"There is, after all, little to explain." His voice was cold and irritable once more. "I am accused of the woman's murder. I know aught else save that I have been forced to forfeit my own manor and have lost ten of my men." He sank back into a scowl.

Hugh's eyes flickered carefully between the woman and de Courcy as he listened to this exchange. "It may be that we can come to an amicable agreement that would benefit both of us." His cold eyes rested on Ghislaine for a moment before returning to de Courcy.

De Courcy stared at the Earl, his distrust of the man barely concealed. Ghislaine rather thought for a moment that he wanted to throw the goblet of wine over him. D'Everard, however, seemed to have sensed that this was not the time to antagonise him.

"We are keen to hear your suggestions, my lord."

D'Avranches inclined his jowly face towards his ward, regarding her blandly with his calculating eyes. Ghislaine shivered a little under his assessing stare.

The man always got what he wanted, caring not a whit if it were by fair means or foul.

"I think," Hugh drawled lazily, "that we require more privacy for this discussion." His eyes turned to de Courcy, who inclined his dark head slightly in deference to the Earl's wishes.

"I believe, Helene, that my ward would benefit from a view of the river to restore her temper and clear her mind." He addressed the grey-haired woman who nodded silently.

As she rose from the bench, Ghislaine glanced at her dark foe. His head was lowered over his wine and his broad shoulders slumped forward as if in complete exhaustion. Suddenly, aware that her hostile eyes were on him, he looked up. For a fraction of a second, those summer-blue eyes compelled her to remain where she was, and then released her when he had taken his fill. Hatred flooded through her and she was glad that he was suffering. Her desire to exit with dignity however, was foiled by her foot catching in some rushes near the dais and she was forced to leave with a flush to her cheeks.

She had a bad feeling that Hugh d'Avranches was about to wreak his revenge on her.

Chapter Two

As they stood outside the wooden doors, Ghislaine turned to Helene. The words she would have spoken died in her mouth as she saw that a deathly pallor had enveloped the woman.

"Is there aught I can do?" Ghislaine took Helene by the shoulders as the lady closed her eyes. She shook her head silently while Ghislaine tried to loosen her kirtle a little. Her bones felt so thin and frail in her strong fingers that Ghislaine feared she would shatter if she held her much longer. "Some wine?" she whispered urgently.

"Nay. It will pass in a moment. Thank you, Ghislaine." Slowly the colour began to return to Helene's soft skin, and much to Ghislaine's relief, a smile touched her lips. "I think some air might help," she whispered, her hand clutching at Ghislaine's sleeve.

Nodding in agreement, Ghislaine gently steered Helene up the stone steps to the top of the keep.

"Do I know you?" she asked the woman curiously as they paused before the last few steps. Few strangers would have used her first name.

"No," came the breathless reply. "But I have followed your escapades about Cheshire with great interest," she added, eyeing the remaining steps with determination. Smiling, the woman turned the most expressive brown eyes on Ghislaine that she had ever seen. "My name is Helene du Beauregard. I have not met you before although I did know your mother." The doubtful look on Ghislaine's face caused her to shrug her thin shoulders delicately. "It was some time ago, but I am sorry for your loss. She was a most exceptional woman."

Ghislaine nodded curtly in acceptance, and breathed in the salty air as they passed through the door of the keep. The two guards who were lounging against the keep wall eyed them with half-interested curiosity before returning to their conversation. Ignoring them, Ghislaine and Helene turned to look at the view. From a vantage point normally monopolised by the soldiers, the women took deep gulps of the air blowing in from the Welsh border.

The last rays of the afternoon sun flitted across the countryside beyond the River Dee that meandered around the ancient city. As Ghislaine stared across the river towards Wales, night clouds gathered on the distant horizon. Thoughts of her brother, Richard, squeezed her heart. He had died fighting the Welsh little more than a year ago, and still she missed him. So many good men had died in those wild hills.

Ghislaine turned back to Helene. The woman was blue with the cold, for her fashionable tunic was made only for the warmth of the indoor fires. Draping her own cloak over Helene's thin shoulders, Ghislaine shivered a little. Her companion gripped her forearm once more and gave it a squeeze in gratitude.

"You are much like your mother in your attention of people," she said quietly, her eyes searching Ghislaine's freckled face.

Her words caused Ghislaine to look sharply at her. "I am nothing like her." Had her father not said as much for the last seven years? Had he not constantly said how much he regretted that she was not more like her mother?

Helene shook her head. "In looks and body, no. But she took care of people, no matter what others thought."

"How did you know her?" Ghislaine asked curiously

For a moment, Helene's eyes trailed over the palisade and beyond, staring almost sightlessly into the distance. Lost in her own thoughts, the older woman pulled the heavy cloak more tightly around her, as if it could somehow protect her from the memories.

"Did you know her well?" Ghislaine prompted, her interest stirred. Above all things her mother had loved people. She had often defied her father to take care of ailing peasants and servants, lavishing attention and her gentle spirits upon them. They had loved her in return. And yet her father had refused to remember that side of her. He had worshipped her memory, albeit a false one.

"Aye. She once attended me for an ailment that would not be cured. It took a long time and we learned much of each other then." She said no more, although Ghislaine waited for her to continue.

"My father did not like her to travel away from the

manor,'' she added, hoping that this would encourage Helene to continue.

"Nay,'' she said rather curtly. "He did not.'' Her lips closed tightly and it was clear that she would offer no more than that, at least for the time being. "Do you have her healing skills?''

Ghislaine shrugged her shoulders lightly. "Some, but I fear I have not inherited her gentleness.'' Her words were spoken with such feeling that Helene laughed gently.

"You have inherited her courage, though. And from what I have heard of you over these last few years, you have needed it to deal with that irksome father of yours.''

Few people had spoken so truly of her father since his death that the irreverence of her statement caused Ghislaine's mouth to lift at the corners. "Aye. I fear that I have inherited much of his temper, too. It is an affliction that caused him much sorrow.''

The laughter that they shared for a moment or two was halted by a sudden gust of wind that buffeted them mercilessly. Standing closer together for protection and warmth, Ghislaine found herself beginning to warm to this woman, despite having known her for a short while. At least she did not criticise nor did she condemn. She also displayed a sense of humour that was sadly lacking in most worthy and pious ladies of the court.

Ghislaine appraised the woman once again. Tall and thin, Helene du Beauregard still retained much of what must have been a great beauty. Her dark eyes were fringed with thick, black lashes whilst her abundant hair had turned grey. Fine lines creased her eyes and her soft pink skin. Ghislaine judged her to be in her forties, a great age for a woman of the court. Her speech and manners were both gentle and confident, not at all what one would have expected from one of Hugh d'Avranches's court followers.

"Do you live in Chester?" The question was direct and pointed.

A glimmer of a smile touched Helene's lips at the younger girl's lack of guile. "Nay. My manor lies half a day's ride to the south-east of Chester. I am come to settle a dispute over boundaries."

A common enough problem for anyone. Ghislaine visibly relaxed a little. "Then you do not live far from Chapmonswiche?"

Helene shook her head. "I live at Omberleigh. It is only a small manor with a few fields and a village, but it is well enough for my needs. A small company of guards protects us from any possible attack, and these days I am glad of the security."

"And your husband?" Ghislaine spoke without thinking, but wished she had said nothing at all as a look of pain crossed Helene's face.

"My husband is dead," came her toneless reply.

"I am sorry," she replied quietly. When would she learn not to open her mouth without thinking?

Helene reached out for her hand and patted it gently. "Do not concern yourself, Ghislaine. I am content now."

Her heartfelt sigh caused Helene to turn her head up to Ghislaine, for the girl was a good head taller than she. "I cannot believe that Margaret is dead."

"Did you know her well?" Helene asked solicitously, her eyes watching Ghislaine carefully.

She nodded slowly, pushing back some loose strands of hair. "Margaret was the only friend I had, really. She was married briefly to my brother, and when he died, she married my father's friend, Peter. How could someone as sweet and gentle as Margaret deserve such a fate?" she asked angrily. "She never did aught but good and look what happened. Both husbands die and she is murdered. There is no justice." She turned to blink away the tears.

Helene looked at Ghislaine's stiff back with sympathy and set her arm around her shoulder for comfort. "How old are you, Ghislaine?" she asked after a minute.

"Nineteen summers," came the muffled reply.

"Whatever Hugh decides," Helene began gently, "you must obey him, for his anger can be ruthless." Her dark eyes scanned Ghislaine's worried countenance. "It will go badly for your people if you do not."

Ghislaine's shoulders drooped at the mention of her villagers. "Aye, I know it. But the thought of spending the rest of my days either shut up in a convent or married off to some loathsome brute does not offer much hope."

Helene shrugged her shoulders. "Few of us have more choice than that. And," she paused to choose her words carefully, "not all men are so hard to bear." The light teasing of her words made Ghislaine's lips reluctantly turn upwards. "Or is there some other reason?"

"What do you mean?" Ghislaine's cheeks blushed suddenly. The question was clear, but she did not know how far she could trust this woman. "If you

mean my manservant, Edwin, I have known him these
past ten summers,'' she began slowly. ''He taught me
how to shoot an arrow, to fish, to ride. He even
showed me how to use a knife.'' Her eyes glanced up
at Helene, their innocence shining. ''Edwin has saved
me from death a thousand times and I have mended
his wounds, revived him from the effects of too much
ale and consoled the women he has cast aside. There
is no more to it than that.'' Ghislaine could have said
that there was, in fact, a great deal more to their friendship, but she was not so sure that Helene would have
viewed their other activities with that humorous gleam
in her eye. Not every Norman lady would consider the
feeding of starving English folk a suitable activity for
one of her own class.

Helene regarded her a little sceptically, for stories
of her scrapes with the Englishman abounded the
county. The man was reputedly handsome. And yet
the girl seemed to be telling the truth. ''Nay, I did not
mean Edwin. I had thought you interested in another.
Perhaps I was mistaken.''

Ghislaine's cheeks coloured even more. ''There is
no other,'' she denied with such vehemence that Helene knew she had hit on the truth.

Warming to the idea of discovering just who it was
that Ghislaine favoured, Helene began to list the can-
didates she knew. ''Most are loud-mouthed, vulgar
louts, as you intimated,'' she began. ''And of the rest,
most are married. Robert of Montalt is probably too
old and ugly; Gerard de Rospernaise shows more interest in his squires; Cadimane de Soubeyron might
possibly turn the head of a girl like you, although his
lack of height might be a problem.'' Helene eyed

Ghislaine slyly to see if she was getting close. "Walter de Belleme is handsome, tall and personable. He is a distinct possibility."

Ghislaine turned almost puce with embarrassment. "I hardly know him. He has been most kind to me, but beyond that, he has been very…circumspect."

Helene du Beauregard frowned. "Walter keeps some strange company, and I think it unlikely that any knight will counter the Earl's wishes," she said gently. "I fear that you will have to face your future alone. It might not be so bad." Her beautiful face saddened a little. "Women must submit to the will of their father or their lord, but you might be able to find some solace in your home or your children. Sometimes an affection can grow in time…" The expression on her face became distant again. Intrigued, Ghislaine could not stop the questions that crowded her mind. "Did you have a choice?"

The question caused Helene to pause for a moment, as if thinking back to that time so many years ago. "Aye. I had a choice. Marriage or the convent. For me it was no choice at all, though. The knight my father had chosen was handsome and young. I was glad to accept him."

"And were you happy?" Ghislaine watched the older woman as she pulled the cloak closer to her thin body. Time seemed to have been kind to her, although there was an aura of loneliness about her that did not leave.

Again her shoulders shrugged casually. "Of a fashion. I had children, a home. My husband…provided well." Despite the brightness of her words, Ghislaine detected a note of sadness. "The convent would not have suited me." Her lips smiled at these words as if she had said something that amused her privately. "Do you like children?" she asked suddenly, her dark eyes intent on Ghislaine.

"A-aye," stammered Ghislaine, somewhat taken aback by so direct a question. "I would like children of my own, God willing."

Her answer seemed to satisfy the woman, so Ghislaine took a chance. Moving over to the edge of the keep wall, Ghislaine's eyes turned to the busy port a little way up the river. Ships from all parts of the world came to dock at Chester, bringing spices, cloth, wine, livestock, furs and many other goods that rich people would pay dearly for. She watched the bustle of activity as a large ship was unloading its cargo.

"My father often used to say that I should have been born a boy, and sometimes I think he was right." She breathed in the soft, salty air slowly, as if savouring this moment of freedom. "Sometimes I used to wish I could fight in the wars or sail across the water." Her eyes remained wistfully on the port. She was sure that even the understanding Helene de Beauregard would be shocked at such an admission. "I wanted to be free to do whatever I wanted, like Richard. And yet, sometimes, I wonder what it would be like to have a child..." Ghislaine's voice trailed off into embarrassed silence.

There was no censure in Helene's voice. "You think no differently from many others, my dear. Unfortunately we cannot do what we like, but sometimes we can try to make the best of what we have."

Helene had come to stand by her side and had placed a hand on Ghislaine's cold arm. "Come. I think that the Earl has probably had time enough with de Courcy, and we are in great need of the fire.''

Ghislaine nodded, a vision of de Courcy's harsh, dark, scowling face rushing oddly before her. ''I can only hope that he has rid himself of that murdering barbarian, but I fear that will prove to be a vain hope.'' A thought struck her. ''Do you know of him?''

Helene sighed. ''De Courcy is well known for his skills on the battlefield and I believe his tactics have outwitted many of William's more persistent opponents. I suspect that Hugh would be more than happy to hire his services.'' She looked at Ghislaine speculatively. ''He is also rumoured to be handsome underneath all that hair.'' The words were spoken with a certain confidence.

Ghislaine gave a most unladylike snort. ''He is a devil. Death would be too good a price for Margaret's murder.'' Her anger spilled from her as she stalked towards the steps.

As Ghislaine descended the steep stone stairway, she was thinking about her future. The convent would at least offer a form of peace and perhaps she could adjust to such a life. A deep shudder went through her body, for the cold and fear had taken its toll. If this barbarian had not decided he wanted her manor, her life would not have had to change. Life was just not fair.

Suddenly she stopped. Walter! She had forgotten about Walter! She conjured up his handsome face in her mind and the thought made her smile. His blond hair was the envy of many of the Norman ladies, but she liked his smile and the way his grey eyes made her feel special. He had been the only one who did not make her feel like a clumsy carthorse. Together they had laughed and talked about a million things, and the feelings she felt for him had grown with the months.

She remembered how her father had disapproved of their friendship to begin with, but Walter had somehow brought him round and became a frequent visitor to the estate. Since the death of his first wife, Walter had become lonely and had often expressed his appreciation of friendship with a woman who did not simper and giggle. Ghislaine had been impressed by his modest courage, for he had continued to hunt there at great personal risk despite the knowledge that the murderous outlaw, Thomas Bollyngton, had made the forest his domain.

Although nothing had been said, she could tell by the way he looked at her that his feelings were engaged. It was only a matter of time before Walter declared himself. Since her father's death, though, the impropriety of him visiting an unmarried girl had prevented him from seeing her much. She had missed him.

When Walter found out what had happened he would be sure to speak out. And yet, despite her belief in the depth of his feelings, Helene du Beauregard's words rang in her ears. Few would ever dispute the wishes of the Earl of Chester. Would Walter? A vague feeling of doubt began to float around her mind as she slowed her steps. He had always been quick to do his bidding, it was true. And yet, he would not abandon her. Nay, he would not.

Fortified by her own conviction, Ghislaine reached the foot of the steps in a more buoyant mood and awaited the slower arrival of Helene du Beauregard with a cheerful smile.

As soon as they entered the hall Ghislaine was aware of the highly charged atmosphere. Something had happened to increase the tension. All eyes were on her as she made her way to the dais.

The mercenary was no longer sitting at the table but was pacing before the fire, his expression even more thunderous than before. He was the very epitome of evil, she thought. He tosssed back another goblet of wine before suddenly hurling it across the floor in a violet temper. Ghislaine gulped. Hugh was still reclining regally in his chair, a raised eyebrow the only outward sign that he had heard de Courcy's outburst. D'Everard just stared at her.

"Ah, Ghislaine," drawled Hugh. "I am pleased you have returned." Ghislaine doubted that, but his words had a dramatic impact on de Courcy. He whirled round to face her, advancing towards the dais in huge strides. Had she not been so afeared, she would have stepped back, but Ghislaine found herself rooted to the spot.

"So you would trade this wench for my services?" De Courcy spat his words out in disgust, his blue eyes staring at her dishevelled, wind-blown appearance with barely concealed scorn.

Ghislaine stiffened in shock. "What do you mean 'trade'?" Her voice was no more than a whisper.

"I have decided that you cannot live at Chapmonswiche with an army of men, and I do not think the convent is the place for you, my lady." The Earl eyed her with an indifferent stare. "Your interests would be better served elsewhere. You will marry de Courcy."

The words penetrated her mind and Ghislaine was

left speechless for a moment. De Courcy looked as if he wished to kill her.

"I choose the convent," she began, her voice trembling. It was very hard to swallow the terror that seemed to be leaping from her throat. De Courcy stilled for a brief second, staring at her with cold blue eyes. Did she detect relief there?

"Perhaps I did not make myself clear," Hugh began slowly. "You will marry de Courcy on the morrow. Your servants are to serve your husband. I have no doubt you will see the advantage of such an alliance." The threat behind his words were apparent to all.

Summoning every ounce of courage, Ghislaine lifted her head in defiance. "You cannot marry me to a murderer. 'Tis not right in the eyes of God. I demand to go to the convent."

Hugh stared back at her, a heavy sigh lifting his chest. "On the morrow, my lady. Or your people will be put to death. Should you and de Courcy find your interests, shall we say, at odds, then I feel certain that you will manage to come to some suitable arrangement." There was a cold gleam in his eyes.

The candles swam about her as Ghislaine tried to focus on the one unchanging thing in the hall. The anger shining from the eyes of Guy de Courcy. At least they were agreed on one thing. A heavy fist smashed down onto the table, causing her to jump from her bemused state.

"She is not willing and neither am I."

"Neither of you has a choice. You need my protection and the lady needs a husband. I am sure you will both see the advantages of such a match by the morning." Hugh d'Avranches was pleased with his decision. He waved to the servant and a goblet of wine was placed in her cold hand.

"A toast to your future."

Ghislaine's goblet fell to the floor and the red wine ebbed unnoticed into the midden round her feet.

Chapter Three

The cold morning light that stole through the cracks
in the meagre shutters broke Ghislaine's fitful sleep.
Neither the heap of fur skins nor the poor fire in the
corner of her tiny dormitory could dispel the blistering
chill of the priory from seeping through her bones. The
corridors beyond her wooden door echoed with the
chanting of the monks at matins. She felt empty. Cold
and empty.

She rose quickly and pulled a heavy skin over her
thin shift, hastily remembering to sketch the outline of
a cross before the crucifix on the wall. Her bare feet
were freezing as she opened the shutters which looked
out over the courtyard. It too was empty in the half-
gloom of the winter morning. What had she expected
to find, she wondered? That Walter would be waiting
for her? Or that Edwin had escaped his chains from
Chester castle and come to rescue her?

She absently rubbed her hands over her arms as she
looked up at the grey, cheerless sky. No doubt a fitting
start to this marriage, she thought bitterly. Slamming
the shutters in frustration, Ghislaine whirled round and

proceeded to pace the short length of her cell. With her mind searching for the most sensible course of action, Ghislaine failed to notice how cold she had grown. It was not until a bitter gust of wind blew open the unsecured shutters and all but put out the poor fire that an idea formed.

Her feet and ankles had turned an ugly, mottled blue, whereas her long fingers were almost white. She remembered then that the priory had the rather unenviable reputation of having to accommodate one or two unsuspecting guests in the graveyard rather than in its spartan cells during the harsher months. Aye, she grinned. Death would be a very expedient remedy for this marriage. Or at least the appearance of her imminent demise. It was possible that the Earl would not insist on the marriage if he thought she was too ill.

The thought of ruining the plans of her murderous bridegroom spurred Ghislaine into action. The fire was doused down, the shutters pulled wide open and the skins heaped in a pile on the floor by the bed. All she had to do now was wait until she was discovered. Hopefully she would be a good shade of blue all over by then.

Easing her body under the thin blanket, Ghislaine soon began to shiver quite uncontrollably. A harsh, dark, unbarbered face made its unwelcome appearance in her mind, the blue eyes staring at her knowingly. She swallowed hard. Marriage to such a monster was sickening. He had murdered Margaret. And yet unbidden she remembered, too, the anger in his eyes when she had asked him why he had killed Margaret.

When their betrothal had been announced, all but the couple concerned drank to the forthcoming mar-

riage. In fact, she reminded herself, they had both ignored each other completely, their dislike of each other
plain for all to see. De Courcy had not bothered to
feign interest in her, and that, at least, was honest. He
had drunk himself into a sotted heap with his blond
companion, and as far as she was aware, he would
have remained on the stinking rushes all night. She
wrinkled her nose in disgust. The man was worse than
an animal.

Sweet Lord, the cold was truly freezing her to death.
It had been Helene's suggestion to bed in the priory
and she had agreed readily. Nothing would have in-
duced her to spend the night on the Earl of Chester's
rushes. The old priory of St Werburgh had been built
in the north western corner of the city, offering respite
to travellers, merchants and visitors alike. The accom-
modation was spartan but clean, each tiny cell boasting no more than a pallet and a fire. The peace of the
place had finally allowed her some sleep, despite her
tortured dreams.

Walter had not appeared and yet as one of the Earl's
close confidants it was a distinct possibility that he
would arrive in time. She pulled the icy blanket
tighter. If she could at least delay the marriage until
Walter could devise a better plan, that would be
enough. He was very adept at shrewd thinking, and at
times she had admonished herself for considering him
a little too clever. Well, he would need all his skill
now.

Ghislaine's breath was icy white in the freezing dormitory before Helene came to find her.

"Ghislaine! What ails you?" Helene took one look

at her before turning to slam the shutters to and hurriedly calling for her maid.

Ghislaine was now so cold that in truth she feared that she might die after all. It would be a poor joke, she thought ruefully. Her body had ceased to feel anything and her chest felt heavy and sore. Speech was nigh on impossible with her mouth frozen.

Helene and her maid worked swiftly. The fire was rekindled and coaxed into giving off some heat whilst more skins were ordered to put on the pallet. Helene chaffed her numb feet, whilst the maid went in search of hot water.

"Can you talk now?" Helene whispered urgently, peering anxiously over Ghislaine's blue-tinged face. "Do you feel any warmer?"

The woman's concern was so obviously genuine that Ghislaine felt a pang of remorse for her dissembling. She would make it up to her later, she vowed. "Nay," came the croaked reply. "I cannot move." That at least was true.

"Then I must send a message to the Earl. The marriage cannot take place today," Helene responded briskly and called one of the monks who was hovering outside the door. He was despatched with all haste and Ghislaine knew a profound sense of relief as the door closed.

Helene du Beauregard's dark eyes studied her for a few minutes. Ghislaine's heart contracted. Did she suspect her?

"If I were your mother, I would put you in a hot tub. 'Tis the only remedy other than a man in your bed that I can think of."

Ghislaine's eyes snapped open at such plain speaking. "I…I think I would prefer a bath," she stammered.

"Very wise," came the dry retort.

The hot water was a welcome remedy that returned Ghislaine to a more normal colour. It was so pleasant just wallowing in a herb-scented tub, so relaxing, that Ghislaine almost forgot her perfidy. Once she was pronounced warm enough, she was dried and reclothed in a thick monk's robe and returned to her warmed bed. The spiced wine heated her gently from within, and Ghislaine began to float away in a haze of drowsiness for a moment or two.

Her peace was interrupted by a loud rap at the door. Stifling her irritation, Helene opened the door and disappeared outside for a moment. The urgent whispering caused Ghislaine to prick up her ears for it was clear that something was amiss.

"Ghislaine," came Helene's entreaty. "You must awake." A stiff hand shook her gently until her eyes opened warily.

"It would seem that your bridegroom is more eager than he appeared last night. His men surround the priory and he is demanding to see you. He fears a trick, no doubt." The older woman's face looked pinched and tired as she smoothed back the wayward curls from Ghislaine's face. "I have sent a message that you are too ill to see him, but I doubt that will delay him for long."

The fear of having to face de Courcy caused her heart to beat more rapidly. Her throat constricted and her chest began to heave. Such a murderous barbarian would not enter these holy walls, she told herself rapidly in an attempt to calm down. He was but a man and she was safe here, wasn't she? The answer to her question was brought by the sound of heavy steps thudding along the stone corridor and doors being thrust open. A loud curse made her heart slam against her ribs. Sweet Lord, he had actually come for her.

"Don't let him in," she croaked to the scandalised Helene. "I cannot see him yet. Tell him…tell him I will see him on the morrow…" The words died in her throat as the door to her cell was slammed open and de Courcy pushed through the doorway. He seemed almost to fill the room, his filthy, dark appearance in stark contrast with the plain white of her chaste cell. His face was still scowling as his eyes rested on the huddled figure in the narrow bed.

"What trickery is this, lady?" His cold eyes stared at the outraged Helene who had pushed herself between him and the object of his anger. Ghislaine was almost certain, however, that the animosity in de Courcy's eyes was fixed more on Helene than herself and wondered what lay at the root of it. As far as she knew, they were strangers to each other. Yet there was something in the air between them.

"There is no trickery, my lord, save what goes on in your mind." Helene's tone was sharp but controlled. "The girl is half-frozen to death and I doubt that the marriage will be completed this day. She has taken a healing draught that will speed her recovery but rest and quiet are necessary."

Guy de Courcy ignored her pointed glance at the open door and walked over to Ghislaine's pallet. His very presence filled her with fear and she had the notion that without a lot of encouragement, she could vomit. At his next words, she almost did.

"You will be in the chapel directly, lady, or I shall see the priory burned and your people exiled at the very least."

To Ghislaine's ears, his threat sounded very ready but she could not forget Margaret.

"I have one question to ask you before I agree," she managed. "If you deny murdering Margaret Staveley, then why is your name linked with hers?"

He had not taken those piercing blue eyes from her pale face and they bore into her silently.

"I wished to marry her, but the lady was not...willing."

Ghislaine stared at him totally at a loss for words. How could such a wretch as this think of marrying a woman as delicate and lovely as Margaret? It made no sense, but looking at him, she doubted whether that was necessary. Somewhere, deep in her mind, she wondered if anyone did not obey him. Her hopes of Walter rescuing her faded in the face of his odious threats. Her head nodded almost imperceptibly as she forced back the anger and the tears of frustration.

"It pleases me to see you can be so biddable, lady. I will await you in the chapel directly." The weary tone in his voice was almost her undoing, but Helene stepped in front of him as he turned to leave.

"So an innocent girl is to be dragged from her sick bed to stand at the altar with an outlaw who stinks of the midden. I had not realised the de Courcys' honour was sunk so low."

Her stinging retort caused de Courcy to whirl round to face her. "And what do you know of the de Courcys' honour, madam?"

"Enough to know that you bring shame to the very

name.'' Helene du Beauregard fairly bristled with anger as she eyed him haughtily, her thin hands placed aggressively on her hips.

Her reply caused him to still fleetingly. "Then it is as well that my parents are dead." He turned swiftly on his heels and left the cell, leaving Helene staring after him. After a moment she turned slowly to Ghislaine who was unmoving on the bed.

"Your bridegroom is eager indeed, my Lady de Launay. It would appear that Hugh Lupus must have been giving him a glowing account of your accomplishments."

Ghislaine groaned into the hard bolster. "He was probably exaggerating the extent of my wealth." Her voice was low and husky "No doubt he is glad to be rid of me." Burying her face in the bolster, Ghislaine prayed hard that when she lifted her head, she would be back at her own manor and that this was naught but a terrible dream. Opening her eyes she found nothing changed except for the expression on Helene's face. Gone was the light-hearted amusement, and instead Ghislaine could only see sympathy and concern.

"I will do it," she whispered quietly. "I have no wish for anyone to die on my account."

Helene nodded her head and helped her out of her pallet.

The small, white-washed chapel was empty save for the priest who had obviously been commandeered into performing the wedding service. When Ghislaine entered the chapel, supported by a monk and Lady Helene, the priest moved forward but was prevented from progressing beyond the first pew by a large hand.

Ghislaine caught her breath as Guy de Courcy rose from his knees and turned to watch her approach. From the damp tendrils of his dark hair that clung to his forehead, Ghislaine realised that he had at least heeded some of what Helene had said. However, a quick douse of cold water was not likely to change his manners or his character.

The fact that she had chosen to remain in the monk's habit told him much about her opinion of this marriage, but his eyes were drawn to the cascade of bright copper curls that hung to her waist. Unadorned, her hair shone with dancing lights picking up the rays from the windows and moving softly in the breeze. His lips tightened. Perhaps he should not have treated her quite so harshly.

As she reached his side, she stopped to look up at him, a mixture of fear, anger and innocence. Guy scowled.

"The Earl took it upon himself to have his scribe lay out the marriage contract," he began, passing her a white scroll with a thick red seal. Ghislaine took it, her hands shaking a little. The marks made no real sense to her, but she did not wish to inform de Courcy of her lack.

When she spoke, her voice was under control. "Would you care to enlighten me?" She would not make this easy for him. After all, he was getting the bargain.

Guy found the parchment casually waved, unread, before his eyes and glared at her. He had no idea whether the woman could read or just couldn't be bothered. Previous experience of ladies and their whims had taught him to expect the worst. Hell's teeth, the woman was difficult. And yet not for the first time did he note her attempt at courage. It would give him a great deal of satisfaction in taming this wild cat. He stopped the thought. Taming—or anything else—did not form part of his plans. Nor did he have the inclination, he reminded himself.

"The terms are the usual ones," he began irritably, "save the parts to do with the payment for advowry."

"I have not married before," she interrupted quickly. "Pray, do explain the 'usual terms'."

His vexed expression afforded Ghislaine some satisfaction but it did not last for long.

"If you try my patience much longer lady, I will be forced to practise my husbandly duties before the marriage is complete. I am no fool and I am done with waiting. There will be no more delays."

So he had seen her ruses for what they were. Ghislaine tightened her lips, knowing that if she said more he would surely carry out his threats. Wife-beating was a common pastime amongst knights of his station. She lifted her head in haughty indignation as he gripped her arm, but despite her best efforts she could not free herself from his hold.

"But know this, lady. When I have cleared my name, I shall put you in the convent as you request and have done with this charade." So saying he turned to the priest and nodded impatiently. D'Everard hurried through the wooden door, accompanied by a lanky youth of indeterminate age, merely nodding at the assembled company and taking his place at de Courcy's side.

The marriage was solemnised quickly and without further interruption. Neither Walter nor Edwin came to rescue her, and Ghislaine had found herself repeating her vows in toneless resignation. Her life was now in the protection of this murdering barbarian, but she vowed that she would find a way to avenge the death of her friend.

In deference to her supposed indisposition, de Courcy had ordered a cart to take her back to the manor at Chapmonswiche. Inwardly, Ghislaine grimaced at the thought of spending so many uncomfortable hours in that contraption, but pride would not let her back down. Biting her lip, she climbed into the cart as gracefully as she could but cursed roundly when her cloak ripped on a nail. The look of amusement that de Courcy bestowed upon her made it plain that he did not for one moment believe her ailment was fact.

Helene gripped her arm tightly. "I shall come to visit as soon as I am able." She paused as if about to say something further, but then shook her head. "Do not push him too far, Ghislaine." Her anxious face smiled gently at her. "If you need me, send word."

Ghislaine nodded wordlessly, too overwhelmed by her sense of impending doom and loneliness to be able to say anything.

As the heavy cart trundled noisily across the wooden bridge that spanned the River Dee, Ghislaine looked back at the walls of the ancient city and tried to stifle her tears. She was married to a murderous mercenary who wished to put her in the convent. Her future looked very bleak.

Chapter Four

As the cart forged along the stony path leading to the manor of Chapmonswiche, Ghislaine's spirits began to rise a little. At least she would be living in her own home. The aches and pains in her jarred bones melted at the sight of the familiar palisade and the stagnant moat that had needed draining for years. If only the ache in her heart would disappear so easily.

Her bridegroom had inexplicably remained with the cart for the entire length of the dreary ride from Chester, his huge black destrier champing to push on. Ghislaine had stared at his stiff, straight back for some of the time, wishing for some awful fate to befall him. They were accompanied by some ten of his uncouth soldiers, the rest having ridden on ahead with d'Everard and Edwin. Escape was impossible, but even so Ghislaine reminded herself of his threat to her people.

As she watched him, the enormity of what had happened struck her anew. She had married the murderer of her friend, knew nothing about him save his oafish manners and surly disposition and could be sharing her bed with him this night. Everything she possessed and held dear was in his hands, and she was greatly afeared.

Never in her life had she truly been afraid, least-ways not of any one man. Her father's temper had been explosive but short-lived, and like as not her clever tongue had aided her to escape the palm of his hand. She had been protected from the rest by dint of her position, although Ghislaine was aware of the harsher realities of married life. Her mother had often treated women for the results of marital disputes, wife-beating being in no way a respecter of rank.

The closer to the drawbridge they moved, the more fearful and nervous she became. Of course she had expected to marry, although her father had never taken any pains to find another partner for her since her be-trothed from the cradle, Robert of Warmundesley, had unfortunately died of a fever some six years before. Since the death of his wife, however, John de Launay had found it more convenient to have Ghislaine look after the manor and see to his needs and comforts, with little thought for her own. Money had been hard come by of late and there had been few suitors for so small an estate. Her reputation as a wild and unbiddable girl who consorted with the villeins and serfs had done little to enhance her bridal worth, even though it was in many ways unjustified.

De Courcy looked back at her over his shoulder and treated her to one of his blacker scowls. At least, she decided, he was predictable. And the thought struck her then, that as he disliked her so much, he was un-likely to spend much time in her company. Were she to give him such a disgust of her, he might spend no time at all with her. That thought was most pleasing.

"Do you need help, lady?"

Ghislaine started as the words pierced her thoughts. Her husband had already dismounted and was standing before her, an impatient frown informing her that he had been waiting for her to get down. As she looked up at his tall figure, a vision of Margaret stood by his side. He had wanted small, delicate, pretty Margaret as his wife. A sweet, god-fearing, clean, well-mannered girl with the experience of two husbands behind her, and, if she was truthful, not a lot of natural intelligence. She would have smiled had she not caught his cold, blue eyes raking her with disgust. A good start.

Without a word, Ghislaine rose awkwardly and attempted to trip out of the cart. She was thwarted by a pair of strong arms which pulled her to his chest.

"I am to ensure that no ill befalls you, lady, for your liege-lord is keen to see you survive the marriage." The words were uttered with a certain twisted amusement that caused Ghislaine's eyes to fly to his face. "Do you succumb in any way, then he has assured me of a place in his dungeon."

Ghislaine gulped. She had never been so close to any man before, let alone a barbarian, and she was unprepared for the strange feelings it stirred in her. He was younger than she had at first supposed, maybe twenty-five or so, but years of fighting in all elements had given him a worn appearance. In fact, Helene du Beauregard was right when she said he was reputed to be handsome. Were it not for those thick, black bristles on his face, he would be very handsome.

She realised that she must have been staring at him as his lips began to curl in irritation.

"If I am too heavy for you, husband, put me down. I am not noted for my delicate size." Her heart was still thudding wildly as those eyes of his bore into hers and it took all her will-power to control the trembling that had inexplicably set about her limbs.

His scornful stare was nearly the undoing of her, for he looked as if he would ignore the Earl's wishes and murder her right there. She found herself sprawling in the mud. His ways with ladies were most appealing!

"Do you wish to die, it can be arranged lady," he growled, the familiar scowl returning. "I am not of the opinion that you are the Earl's favourite ward."

"My wishes count for little in this arrangement," she retorted angrily from the ground. "What I wish to do is to enter the convent." Ghislaine stood up, momentarily forgetting her plan as she brushed the dirt from her cloak.

"That, too, can be arranged," he murmured as he turned his back on her to survey the manor. His only comment was a grunt, before he set about ordering his escorts to dismount.

Further conversation between them was brought to a halt by the arrival of Arnaud d'Everard in the company of Sir Brian de Ferrars, her household steward. Sir Brian had been with the family a good ten years and, although approaching middle years and a little unreliable as a result of his fondness for ale, was loyal and good natured. In truth, the manor was too small to require his services, but Sir Brian had been a close friend of her father's and even the normally hard-hearted Sir John had not been able to turn him off.

"A relief to see you returned in one piece, Lady Ghislaine." Sir Brian's bleary blue eyes surveyed his mistress closely, but seeing nothing amiss, turned to the tall stranger at her side with a look of suspicion on his face. Being only of medium height, Sir Brian had to look up to the newcomer, a fact which clearly annoyed him.

"I bid you greet Sir Guy de Courcy, my husband, Sir Guy, the head of my household, Sir Brian de Ferrars." Ghislaine's voice sounded far more controlled than she felt. Her relief, however, was short lived for she could see from his expression that Sir Brian had already made up his mind about the new lord of the manor.

"I believe in plain speaking Sir Guy," stated the older man baldly. "Your reputation is not an enviable one, and you are not the choice I would have made for Lady Ghislaine."

Ghislaine held her breath, waiting for the sword to fall at such a pompous greeting. Sir Brian was apt to take a paternal attitude when he deemed it necessary. Her eyes widened when they saw de Courcy nod his head in agreement.

"In your place I would feel the same, but the match was arranged by the Earl of Chester. He felt that Lady Ghislaine and I would be...well suited." The last statement was made with more than a touch of irony.

Sir Brian raised his eyebrow in question.

"I have wealth enough to bring to the property and a loyal army of twenty men. Lady Ghislaine has seen the wisdom of the alliance," he added with a faint smile in her direction.

Ghislaine's face suffused with pink at such familiar

talk, but although Sir Brian clearly remained suspicious of Sir Guy, she decided this was not the time to create a fuss.

"I see you have met Sir Arnaud d'Everard. He will have given you forewarning of our arrival, no doubt?"

"Aye, Lady Ghislaine. We have done what we could under the circumstances." The gloomy look that the hapless Sir Brian gave her told Ghislaine all she needed to know. The kitchens were run by a domineering woman whose swings of mood were as notorious as her morals. Elfrieda had turned up at their gates one freezing, wet day last winter. She had been heavily with child. The mercenary who had dumped her there had muttered that her only talent was cooking. He didn't return, but Elfrieda's skills in the kitchen had more than repaid her debt of gratitude.

Sir Brian had always found Elfrieda most intimidating and Ghislaine suspected that if they were to eat that night, then she had best sort it out herself.

"In that case, I shall see you in the hall when you have made the necessary arrangements with the men." And with those parting words, Ghislaine escaped through the gate house and disappeared into the bailed, leaving the three men staring after her.

"Edwin!" Ghislaine stared in horror at the sight of his handsome, battered face. "Did de Courcy do this?" she demanded, delicately probing his angry swollen bruises for any serious injury. Finding none, she took a step back to survey his scowling countenance. Sweet Lord, did all the men she knew scowl?

"Nay," he replied calmly, picking up a small cup of usquebaugh from the table before him. Clearly Effie had provided him with this from her father's stock. "This was the work of the Earl's men." His grey eyes continued to stare at her as he drained the cup quickly, and Ghislaine began to feel uncomfortable. They had grown up together and she recognised anger in him.

"You were right," she grudgingly admitted, finally able to take no more of his accusing looks. "Had I heeded your advice we would not be in this position. However, I did not and that's an end to it. At least you're not the one married to him."

Edwin uncurled himself from his spot on the bench and stood before his mistress, his long braids matted and filthy, his tunic badly torn. "This man is no fool, Ghislaine. Do not attempt to trick him or it will not go well for us." This speech was delivered gravely and Ghislaine knew that he was worried. He had been her sole protector for years. No one else save Richard had ever bothered overmuch for her safety.

She sighed heavily and turned to the fire. "I know that, but there must be some way to get rid of this oaf. Mayhap an accident?" Her hopeful tone caused Edwin to take a step closer and grip her shoulders in his hands. Gently he turned her back to face him.

Edwin had been the one constant person in her life. There had been a time when Ghislaine had thought of him as more than a friend, but that had passed years ago. They had settled into a relationship based on trust and respect. It didn't blind them to each other's faults, however. For some months, Ghislaine had sensed a change in Edwin. A restlessness seemed to have taken a grip on his soul and she had often caught him staring into the distant hills.

His anxiety was mirrored in his fathomless grey

eyes. "You would be dead before you finished the thought." His grim expression softened a little as he saw the fear that lay behind her suspiciously bright eyes. "Do not anger him, lady. He is a knight with rough ways and a bad temper. If you value your life, look to his needs quickly."

"Good advice, lady. I hope that you heed him this time."

Ghislaine whirled round to face her husband smiling down at her benignly. "You were listening," she accused, glaring at him.

"Did you have something to hide? There will be no secrets between us, wife." His gaze travelled to Edwin. "And this, I take it, is your partner in crime?"

Ghislaine did not even deign to reply, but watched in fascination as the two men assessed each other thoroughly. They were matched in size, although as Edwin was younger his body did not have the same strength as de Courcy's. Her husband did not scowl, but seemed to have come to some decision.

"The Earl informed me you were a skilled marksman. Does he have the right of it?"

Edwin crossed his arms over his chest and nodded.

"He was also under the impression that you had some...er...difficulty with our language."

Edwin sniffed derisively. "There was never anything I could say that would have changed his view of me," he said finally. "His men had no problem communicating with me."

His pride was shining from his swollen eyes, but he did not seem much like a man in love with his wife, concluded Guy. In fact, he appeared to treat her much like a brother would. With this thought in mind, he voiced his decision. "You would swear fealty to me this night?" he demanded. "I would ask no more of you than Lady Ghislaine does, except that you would ride with my men when I need you."

"And his alternative?" Ghislaine demanded angrily.

Guy shrugged carelessly. "I would send him to the Earl for trial for crimes of the venison. I am sure that evidence could be produced."

Edwin rubbed his hand over his beard and looked at him speculatively. "Would I be paid?"

Ghislaine gasped. He was going to accept the outlaw for a few coins.

"Aye. The same as my men. A silver mark a month, with food and a share of any treasure taken." Guy smiled slowly. So he had his price after all. Ghislaine, he had to admit, looked more thunderstruck than heartsore.

"I accept." Their eyes locked for a moment until Ghislaine, incensed by what she saw as Edwin's defection, interrupted.

"Excuse me whilst I go to organise the servants. No doubt there are still some who wish to do my bidding." With her eyes full of anger and her cheeks pink, Ghislaine whirled around. Her flourish was marred somewhat by her tripping on the long monk's robe she still wore, but she cared not.

Edwin watched Ghislaine's stiff and clumsy retreat before turning back to his new liege-lord.

"If you harm her, I will kill you myself." So saying, he picked up his bow and quit the hall.

"It would seem that your bride has made a full re-

covery,'' stated Arnaud with an impish grin. He was
lounging idly against the wall, watching Guy's face.

Guy half turned towards him and grunted in response, pondering a little more on the curious relationship between his wife and her man-servant. He had
a feeling that the Englishman was going to be less
trouble than his wife.

"She inspires much loyalty, this wife of yours. If
two grown men are so keen to defend her, it may be
wise to treat her with perhaps a touch more...ah...
courtesy."

"Do you think I am afeared of them?" Guy asked
impatiently.

"Nay," came the guarded reply. "But it would not
harm you to scowl at her less."

"She does not appear afraid," Guy pointed out
gruffly. He did not like his shortcomings being em-
phasised quite so obviously.

Arnaud's silence was most eloquent.

"I had no choice," he continued, his growl returning. "Were her behaviour and tongue more ladylike,
she would not be in this position either."

"Aye, true enough," agreed Arnaud amicably.
Clearly he would win no ground with that approach.
He decided to change tack. "It would do no harm to
keep the lady sweet, though. We do not want to sniff
the ale every time we have a thirst." That found its
mark, and Guy sighed wearily.

"I did not want to be married to her. She was not
my choice."

So that was what irked him. He had gained a good
estate but the bride was not to his taste.

"She is not that sore on the eyes," he pointed out

pleasantly. "The girl is perhaps not young but seems healthy enough."

"She has red hair," growled Guy, pushing his black hair back off his face in frustration, "and a tongue like a viper."

"Ah." Arnaud smiled to himself. It looked like things were going to be interesting. If his memory served him aright, Guy had never hesitated to choose a willing wench with red hair to warm his bed before. But perhaps the root of the problem lay in a slightly different direction. Lady Ghislaine was, after all, no camp follower and Guy was not used to dealing with ladies. It was possible that his friend felt very much at a disadvantage. No doubt the rejection from Lady Margaret had played some part in all this. "Then maybe we should search out some of that ale before she fills it with her venom," he grinned, pushing himself away from the wall.

Guy grinned back before slapping him on the back in good humour. "Maybe she would prefer your silver tongue. The Earl mentioned she prefers blonds."

Guy held his tongue throughout the ordeal of being presented to all the servants and vassals that inhabited the manor. His wife appeared reasonable, although he could tell from the noises her stomach was making that the girl was starving.

When they finally sat down at the lord's table in the plain, square hall, Guy knew relief, although he did remember to sniff the ale before he tasted it. As he did so, his eyes locked with those of Arnaud's. Each raised a cup in toast before tossing the spicy liquid back.

Amazed that he still lived, Guy tasted the venison and boar at his wife's bidding, as well as the fine white bread and nuts that she had brought to him specially. Grudgingly he admitted that the food was most acceptable, and with Arnaud's warning still ringing in his ears, Guy complimented his wife on the banquet.

"I am most impressed with the fare, lady. It is some time since we have eaten so well." He managed a nervous smile.

His words were received with little more than a raised eyebrow. "Most gracious, my lord."

As his wife was clearly not going to continue the conversation, Guy racked his brains to think of something else to engage her interest. He was pleased to see her drink freely of the ale.

"A fine brew, lady."

"I made it myself, sir. I am most pleased you find it to your liking."

He did not miss the sarcasm behind her expression, but was surprised to see her toss back another skinful of ale.

"What other accomplishments do you possess, lady?"

His question caused a deep flush to steal upwards from her neck. "I...I had thought the Earl would have given you a complete inventory of my...accomplishments, Sir Guy." Her eyes remained fixed on the table before them and it irritated him that she would not look him in the eye.

"Aye," came his grave response. "But I do not always set much store by what Hugh d'Avranches says."

Such treasonable words caused her dark eyes to fly

to his face. And they were very expressive eyes, Guy noted. At the moment they were trying to suppress what appeared to be amusement.

"I will confess, sir, that most of what he says is true. You have, I fear, landed yourself with a most unladylike wife." To his complete surprise Ghislaine rounded off her words by drinking more ale.

Guy looked at her flushed cheeks. Arnaud was right. She was quite comely, and he remembered thinking when he had held her earlier that she had felt good. He turned his attention to his food to divert the train of his thoughts. This was one woman he would not be bedding. He wanted no wife and she wanted to be in the convent. Well, so be it. Once this charade was over, the marriage could be annulled and they could all return to normal.

Despite his best efforts to entertain his wife, the girl proceeded to drink greater quantities of the ale. Somewhat deflated by being so ignored by a woman, Guy turned his attention to Sir Brian, who regaled him with tales of Ghislaine's father.

From the corner of his eye, he watched Ghislaine sink into a most unladylike stupor, and if he guessed aright, she would soon be collapsing into oblivion. Arnaud was right again, it seemed. The girl was so afeared of him, she would drink herself to sleep on her wedding night. He ought to have put her fears to rest on that point before now. Well, that would have to wait till the morrow.

He rose quickly and picked up his wife in what seemed to the assembled company to be a lover-like gesture of consideration. Sir Brian tottered to his feet, clearly unsure of his move.

"Rest easy, Sir Brian. My wife has had a long day. I will see to her comfort." Guy tried hard not to scowl and after a moment, the knight nodded curtly and sat down.

Guy reached the steps that led to the lord's room in three strides but was prevented from mounting them by Edwin. From his expression, the Englishman was not to be so easily dismissed. Guy sighed heavily.

"Your loyalty does you credit, but I can assure you that she will have no hurt from me." They both looked at the sleeping Ghislaines and Guy could have sworn that he saw a glimmer of regret cross the cold grey eyes of the Englishman. Silently, Edwin stood back to let them pass.

Chapter Five

A loud groan brought Ghislaine unwillingly from her strange dreams. It was a moment or two before she realised that the noise had come from her own lips, and that the terrible throbbing in her head and sick feeling in her stomach made her want to retch. Had she truly done this to herself?

A sound beyond the bed caused Ghislaine to lever the upper part of her body gingerly into a sitting position. She wished she hadn't.

"Awake at last, my lady?" Effie's normally soft tones grated violently against her aching head. Ghislaine raised her hands to her head and thought she was going to be sick.

"Sir Guy said to give you this when you woke. He thought it would help." That her maid sounded dubious was an understatement, but at that moment, Ghislaine would not have cared had the girl said it contained lethal poison. She took the goblet and swallowed the contents. It tasted disgusting.

"He said you would most likely be sick, but that you would feel better for it."

"Sir Guy is not here?" Ghislaine's bleary eyes slid around the bare room suspiciouly, noting a heavy dent in the mattress by her side.

"Oh, no, my lady. He was up some time ago." Effie tossed back her thick blonde braids and her blue eyes regarded her in a thinly veiled rebuke. "He went to the kitchen himself to make the potion." Admiration was shining from her eyes and had Ghislaine felt less like death, she would have done more than give her a sickly moan. She refused to contemplate how he had managed the volatile cook, Elfrieda.

Guy's prediction about her condition was sadly accurate, and when she was finally able to quit the privy, Ghislaine could do no more than sink back into a few hours more of dreamless relief.

When next she awoke, the sun was much higher and from the sounds outside, Ghislaine could tell that she had stayed abed far longer than usual. Dappled light shone through the rickety shutters, penetrating the thick gloom of the lord's room. She was alone.

The violent nausea and throbbing headache had been replaced by symptoms that were easier to cope with. Stretching back on the hard bolster, Ghislaine pondered her state. She had absolutely no recollection of how she had arrived here, and, far worse, what had happened to her when she had. The large dip in the bed by her side informed her that Guy had slept there too. There was an aura about the place that even smelled of his black soul. Hesitantly, Ghislaine drew back the blankets, and it was with some relief that the white sheets proclaimed her innocence. At least he had spoken true about his intention to keep her for the abbey. It seemed, for now at any rate, her innocence was safe, but how long that would endure she could not guess.

Slowly she slipped from the sheets of the large bed and pulled a threadbare blanket about her shoulders. Her eyes were drawn back to the bed. She knew what happened between a man and a woman, and judging by the whispered giggles of her servants, it was a pleasurable experience. But the thought of experiencing pleasure in the arms of that murderer drew a shudder from her cold body.

A shout outside made her venture to the window and pull back the shutters a little. Judging by the sun, it would be close to midday and she should be about her duties. Consumed by curiosity Ghislaine leaned forward to watch the activities below without being observed.

Small groups of unfamiliar men were setting to the repairs of the palisade, clearing rubbish and rethatching the stable roof. All of these were vital jobs that her father had refused to take in hand, and Sir Brian's indifferent health had allowed the state of the manor to deteriorate over the course of several years. Despite her pleas for many improvements and repairs, little had been done. Ghislaine watched with open-mouthed amazement at the scene below her. It was hard to believe that the instructions had come from her husband, for she was certain that he had little personal experience of running a manor. No, she decided finally. The orders were most likely to have come from Sir Arnaud, but Ghislaine found it intriguing to think that Guy de Courcy would allow his trained mercenaries to expend their energies on such lowly tasks.

A sudden glimpse of Arnaud d'Everard caused

Ghislaine to step back quickly and retreat into the
safety of the bedchamber, reminding herself that she
would have to face them all soon. No doubt she looked
and smelled as if she had spent the night in the byre.

Despite her plan to give Guy de Courcy a disgust
of her, Ghislaine could not deny herself the comfort
of a bath. When she sank back into the tub, a sense
of well-being and comfort stole through her. This was
a luxury she had not often been permitted by her father, but for once Ghislaine had been determined to
choose something for herself. If Guy de Courcy did
not approve, he would have to tell her himself. Sighing, Ghislaine attempted to put all thoughts of her husband to one side. It was not to be.

"You are recovered, I see."

Ghislaine turned rapidly, causing water to splash
over the edge of the tub and her cheeks to flush. The
object of her thoughts had materialised silently at the
door of the bedchamber, an expression of cool indifference on his dark face.

Ghislaine's lips tightened and her brain desperately
tried to work convincingly. "Your concern is most
gratifying, Sir Guy, but not at all necessary. My par-
tiality for ale is well known and my body used to the
effects." She then proceeded to affect complete indifference to his presence and smeared dollops of the
sweet-scented soap onto her arms before sinking as
low as she could into the tub.

Guy's lack of interest wavered somewhat on hearing
those words. His wife's voice was attractive when she
wasn't shooting venom at him. Low and husky. But
why she should tell him a blatant lie about her drinking habits had him foxed. The girl could be most vex-

ing. He closed the stiff door behind him and took a few more paces into the semi-dark room. The two candles flickering in the prickets offered little light. Her frugality, at least, was a welcome sight.

"I had not realised that drinking ale was one of your vices, lady." His eyes fixed on the soft white curves of her shoulders. "Have you any others?"

Unwilling to look up at him, Ghislaine missed the glint in his eyes and the underlying meaning of his question. "Oh, many," she replied airily as she splashed the water over her shoulders. "I am known to be a...glutton, too."

Guy raised an eyebrow. "There was not much evidence of that last night." He tried to picture his wife's figure but could only recall her telling him she was not noted for her delicate size. She had not felt a great weight in his arms either, but even as he puzzled over her words, he took another step or so forward.

"I was hoping that you would be...er...rested enough to show me the estate." His eyes followed the hand that was busy soaping her shoulders in gentle, almost caressing movements. As her hand moved lower, so did his eyes. Just below the water-line he could see the swell of her rounded breasts. His throat went dry as he recalled that it had been some time since he had tumbled a woman. His black scowl returned. He was acting like a young boy.

"I am sure that Sir Brian would be most happy to show you Chapmonswiche," she said coolly, still refusing to look at him.

His scowl deepened. He was not going to be dismissed like a lackey in his own home by this arrogant wench.

"Given the sudden nature of our marriage and my reputation, I had thought you would prefer your people to see you unharmed at my side. No doubt you know them better than I."

His words caused her to still and finally to look up at him. "Are you afeared that they will balk against the Earl's choice of husband for me?"

His lips tightened in anger at her superior tone. He should have known she would parry words with him and it was irritating beyond belief. "I have naught to fear," he snapped, "but should you do aught to incur my wrath, then you will have my hand to fear, lady."

So that was how it was to be. The cool way her eyes regarded him and her quick tongue had riled him so much he had let his temper take over. Were he to stay in the chamber a minute more, he would surely put his threat into practice. No doubt even the befuddled Sir Brian would have a better understanding of the estate anyway.

Ghislaine heard rather than saw Sir Guy's angry exit and she released the breath that she had been holding. For a few moments in his presence she had forgotten that he was a murderer of women, and his threats had sounded no more serious than those of her father. But if she valued her life, she must be more wary of him.

The rain had started to fall not long after she had slipped away from the manor and ridden into the village. There were the ploughing arrangements for the coming months to be discussed with the head villager and Ghislaine had also convinced herself that she wanted advice on herbal remedies from the old Angle crone, Hulda. She had thought Sir Guy unlikely to interfere with the general running of the estate immediately, and had seized on the excuse to escape the manor for an hour or so. She doubted that her presence would be missed for some time, everyone believing that she was closeted in the bedchamber.

She had donned her oldest tunic and braided her hair deftly in a style more practical than becoming. Briefly, Ghislaine wondered if she should take more care over her appearance in deference to her newly married status, but finally decided against it. All her gowns were old and worn and she was certain that her husband was indifferent to her looks in any case. He had married her for her value as ward of the Earl and for her estate after all.

Pulling on her leather shoes, Ghislaine noticed a new hole in the seam and sighed. Well, it could not be helped. Her father had believed any spare money better spent elsewhere. She had no reason to suppose that Guy de Courcy would think differently.

It had been easy enough to slip unnoticed from the hall, and as few of de Courcy's men had cast barely a glance in her direction, Ghislaine was able to lead her grey palfrey from the stable to the gatehouse unquestioned. To her own guard she only needed a smile and a nod and she had been given her usual free passage. Her husband had not forbidden her to leave exactly, but she knew that he would not be pleased by her absence. Still, as he would never know, it would do no real harm.

The village was sited no more than a short ride due south from the manor, close by a stream of sweet water. Boasting no more than about twenty families, the inhabitants provided little revenue for the manor, but were peaceful and friendly. Survival was based largely on a mixture of crops, cattle and pigs. Last year her father had bought some sheep and Ghislaine was hopeful that they would breed successfully and bring in some money for the woolclip.

The village huts were clustered around the muddy track that led directly to the old Roman road linking Chester with the North. The villagers muttered their congratulations to her but were plainly at a loss as to why her husband was not at her side. Offering a few hasty excuses about Sir Guy being detained on personal matters, Ghislaine hurried about her business.

Hulda lived at the far end of the village, a little apart from the rest. Respected by the others for her knowledge of cures and herbals, she was also a little feared. Some believed her to practise the old pagan rites of the Angles who had settled here before the Normans came, but Ghislaine dismissed such views as foolish. She had harmed no one and saved many. She had saved Edwin.

According to her brother, it had been Hulda who had saved the ten-year-old Edwin from the swords of the Norman soldiers whilst they hunted down any land-owning Englishmen who opposed the Conqueror. They had attacked the village ten years ago, killing the Angle thegn and his two elder sons. The youngest, Edwin, was left writhing in agony from his vicious wounds. When the soldiers had finished burning and looting, they took turns in raping his mother and sister. Both died from their injuries. Were it not for Hulda's skills, Edwin would have also succumbed.

When John de Launay had been made lord of the manor two years later, Edwin had already grown into a strong, surly lad who had been brought up by Hulda as if he were her own. No one in the manor knew of his aristocratic parentage, nor of his vow to kill the Norman dogs who had violated his mother and sister. No one except Ghislaine and her brother, Richard, and they had come by that knowledge painfully.

What had started off as a childish game had ended in unexpected violence. Ghislaine and Richard had often roamed the forest beyond the village, exploring, trapping and indulging in youthful fantasies of adventure. One day, Richard had discovered a thin youth tampering with their traps and immediately challenged him. Instead of turning tail and running, the boy had launched himself at Richard. All the venom and hatred Edwin had bottled within him had poured out, and Ghislaine had been certain that he truly would kill Richard. But when Richard's arm had snapped Edwin had turned pale. He had carried Richard to Hulda's hut where she had done what she could for the arm. It was there that they had learned of Edwin's past and his vow. It was there the three of them had forged a bond that would endure.

Ghislaine still remembered that first afternoon inside the dark hut. The smell of the herbs was overwhelming, pungent and yet wholesome. Everywhere there were bunches of the different plants drying, boiling, steeping. Strange pots crowded the table and floor, and it was hard to know where to stand.

As she looked through the open doorway, it was as if she were once again that tearful maid of eleven. Little had changed except that Ghislaine was older and, of course, married to a stranger.

"So. You've come, then?" A thin voice floated out from the gloom. "I wasn't expecting you so soon."

Hulda's grey, lined face peered up at her, the dark eyes missing nothing. She had few teeth left and rarely smiled, so a curt nod was an affectionate enough greeting. "You'd best come inside afore the rain sets in."

"Elfrieda thinks she's with child again, so she'll be needing some of your potion." Ghislaine idly picked up a bunch of herbs and sniffed them appreciatively. It was a comforting, homely sort of a smell that reminded her of her mother.

Hulda grunted, shuffling to the back of the hut. "What she needs is a husband."

Ghislaine shrugged her shoulders. "Aye, but none will have her now. Besides, she's a good cook." She replaced the herbs carefully on the table.

A deep sniff was the only answer Ghislaine received as the old woman sorted through her jars. "She cannot use it again, tell her. She may not carry her full time else."

"Aye. I'll tell her," said Ghislaine dubiously, taking the potion offered.

Hulda said no more, but carried on with her chopping and steeping, her face cloaked in the darkness of the hut.

"Have you spoken to Edwin since yestereve?" The question seemed innocent enough, but Hulda smiled to herself.

"Aye. He was here not long afore you came."

"So you know?" The disappointment was genuine.

"That you married a Norman and that Edwin takes a silver coin each month to buy his freedom? Aye."

"Why should he want his freedom? He has all he

needs with us." Ghislaine frowned, knowing the answer and knowing she sounded like a petulant child.

"His destiny is not with you, girl. He has always known that and it has not gone easy with him. Let him be now."

Pushing her braids back over her shoulders Ghislaine turned to stare at the chickens squawking outside the hut. Edwin had always been there, watched over her, aye, and had always loved her. Her feelings for him, however, were those of a sister for a brother, and Edwin had never tried to change her mind. Sometimes though, she had caught him watching her. There had been such longing and passion burning in his eyes and she had been so lonely that once or twice Ghislaine had been sorely tempted to find out about passion in his arms. Yielding to the temptation, however, would surely have signed his death warrant, since the Earl would brook no such liaisons and marriage would have been out of the question.

Catching her bottom lip between her teeth, Ghislaine turned back to Hulda. "I will miss him sorely. He is my only friend." Her voice was full of hurt and misery and Hulda was not proof against the young girl's anguish.

"He has to go, girl. It is time for him to start his journey, but he will return when he is at peace. You must be strong for him." Hulda's dark eyes burned into her and Ghislaine knew the woman was right. "There is much for you to do here."

Grimacing, Ghislaine looked across at the old woman. "You have the right of it. Sir Guy's men are little more than a pack of wild animals and I have no doubt that trouble will come soon."

Hulda paused for a moment and looked across at her. "It seems to me they've done more in a day than your father did in years. The blacksmith says his roof has already been rethatched and there's plans afoot to take a look at that stinking moat. Don't be too quick to condemn, my lady."

Managing a wan smile, Ghislaine picked up the potion for Elfrieda and left the hut. She was heartsore and in need of a friend. Knowing that Edwin was planning to buy his own freedom made her feel even more trapped. The only freedom she would find was in the convent.

The effects of the previous night's indulgence were beginning to take their toll on her once more, and Ghislaine found herself loathe to return to the manor just yet. The rain had stopped and the cool silence of the forest beckoned. According to Hulda, Edwin had taken the path in that direction and, if he was not going too fast, she could probably catch him. Ghislaine knew all his secret hiding places and she wanted to talk to him without her husband's eyes on her.

She had reached the first line of trees when the rain came suddenly in thick gusts of wind that soaked her cloak and her tunic within moments. The bitter cold froze her skin, and Ghislaine knew that she would have to find shelter or she would catch the fever that often killed travellers in this area.

The large, bare trees overhead offered little protection from the rain but did prevent the light from penetrating the darkness of the undergrowth. Ghislaine could see only a few feet in front of her with the rain driving into her eyes. Cursing herself for her foolishness, she made her way towards the stream where there was a woodcutter's bothy nearby.

Gratefully she took refuge in the meagre hut but was disappointed not to find Edwin there. Despite the holes in the thatch and broken shutters, Ghislaine was able to keep out most of the wet.

It was nigh on an hour later when the rain finally abated, and the light was failing. She felt so cold that all she could hear was the chattering of her teeth.

Her horse, Morwenna, greeted her with a friendly snicker as she patted her gently on the neck. For a brief moment, Ghislaine listened to the sounds of the forest, but all she could hear was the stream and the dripping of the raindrops on the sodden earth. The fresh smell of wet vegetation was everywhere. She was impatient to get back and worried that Guy de Courcy would discover her absence. He had threatened physical punishment if his commands were disobeyed and she was certain he would carry them out.

The mud prevented her from pushing on at speed, and as the dark gathered in, Ghislaine became increasingly concerned. Her impetuosity had once more landed her in a potentially dangerous situation, although she did not really imagine herself to be at risk.

Her position had always been a form of protection, for most knew of their lack of money. Few robbers would risk their lives on her. Yet, as the wife of a mercenary, Ghislaine realised belatedly that she now had much greater ransom value. Fear began to creep into her mind. It would also be one way of eliminating an unwanted wife without troubling the Earl's conscience. Would Guy de Courcy stoop so low?

Ghislaine did not know but a tiny voice inside her

said he was not to be trusted. He had murdered Margaret. At least, he had not denied it as vehemently as she would have expected an innocent man to do. She shivered, for suddenly she was very cold.

Behind her a twig snapped and Ghislaine froze. She could see nothing but she sensed she was being watched. Her heart was thudding as she drew her horse to a standstill, afraid of plunging headlong into an ambush. To her right, a bird fluttered suddenly from the undergrowth and she almost jumped out of the saddle. Icy fear crept along her spine. No one knew she was here and she would not be missed if she were attacked. Was this how her father had been killed?

Turning her head nervously to the place the bird had flown from, Ghislaine was sure she had picked up the furtive movements of her hidden enemy. Dismounting carefully, she peered into the undergrowth. The indistinct outline of two shadowy figures darted from place to place. Dressed in green and brown, they blended in well with their surroundings, and Ghislaine felt the cold hand of terror squeeze at her pounding heart. Should she risk riding on or try to slip silently from their grasp by playing them at their own game?

The decision was wrenched cruelly from her hands by a sudden whinny from her horse. Clearly unsettled by the tense atmosphere enveloping them, Morwenna stamped skittishly amongst the leaves and mud, her head rearing anxiously. Even as Ghislaine turned back to calm the horse, she could hear the men advancing quickly upon them. She had no choice but to mount and ride, despite her lack of time. Trying to haul herself clumsily over Morwenna's back, Ghislaine looked over her shoulder to see the first man emerging from the undergrowth, his arrow already poised for flight. She knew she was doomed but still reached desperately to pull herself up.

Quicker than she had expected, the low hum of an arrow in flight reached her ears and Ghislaine braced herself for the inevitable pain. But it never came. Instead, a piercing shriek broke the eerie silence of the forest, followed by a heavy thud. Risking a glance, Ghislaine saw her attacker felled by an arrow in his back. There was no sign of his companion, but she did not wait to find out what had happened to him.

Her palfrey bolted from her hiding place as if the devil himself were behind her. Twigs and branches tore at Ghislaine's hair and cloak. Behind she could hear shouts and then the steady thud of a horse in pursuit. As she looked over her shoulder, she saw them. A dark cloak atop a dark horse. There was naught else to see, but she would not stop to look further for the distance between them was closing.

She did not see the low-hanging branch that knocked her from the saddle, but she felt the pain in her arm and shoulder as she hit the ground with a heavy thud. For a moment she heard and saw nothing save a soft whirring before her eyes and a light-headed feeling that lifted slowly.

Two blue eyes bore into her, a mixture of relief and anger apparent.

"This is not so easily remedied, lady," came a low threat.

Ghislaine raised an eyebrow. She was most surprised to find her head propped up on her husband's lap, his strong arm under her neck. She did not immediately feel the need to move away for his huge hands had started to move along the length of her arms and legs, presumably to locate any serious injuries. She could not prevent her cheeks from burning; no man had ever done such a thing before.

"I am not hurt," she assured him, unable to look him in the eyes. When Ghislaine attempted to sit up, however, she saw stars before her eyes and the buzzing in her ears grew louder.

"You will be," he muttered as he picked her up, far more gently than she had thought possible for such an oaf. Her weight seemed no great thing to him as he strode towards his warhorse. There were eight of his men in the clearing, their eyes taking a good look at her this time. Edwin stood by the destrier, the expression on his face implacable. She was dumped less gently into the Englishman's arms whilst her champion eased himself into the saddle. Edwin regarded her steadily without a word, and his rebuking silence was worse than his bite.

Ghislaine began to shiver, whether in fear or as a result of the cold it did not seem to matter. Her desire to have some time to herself now seemed so childish and pointless, but she was sure that she was going to pay for her foolishness nonetheless.

"I would thank you for your timely arrival my lord. Had you not killed the brigand, I am sure I would now be dead."

Guy's eyes narrowed. "I killed no one, lady. Where was this?"

Ghislaine frowned in confusion. "Back down the path. I thought..."

Her words were interrupted by de Courcy's swift orders to five of his men. They charged off in search of her attackers. If the mercenaries had not saved her, then who had? She was passed back to Guy as if she were no more than a sack of grain. Her husband's arms gripped her like wet leather straps as they rode swiftly back to the manor. Dark was setting in as they crossed the drawbridge. Guy had said nothing to her on the journey back and she surmised that he was going to say it all on their return.

When her husband had dismounted, he pulled Ghislaine once more into his arms and stormed into the hall. She saw nothing save the lights of the wall sconces and concerned faces. The smell of cooking food permeated the entire building but she guessed aright when she thought she was not to savour any this night. Guy crossed the hall to the steps leading to the lord's bedchamber, but Sir Brian was there before him. Whatever he had been about to say, he did not say it; the look in Guy's eyes told him all. A look flashed between them and Sir Brian stepped aside.

As they mounted the stairs, Ghislaine's heart began to thud. He had threatened her with a beating if she did not behave and it looked as if he were going to show her the mettle of his words. Daring to look up at his grim face, Ghislaine's fears grew.

She was dumped on the bed as Guy paced the room. A good fire burned in the stone grate and yet another tub of hot water steamed in the corner. Three baths in two days!

"Why did you leave?" The question was spat out as her husband stared down at her, hands on his hips.

Ghislaine gulped. Her throat had constricted and her brain seemed to have ceased functioning "I...I had thought to spend a little time on my own." His black frown was not encouraging. She sighed nervously and began to push her wet hair from her face. "If you want the truth," she began, deciding he at least deserved the truth, "I was afeared and I had gone in search of Edwin."

He looked huge, looming above her, his dark hair wet and curling at the edges, his unshaven face rough and threatening. "Afeared? I had not thought it, lady."

Did she detect a hint of irritation at these words? He was glaring at her, his anger barely kept at bay, watching as she pulled herself to her feet. At least she was on a level with the man and could face him as an equal.

"If I did wrong, then tell me now, for I am unused to dealing with men such as you." Such plain-spoken words had an instant effect on her husband.

"I mean to do more than tell you, lady. You had fair warning earlier this day." He advanced towards the bed, his mouth set in a hard line. Ghislaine backed away, her heart racing.

"I had not thought to anger you," she replied with less confidence.

"It would seem you did not think at all. There are all manner of men searching for me, including Margaret Staveley's family. Dettingham is baying for revenge and as my wife you would make a good substitute. Nowhere is safe, girl. Were you hacked to pieces in the woods, no one would know."

His concern took her by surprise. "I did not think I would be missed," she whispered miserably.

That earned a derisive snort. "My protection depends on your well-being, lady, and I do not intend to lose what I have due to your whims and carelessness."

That put her in her place. Ghislaine gave him a fulminating stare but the effect was marred somewhat by her bedraggled appearance. She would take her punishment with grace and dignity and in no way would she give him any satisfaction.

"Now, do you set yourself on my knee or do I force you?" From the look on his face, her husband was perfectly serious. The choice was hers, and much as she did not like giving in to him without a fight, it would go ill for her otherwise. Ignoring his hand, Ghislaine stomped to stand before him, her chin high in indignation.

He sat on the edge of the bed and pulled her over his thighs. Distress and shame burned through her whole body. He would regret this, she vowed with heartfelt anger.

Suddenly she felt his hand lifting her skirt. "Nay," she gasped as she realised his intention. "Do not do this." Her voice told him of her misery and her complete distress. Her hand tried to pull her skirts back down, but he held her still. It was not until he had pulled her skirts up to her waist that he realised why she had suddenly begun to struggle.

The sight of her uncovered bottom stilled him as nothing else would. The girl wore no undergarments and he had not expected it. Aye, he had seen how poorly she was clothed, but he had not thought she would be as naked as a servant under her dress.

His eyes were drawn to the sight of her soft, rounded hips and shapely legs, and he held his breath. How could he have known that under those ugly garments, the woman hid such a body? He gave into the desire to touch that soft, white skin and felt her shudder. His reaction was instant.

Ghislaine found herself sprawling in the rushes at the foot of the bed, completely confused by her husband's actions. He had done nothing other than stroke her so gently she could hardly feel it, and then he had pushed her roughly to the ground. In that, at least, he was consistent.

"If you leave the manor once more without an escort, lady, you will surely feel pain the next time." His threat was issued as he strode towards the door, and without a backwards glance, stormed down the stairs. Ghislaine was left on the floor to contemplate her husband's strange behaviour

Chapter Six

Effie's gentle hand roused her from her sleep, and as the mists cleared from her mind, Ghislaine's eyes flew to the other side of the bed. The fact that it was empty told her much.

"Sir Guy bade me bring you this, my lady." Effie handed her the posset with a tight smile. No doubt she knew everything that had transpired the night before. "He was afeared you had taken a chill and says you are to rest in bed until he gets back."

"He ordered me to stay in bed?" Ghislaine stared at her maid incredulously. The man's arrogance knew no bounds. "There is naught wrong with me, Effie," she said briskly, attempting to rise from the bed.

Effie stared at her as if she were mad. "But he bade you stay there, my lady," she began.

Ghislaine gave her a look that told the girl what she thought of that particular piece of information. "Would you bring my clothes, Effie, and stop prating on about what Sir Guy said?"

Effie's eyes did not look up, and the girl looked

embarrassed. Ghislaine stared at such odd behaviour, and then narrowed her eyes in suspicion.

"My clothes, Effie. Where are they?"

"He took them, my lady. He took them all."

Ghislaine looked at Effie, aghast, It was clear from her expression that her husband had done just that, but the reason behind such behaviour was a mystery. She sat back in a huff, her arms folded across her chest, and sighed heavily. She would have to stay there until he decided otherwise, and it was most vexing.

"Did he say when he would be back?" Ghislaine demanded with as much authority as she could muster, for in truth she did not feel as if she carried much weight now. She remembered he had wanted a compliant, obedient wife.

Effie shook her head as she busied herself about the bedchamber, but did not volunteer any more information about her husband. That, too, was most odd. Seemingly loyal servants appeared to have traded their allegiances with little hesitation. She yielded to an unladylike outburst which earned her a reproving look from Effie.

Her empty stomach reminded Ghislaine that she had not eaten since early the day before. Her supposition that she would be allowed none of the evening meal turned out to be correct. She had bathed and then fallen asleep the minute her head nestled into the bolster.

"Am I allowed to break my fast?" Her tone was most haughty. Prisoner or no, she refused to act like one.

Effie's round cheeks coloured just a little. "He said

something about you weighing so heavy that missing a bit of food would do you no harm, my lady.''

Ghislaine received this piece of information with wide-eyed disbelief. And then her lips twitched a little. Guy de Courcy had thrown her words back into her face. So, he liked playing games. She nursed this thought for a while, deciding that it seemed most at odds with her perception of him so far. That a cold-hearted, oafish mercenary with a growl like a bear could have a sense of humour seemed very unlikely. And yet she could not prevent the smile from tugging at her lips every so often.

The next few hours were spent in mending and re-pairing the stockings and shoes that had been left, but as sewing had never held much interest for her, Ghislaine found it hard to concentrate. Effie and several of the women servants came to complain about the un-tidiness and the lascivious behaviour of her husband's men and she promised to broach the matter with Sir Guy when she had the time. It was not a conversation she would look forward to since her husband did not appear to take criticism well. It would be best to choose the right time.

Idly, she looked in her mother's carved wooden chest, which contained her own meagre possessions. There was not much to look at since her father had never bestowed gifts upon her and somehow the gath-ering of pretty objects seemed unimportant.

Carefully she laid each thing out on the bed before looking at them in turn. Her mother's comb was made of a delicately carved ivory, chased with gold. It was so fine that it would never survive combing her thick curls. She had also inherited a set of fine needles and thread, but these remained wrapped in their leather case. Amid the muslin parcels of sweet-smelling lavender, Ghislaine found the leather case that had contained her mother's jewels, all long since taken by her father.

Next came her mementoes of Richard. His thick blue tunic that had made him look so handsome and the bow and arrows he had used as a young boy. As she stared at these reminders of her family, memories flooded through her mind and her eyes began to prick with tears.

So absorbed was she by this task that Ghislaine did not hear the door open and she jumped a foot off the bed in surprise.

"So, lady. I take it you are restored and suffer no ill effects?"

Ghislaine whirled round, her anger mounting. "I am like to be lighter without food or clothes. You have kept me prisoner in my own home and I would like to know the reason." Her eyes glinted with fury as they rested on the object of her dislike.

She stood before him, hands on hips, dressed in a thin, well-patched chemise that had been clearly made for a smaller girl. Looking for all the world like a woman possessed, Ghislaine's thick red-gold curls tumbled over her shoulders in abandon and her eyes, dark and accusing, bore into him. Guy was rendered silent as he looked at the angry figure of his wife. His eyes were drawn to the chemise and he was certain that she could have no idea how worn the material was. It hid nothing from him, for he could see the clear outlines of her generous curves. His mouth dried at the sight.

"The reason? I had no desire to waste another day in the forest searching for you." He watched as she saw the direction of his eyes and the sudden rosy flush that stained her cheeks. Hastily she bent to snatch a blanket and all but disappeared under it. Her eyes narrowed accusingly as a lazy grin broke his scowl.

"I did not ask it of you," she replied bitterly her embarrassment diminishing. "I had merely gone to the forest to talk to Edwin." She paused. "Did you find the men?"

He shook his head. "Only a body, but that could tell us naught." He slumped down on the bed and eased his boots from his feet. "The forest is dangerous. Was your father not murdered there last year?"

"Aye, but we had never felt in danger before. My father would often go hunting and never come to any trouble."

Guy looked up then, alert, watching her fiddle with the edge of the blankets. "You doubt something?"

Ghislaine shook her head slightly. "It's nothing much, except that fewer attacks had happened here of late. We had thought the outlaws had moved further north for the richer pickings. There are never many travellers round here."

What she said made sense with the information he had managed to gather so far. Perhaps the girl's wits were not so addled as he had thought. "How many men were with him?"

"Three men-at-arms and Peter Staveley." The accusing tone in her voice made him frown. "They were all killed."

"Peter Staveley? Kinsman to Margaret?" His eyes held hers.

Ghislaine just nodded. It had been no more than an unfortunate coincidence, she was certain.

"And no one was ever caught?" Guy's voice had taken on a speculative tone.

"Nay. The Earl did not seem much concerned, although Walter spent many days investigating."

"Walter?" He sensed a softening of her voice when she mentioned the name.

"De Belleme," she finished. "He was a...friend of the family."

His eyes bore into her as she stammered out the last sentence. It was clear that he was more than a family friend. "He found nothing?"

She shook her head. "He believed the outlaw was Thomas Bollyngton and his men, but there has been no sight of them these many months."

"I have heard that name before, but who is this Walter de Belleme?" His dark face was now harsh and the dark scowl had returned. Whoever the man was, he would not be bothering his wife again.

"I told you. He was...is a family friend. He is close to the Earl and has an estate some ten miles to the north of here. He visited frequently after his wife died."

Guy digested this information in silence. So far the man had made no attempt to contact Ghislaine, unless she had lied and had ridden out to meet him in the forest yesterday. It would be interesting to see the man that had seemingly captured his wife's heart.

His eyes strayed around the gloomy chamber. In truth, there was not much to see. The tapestries on the walls were darkened and frayed, and the two seats before the fire were old and wobbly. There were no rugs nor floor coverings save the rushes, but these were sweet-smelling. Noticing the chest was open and that some fripperies lay on the bed, Guy stood up and sauntered closer.

"Is this yours?" He picked up the box.

Ghislaine looked at his unshod feet with contempt. "Nay. Richard used that before he went to foster."

"Richard? Another friend of the family?"

She shook her head before snatching the bow from his hands. "My brother."

The pain in her voice was there for all to hear, and Guy was not impervious to it. He watched her jerky movements as she stuffed her pathetic belongings back into the chest.

"How did he die?"

"Against the Welsh. He was caught in an ambush nigh on a year now." The words she uttered sounded like a sharp rebuke, but Guy had heard too many bereaved mothers and widows to be fooled.

"You miss him?"

Ghislaine looked at him then, before nodding her reply. The dark face was not scowling, but was softer than she had ever seen it before. "He was the only one who ever talked to me." The words were said simply but with such feeling that Guy almost gave into his instinct to soften a little towards her. But comfort was not what his wife needed.

"Was he a better shot than you?" Guy indicated the bow.

Ghislaine struggled for a moment about the impropriety of admitting she could use one more than adequately. "Absolutely not."

Guy's lips twisted in an attempt to repress a smile. "Maybe I should be enlisting you to my army."

Ghislaine could not help a tiny smile from breaking her resistance, for she was not proof against the most dazzling smile she had ever seen in a man. The blue eyes were alight and his teeth were perfect. Helene had been right, for underneath all that hair her husband was very handsome.

For a moment their eyes locked and Ghislaine found that her heart began to beat faster. She also found that her stomach began to protest loudly.

To her profound consternation, Guy just laughed. "I think your punishment has lasted long enough, lady. I bid you come to the hall to break your fast."

Mortified by her stomach and by his humiliating reaction, Ghislaine glared at him, her cheeks pink.

"Do you wish me to parade myself as I am?" she hissed. "Or will you return my clothes?"

Guy pulled her drabbest tunic from under his cloak and threw it at her, his expression blank once again. He was most changeable in his mood this husband of hers. "I will give you this one...gown, the others when I see fit."

Ghislaine stared at him open-mouthed. "So I am still a prisoner?" She did not think she could contain her anger.

He looked at her and raked his hands through his black hair. "You have been more trouble these last few days than my entire army. I doubt that either of us will survive."

He looked so perplexed that Ghislaine felt immense satisfaction, but it lasted only seconds.

"You will not leave the manor walls without my

permission first and only then accompanied by two of my men-at-arms. And do not think you will be able to smile your way out, for your men have been warned that should you ever slip out again the guard responsible will be hanged.'' He returned her defiant stare with a tight-lipped observation. ''You will obey me in this.''

''I do not understand,'' she began. ''Why must I leave with your men? If it is a question of safety, my men have always protected me.'' Ghislaine raised her chin a little, defying him to challenge her words.

''Precisely because they are your men,'' he retorted, taking a step closer to her. ''I need to be sure of your safety and your...loyalty.''

His meaning was not lost on her. ''Loyalty!'' she spat. ''I am not at all sure what I am supposed to be loyal to as your treatment of me hardly deserves my unquestioned obedience either.''

Why those words had slipped out, Ghislaine had no idea, but they propelled her husband into action. She suddenly found her wrist gripped by an iron fist and pulled into a solid chest. He smelled of the forest and horses, and it was not as awful as she had thought. His free hand came to rest under her chin and her head pushed back as he looked deep into her eyes.

''I had thought that you preferred the convent to the pleasures of the flesh, lady, but if you wish me to make you truly my wife, it can be arranged.'' His shadowed face lowered menacingly as he pulled her body flat against his. There was nothing between them now save a few layers of cloth. Breathing seemed to have ceased for both of them, and it was with great difficulty that Ghislaine managed to draw back a little.

"Take your hands off me, you great brute. I do not deserve this treatment."

"Do not deserve this? Lady, you push your luck." As he looked down at her, his eyes caught hers again and he could feel her soft curves pressing into his body. His body responded as if it had been lit on fire, but this time Guy de Courcy could not fight it, nor did he want to.

His lips touched hers with a softness she did not expect. They brushed her mouth again and then, without warning, his hand slid up to the back of her neck and lifted her mouth to his. Ghislaine found her lips being stormed relentlessly, his lips moving possessively over hers, exploring, tasting. His other hand lowered to pull her hips tighter to his, and Ghislaine could hardly breathe, her pulse racing.

Dazed by such strange sensations shooting through her body, she was powerless to deny his tongue the access it was demanding. Somehow, instead of pushing him away, her hands had curled around the nape of his neck, her fingers entwined in the thick, black locks, allowing her body even greater intimacy with his. Her mind was sent spiralling off into a world of darkness and sweet pleasure whilst his tongue danced with hers. Leaning even closer into him, Ghislaine felt his hand slide lower, caressing and squeezing, pulling her even tighter to him.

With a silent groan, Guy pushed her roughly away. He had been carried away by the sweetness of her response, and by the soft invitation offered unwittingly by her body. He closed his eyes remembering the feel of her, remembering her racing heartbeat, the shy touch of her fingers on his neck. Lust. Pure, simple lust. It was no more than that, he reminded himself as he put his confused wife at arm's length.

"Truly it would be easy to take you right now, lady, but unfortunately I have more pressing engagements elsewhere."

Ghislaine's cheeks fired with humiliation and confusion, for he spoke true. Had he carried on with this magic she would have surrendered with no real struggle. That he should dismiss her so lightly was very cruel.

"You are nothing but a scheming, stinking brute with no regard for anything but your own ambitions." Her true feelings were written on her face as she turned her back to him and attempted to get some control over her shaking body.

"Were you so perfect, lady, you would not have been...ah...available." His cruel response brought a sudden desire to fight back.

"Had you not captured me for your own evil ends, I might have married elsewhere. Despite what you think, my lord, I am not totally without attraction."

"And who was this paragon that so timed his absence to coincide with your wedding?"

The jibe came very close to the mark and Ghislaine tried hard to ward off the tears.

"His name is unimportant, for I will never be able to marry him. He is all that is good and kind, and is able to make me laugh. He listens to me," she finished in anger. "And he is barbered regularly," she added for good measure.

"Let me warn you, lady. If I find you alone with this man, or any other man, then I will surely kill you before you ever reach the convent."

Ghislaine stared at his retreating back as he left the bedchamber. The man was not destined for a long life.

The midday meal was a silent affair, enlivened only by d'Everard's light-hearted flirtation with Effie. Guy sat in sullen silence and Ghislaine followed suit, determined not to engage in conversation with her husband unless absolutely necessary. Their mood was visited on the rest of the men and servants who took their meal there, and conversation between them was unusually quiet.

Ghislaine took little interest in the spicy pottage or meats that were served, preferring the simple bread and cheese that was her usual fare.

"You do not drink the ale today, Lady Ghislaine?" Sir Arnaud's blue eyes twinkled at her in amusement.

Ghislaine gave him a withering look and proceeded to sip at the water. "Do not let my preference inhibit your own, Sir Arnaud. Our ale has a good reputation for its flavour. Sir Brian can vouch for it, at any rate."

"Aye, I have noticed." He glanced briefly at the worthy Sir Brian. "My compliments to your brewer, my lady. And the food is more than acceptable." Arnaud's blond head turned to Guy. "As your husband has done naught but fill his mouth since our arrival, you must regard it as total approbation. It is not often he is so silent over his food."

That dig earned Arnaud a black scowl which caused him to laugh. "Do not mind his lack of manners, Lady Ghislaine. It is not meant personally."

"I am most gratified to hear it, Sir Arnaud. I had been losing sleep over the matter, you can be sure."

Her words were delivered with such a haughty tone, that even Sir Brian blinked hard.

Arnaud noticed his friend's lips tighten at that retort and watched him thoughtfully for a moment or two as Guy sank his teeth into the sweet curd tartlets. He recalled that it had been a long time since Guy had relaxed enough to eat such food, and though his mood was rather sour at the moment, Arnaud had observed a general lightening of his usually sober spirit. Perhaps it had something to do with this new wife, since the man was constantly watching her when she was not looking and irritable when she was not in sight. He had been ready to kill the guards ere he found out she had left the manor yesterday.

"I am sure we would welcome the chance to visit your kitchen and buttery so that we could thank your people ourselves." Arnaud smiled at her with such sincerity that Ghislaine could not turn him down.

"Of course. Should you wish to make your preferences known, then please tell me. I will do all I can to make you feel comfortable." Ghislaine addressed her sarcasm to her husband, but he appeared not to hear her. The oaf was biting into his third tartlet. An oaf with a sweet tooth, then.

When the meal was ended Ghislaine did as she was commanded and led the way to the buttery. It was a small, dark room off the great hall filled with wooden barrels and the sour smell of brewing ale.

"We brew twice a month," she began, "depending upon our stocks. There are not often visitors or travellers here, but there is not much else for the men to do."

"And your wine, lady? Do you make your own?"

Guy glanced around the room but could see no evidence of the wine. "Or perhaps you have drunk it all?" His grin was positively childlike and Ghislaine swept past him with her nose in the air and a disdainful sniff.

The tour of the kitchen and the gardens passed without incident, with Guy relieved that his wife did not choose to display her venom before her people. At least she could be reasonable, although he did not trust her. Ghislaine was probably the same as all the other women he had known, but as yet had not shown her true colours. She was, in fact, most knowledgeable about the running of the manor and the estate, answering his questions quietly and thoughtfully, and he was impressed with her quick understanding.

As they approached the blacksmith's hut in the bailey, Arnaud was summoned to settle a dispute between two of the men. Ghislaine watched the heated fight with barely concealed dismay.

"There is something I have been meaning to discuss, Sir Guy. Since your men have had several days to adjust to living at Chapmonswiche," she began uneasily, "I would like to point out that their behaviour within the manor leaves much to be desired." She lifted her chin more firmly. "They are noisy and untidy and my servants have had cause to complain on several occasions. I would be grateful if you could perhaps discuss the matter with Sir Arnaud."

Guy stared at her. "My men are trained soldiers. I have noticed no deterioration in their behaviour. Besides," he added stiffly, "as far as I am concerned, it is my men who seem to be plagued by your women. You would be better advised to discuss the matter with

Sir Brian, I think, although the poor man appears to be overly stretched.''

"Poor man!" Her temper exploded. "He is lucky to have lived so long, for I have often been tempted to add to the ale he is so fond of."

At those meaningful words Guy burst out laughing, the anger between them dissipating. It was a deep, attractive sound that had many of the men turning to look at them. "And what prevented you?"

"Father Thomas did not think it would aid my case with God." Her lips had formed a tight line.

Her indignant reaction brought another burst of laughter from him and this time it was impossible to ignore such an infectious sound without grinning ever so slightly.

"I take it that Father Thomas lives close by to ensure that men continue to survive your ale?"

"He does. If you wish to avail yourself of his services, he will come on Friday to hold mass."

"I fear my soul is beyond redemption," he sighed.

"You are not alone in that supposition, my lord." The words were delivered with such arch haughtiness that Guy was rendered speechless once again.

Deciding that retreat was her best policy, Ghislaine flounced off towards the hall, leaving her husband pondering her last sentence.

As he watched her leave, Guy's mouth curved into a broad smile. The woman was spirited, there was no doubt about it. Nor did she mince words and that pleased him too. What else caught his attention was the way her hair glinted in the sun and, despite what he had told Arnaud, he found it most attractive. In fact, Guy was beginning to find himself increasingly looking out for her whenever he was near the keep. Memories of her fragrant white skin and soft lips crowded his thoughts far more often than he would have thought possible. He raked his hair back from his forehead. No matter that his mind insisted he did not want this woman, his body told him otherwise. And that was a problem.

Chapter Seven

"I see him, Lady Ghislaine," squealed Effie in delight as she leaned from the window of the hall. Her plumply pretty body was wedged into the narrow opening as she strained to watch the men training in the bailey.

"He would not thank you for embarrassing him before Sir Guy's men," replied Ghislaine tartly as she laboriously stitched new blankets for the men. The completed heap did not seem so large and they had been sewing for days. A heavy sigh from the window caused Ghislaine to look up.

"Perhaps you are right. He has taken a hit. Do you think he noticed me?" The hopeful note in her voice caused Ghislaine to smile to herself.

"Edwin could not fail to notice you since you have been hanging out of that window and making enough noise to attract the attention of the whole manor." The reprimand was received with a pout as Effie flounced to her seat.

Guy had spent the past few days training the men hard, with daily sword practice, body fighting and mock jousting. Ghislaine had seen little of him save at meals; even then he was too tired to communicate more than the bare minimum.

She supposed he was sleeping with his men in the keep for he had not returned to her bedchamber. It should have pleased her since he was keeping to his word, but Ghislaine knew that his lack of attention irritated her and she could not for the life of her think why. The fact that she thought of him at all was annoying for the man was no more than a common outlaw.

Taking pity on Effie and determined to escape the confines of the walls, Ghislaine decided to brave her husband's wrath. Elfrieda needed some herbs, and the first shoots were already looking strong. The weather was cold but fine and it would be an ideal morning to go to the forest. Putting down her sewing in relief, Ghislaine went to put on her cloak.

"I doubt it will last another winter," she said, staring at it ruefully, her fingers searching the material for other holes. Had she not said the same last spring?

"That's what Sir Guy said about it, too." Effie's mumbled statement took Ghislaine completely by surprise.

"He said that? When?"

"The other day when he was looking at your things."

"Why was he doing that?"

Effie looked up from her sewing, a frown on her face. "He didn't say."

Ghislaine shrugged her shoulders as she slipped the cloak around her. It did not matter that the cold would seep through the thin layers of wool for she was desperate to walk in the fresh forest and breathe the pure air. At least there she could be herself.

"Come. With all this training, maybe Sir Guy will look favourably on a request to go to the forest?" Ghislaine raised her eyebrows in a question, and Effie, after a moment or two's hesitation, smiled her acceptance.

The bailey was awash with men and their war paraphernalia, and the two women had to dodge between swords and lances to reach Guy de Courcy. Ghislaine found her eyes drawn to the tall, dark-haired figure in the centre of the yard. Her husband was fighting in hand-to-hand combat with a massive blond warrior.

Dressed only in his braies, Guy de Courcy was a magnificent sight. His skin, Ghislaine noticed in embarrassment, shone nut-brown under the weak March sun. Taut muscles rippled in his arms and shoulders as he drove the stick up and down with agile determination. Long strands of his thick black hair trailed down his back as he lunged forward into attack, and she wondered what it would feel like to touch his bare skin. Her cheeks blushed with the sin of such thoughts and Ghislaine sternly reminded herself that she was bound for the convent.

As she approached the men somewhat apprehensively, Ghislaine sensed their eyes on her. Arnaud d'Everard, courteous as ever, was the only friendly face in the crowd. He, at least, managed a passable smile although, from the blush on Effie's cheeks, Ghislaine was not absolutely certain that it was meant for her.

At her bidding, the lanky youth she now knew as Raoul ran to inform Guy that Ghislaine wished to see him. From the grim expression on his face as he strode towards her, Ghislaine half wished that she had waited until he had finished his fight. Steeling herself against his irritation, she decided to try a different tack.

"A lovely day, Sir Guy," she began brightly. His expression remained implacable as the blue eyes stared at her with polite disdain. In one hand he carried his crumpled tunic but had clearly dismissed the idea of putting it on to save her blushes. Embarrassed to look at him, Ghislaine turned to look at the men who continued to practise. "You have been training them hard. Are you preparing for any particular target?"

"Should Margaret Staveley's relatives decide to pay me a visit to settle the score, there seems good reason for being well prepared. I am sure that the Earl also has plans which will require my services sooner or later," he replied stiffly. "Gratifying though it is," he continued, "I am sure that concern for my men was not the reason you asked to see me."

The expression on his face was not encouraging, but Ghislaine was determined to get her way this time.

"You are right, my lord. The truth is that the kitchens require some vital herbs and that I am in sore need of some fresh air in the forest." She looked at him then. "You said I could not leave the manor save with an escort of your choice." Ghislaine eyed him with a defiant toss of her braids.

Despite his irritation at having his practice curtailed, Guy could not deny the truth in her words.

"Herbs at this time of the year?" he queried suspiciously.

"Aye. There are a few near the stream." She did not like the scowl that was deepening on his face.

"Where I found you last time you made a foray beyond the manor?"

Realising the track of his thoughts, Ghislaine's spirits plummeted. She nodded her head with grudging resignation, knowing that she would be returning to the growing pile of sewing.

"I will take you myself."

Ghislaine was so surprised at his words that she was rendered speechless for a moment.

"You do not trust me." Her cheeks coloured in indignation.

"Nay, but then I find few women trustworthy," he replied flatly, wiping his brow with his tunic. "However, I am still prepared to accompany you."

Ghislaine gave him a withering look as she swept towards the stables. She would have to be content with his company then. Strangely she did not find that thought as distasteful as she had imagined, but it did make her feel rather nervous. Anyone, she decided, would be foolish indeed not to feel apprehensive in such company.

The ride to the forest was a pleasant one, despite Ghislaine's misgivings about her husband and the fact that he would not let Effie accompany them. When he joined her at the stables, the man had at least had the grace to put on his tunic and cloak so that her heart did not thump so fast as before. He rode before her on his destrier and thankfully made no attempt at conversation. The two men-at-arms who accompanied them rode behind her.

The sun had reached its high point by the time the party reached the forest and to Ghislaine's consternation her stomach began to protest at having been denied food for so long.

"I hear that you are in need of sustenance, lady."

Ghislaine glared at him, her chin high. How could he mention such things? The man was really an ignorant oaf.

"Perhaps we should sit and eat. I persuaded Elfrieda to pack some bread and cheese. An interesting woman, that." He signalled to his men to draw to a halt.

The demands of her stomach got the better of her and Ghislaine agreed with a curt nod. Elfrieda's acquiescence to packing any food was most strange. Not for the first time did she wonder at her husband's powers of persuasion. He had very little difficulty with other women, it seemed. They dismounted at a clearing by the stream and much to her surprise, her husband placed his cloak on the ground for her to sit on.

"There is no need to spoil your fine cloak to protect mine," she pointed out prosaically.

Guy straightened up and smiled at her lazily. "I was thinking more of your health than your gowns."

Such a nicety of manners wrongfooted her completely and Ghislaine could feel the blush stealing over her cheeks. Again! Was she never to remain normal before the man! Mumbling her thanks she sat down at his command and took the food he offered.

"Your wardrobe is not extensive, lady. Have you a dislike of gowns or do you prefer running around like a village hoyden?"

His softly spoken words caused her to cough violently and Ghislaine was glad that Guy had had the foresight to send his men-at-arms on guard out of earshot.

"There is not much call for finery hereabouts. Practicality is of far greater importance." Even to her ears she sounded very righteous, but nevertheless she was not going to admit her father's meanness to one such as this.

"A very commendable attitude which gladdens my heart, lady, as well as my purse. I do not relish spending on feminine fripperies unnecessarily."

Ghislaine peered at him, uncertain whether she had detected a note of sarcasm in his voice. He had stretched himself out at her side, his head propped by his hand, his eyes watching her carefully. His eyes, she noticed, were a wonderful blue, a summer-sky blue.

"I had not realised that my wardrobe held any interest for you." The words came out a little muffled as she had just bitten into a small loaf of grey bread.

He looked at her with interest as she gazed into the depths of the forest, long red wisps of hair escaping from the repressive braids she favoured. She was not pretty exactly, but there was something there that made him want to watch her. And he liked the way she chewed with such obvious relish. Remembering then those soft curves of her body caused a warmth to flood through his veins that had naught to do with the sun.

"Anything that is mine interests me," he replied finally with such an arrogant tone that her cheeks flushed in indignation.

"I may have been part of your agreement with the Earl," she retorted tartly, "but I do not consider myself to be yours." Her eyes were suddenly alive with contempt. "You promised to send me to the convent."

Guy paused in surprise at such a bitter outburst. It would seem that his wife had still not accustomed herself to her status. Yet with one look at her flushed cheeks and dark, glowering eyes he realised, rather belatedly, that she probably did not deserve such treatment as she had received at his hands.

"I always keep my promises," he replied somewhat gruffily.

"That is so reassuring."

"You still have not answered my question," he prompted mildly, his blue eyes holding her gaze. Ghislaine almost felt that she was being held by force and then gently freed as he turned his attention to the handful of nuts at the bottom of his pouch.

"Oh." It was suddenly hard to concentrate as her pulse began to quicken.

"Your gowns," Guy reminded her with a perplexed smile.

"Aye," she stuttered. "Well, I dare say your knowledge of appearance is far greater than mine." The contemptuous look she offered him as she looked over his attire caused his lips to twist into a grin.

"Most women seem to spend a great deal of their time and men's money on clothes," he remarked rather cynically.

"I have no need of them for there is rarely anyone to see me in them," she shot back suddenly. Her irritated silence and tightly drawn lips told him not to press the point.

As Ghislaine brushed the crumbs from her lap, Guy rose to fill his water bag from the stream. His stride was long and easy and she found her eyes drawn to his retreating figure. He was tall, much taller than her

father or even Walter, and she admitted to liking the
way his dark hair trailed down over his shoulders in
a thick, black mane. Somehow it gave him an aura of
pagan strength that made her shiver.

"How long have you been living here?" The question was so unexpected that Ghislaine had to pull her
thoughts back to reality.

"About eight summers. My father was given the
village by Hugh d'Avranches for his services in Normandy. We were sent for shortly after."

Guy passed her the water pouch and Ghislaine
gratefully accepted. The cold water trickled down her
throat.

"Do you desire to return to Normandy?" he prod-
ded, his eyes roving over her face. He found the freckles rather endearing.

Ghislaine shook her head. "I remember little about
it. This is my home." A gleam of pride lit up her eyes
and Guy felt oddly touched by it. There was precious
little wealth here and the girl barely had enough rags
to cover her back, and yet she wished to stay.

"Have you other family?" Guy remembered that
Hugh d'Avranches had been her guardian, so it was
unlikely.

"Not that I know of," she dismissed lightly. "And
if I had, I doubt if they would be much interested in
having an extra burden placed on them."

"Ah," he began, the light clearly dawning in his
mind. "Hence the convent."

She shrugged her shoulders dismissively, unable to
look him fully in the eye. The man was sitting so close
to her that she could feel the warmth of him, smell
him even. It was decidedly uncomfortable as she was

unable to think straight and would have risen to leave
had a large, tanned hand not clamped down on her
arm to prevent her.

"Is my company so awful?" He paused for a moment to clear his throat. "I am not used to speaking
with ladies and I had not meant to cause you upset.
My words are perhaps too blunt."

Expecting to see amusement glittering in those blue
eyes, Ghislaine looked directly into them, a sharp retort on her lips. But what she saw there made her
hesitate. It was a genuine admission of weakness without any hint of sarcasm. Guy was so close that she
could see the tiny scars of battle on his face and the
way his newly shaven chin was already growing dark.
Lines of fatigue were etched lightly round his mouth
and darker circles below his eyes.

"Awful?" she repeated with difficulty. Her throat
seemed to have constricted. "Nay. I...I...am not used
to you," Ghislaine blurted out quickly. "As for the
rest, I think I prefer the truth."

Guy looked up to watch the darkening clouds gather
above. He suddenly turned his face towards her and
placed a forefinger below her chin, forcing Ghislaine
to look at him.

"If I have treated you badly," he began gruffly, "I
apologise, for you deserved none of it." He drew in
a deep breath, as if drawing courage from it. "I would
not send you from your home unless you truly wish
it. Will you think about it?"

The unexpected question hung in the air between
them as their eyes locked together. Ghislaine could
feel her heart pounding faster beneath her cloak as his
finger moved to push back some of the wisps of hair

that floated across her face. Warmth from an unknown source crept through her body as his finger traced a gentle path along her chin. Had he tried to kiss her, she would have pushed him away and stormed off, but he did no such thing and she was not proof against that deep, gruff voice asking so simple a question.

"Why?" Her voice was almost a whisper as she looked into the fathomless blue of his eyes.

Guy ignored the question as he did not rightly know the answer himself. Because she was an innocent? Because he had changed the course of her life? He had known what he was doing when he started this and it had not bothered him then. Somehow this girl with the sharp tongue and her red hair had gotten under his skin. He had no desire to hurt her further and if he could repair some of the damage, then he would.

"I do not believe that you have a vocation." His eyebrow was raised in question, a grin lurking about his lips.

Ghislaine returned his grin with a reproving sniff.

"You do not know me at all, Sir Guy."

His laughter at such a proud response drew a twitch from Ghislaine's lips.

"I can see why the Earl was keen to rid himself of such responsibility, for you and your tongue are more trouble than a besieged keep." Guy watched as she laughed at that. It was a husky, most attractive sound that pleased him greatly.

Ghislaine smiled at the thought of proud Hugh d'Avranches being bedevilled by herself. "My father was of the same opinion. He would, no doubt, have approved of you."

There was not a trace of vanity in her, no coy looks

nor angling for pretty words. Guy felt the tension slide from him as he stretched out on his back, his hands behind his head and closed his eyes. "I doubt that," he said soberly. "According to Hugh d'Avranches, John de Launay was an honourable knight of great courage and honesty."

Ghislaine stared down at the body lying at her side. In repose he looked younger, less…threatening. Aye, that was the word. She drew her legs up against her chest and wrapped her arms around them as she thought then of her father. Well? Would he have approved of this outlaw and mercenary?

"Did you do all those things you are supposed to have done?" She was suddenly curious about this murderer who could laugh and tease her like any brother.

"Some." His answer was delivered with complete indifference and Ghislaine realised that she was heading for difficult waters. She could not stop now.

"Did you kill Margaret?"

He sat up at that, his eyes upon her. After a moment or two, Guy shook his head slowly. "No." It was such a simple word, uttered with complete finality. And she wanted to believe him.

"Will you tell me?"

Guy sighed and shrugged his shoulders, his fingers busy picking twigs off his cloak. "After I left her keep, I received a false message to finish a siege near Stafford. In the mood I was in, it was a very welcome distraction. As it happened, it provided the perfect cover for the real criminals."

Behind the seemingly indifferent words, Ghislaine could sense the anger and resentment that had taken hold of him, that threatened to eat him from the inside. She found herself wanting to believe him.

"But why did you not leave England and go back to your home in Normandy?" Guy's shoulders were stiff and unrelenting as he tossed the twigs away to the side of him.

"My living, and that of my men, depends on the strength of my reputation. People are quick to condemn without hearing all the facts," he added on a bitter note. "Besides, there is nothing in Normandy for me. This is as good a place as any."

Ghislaine wondered at that. For a man of his worth and skill there would always be someone willing to open their arms to him. And yet Margaret had not. Margaret. Sweet, gentle Margaret.

"Why did you choose Margaret as a wife?" As soon as she had spoken the words, Ghislaine regretted them but could not unsay them. She returned his gaze with steady eyes. For a moment she thought he would not answer, but then she remembered his habit of thinking carefully.

"I needed a wife," he said simply. "I was tired of bad food, cold pallets and stinking clothes." A wry grimace fleetingly touched his lips. "Margaret Staveley seemed to fulfil my requirements." His lips tightened into a straight line. "Unfortunately it would seem that I did not fulfil hers."

It was the words he did not say that tugged at her heart. Despite his gruff, cool exterior, the man was capable of feelings and desires just as the next. There was something about the way he stared sightlessly into the distance that made her want to put her hand on his arm. For comfort.

"And now?" She stole a look at his hardened face which once more sported his scowl.

"Now?" Guy turned slowly to look at her, his eyes colder than the winter sea. "Now I must fight to protect my name and to win back what is rightfully mine. I paid more than one thousand marks for a manor which now resides in the hands of Henry Dettingham with the blessing of the King's men."

For a moment, Ghislaine was uncertain whether Guy was upset more because of the loss of his one thousand silver marks than the loss of his reputation. And yet such admissions had shown her a different side to him. A side that she found vulnerable and human, and had wanted to trust.

"My father would have said exactly the same," she sighed as she stood to shake the crumbs from her lap. "I am sure you would have understood each other well."

"And why do I feel that was not altogether a compliment?" he responded mildly, gathering up his cloak.

"You fire the same black looks at anyone who displeases you," she ventured, a delicate brow raised in disdain.

"We have both been plagued by the same wench," came his instant retort.

Ghislaine smiled at him then, encouraged by his lightening mood. "That," she pointed out, "does not sound like a compliment either, my lord."

The forest was cool and smelled of the fresh mixture of decaying earth and budding greenery and Ghislaine found herself smiling as they made their way to the herbs that grew near the stream. Guy asked her many questions about the estate and the land about, showing her another side to his character. His manners might be lacking most of the time but his wits were not. The man knew much more about running a manor than she had imagined. She was curious about him.

"Do you have family, Sir Guy?" Ghislaine stooped to pick at the herbs carefully.

"Aye. Three brothers in Normandy."

Encouraged by his lack of aggression, Ghislaine looked up. "You must miss them."

A veil seemed to draw down over his face at that and she knew she was stepping on stony ground. Ghislaine knew the answer before his lips formed it.

"I never think of them."

As she tugged at the difficult stem, Guy handed her his knife. It was a handsome hunter's knife with an ivory handle chased in gold. She took it with a grateful smile.

"Never?"

Guy looked at the knife in her hands. "Keep the knife. You may have need of it."

She nodded silently. This was certainly a different side to her husband.

"Do you ever think of your brother?" He had sidestepped her question with an irritating lack of conscience, but Ghislaine wondered why. She stored the information for another time.

"A lot of the time I talk to him. As if he were still here," she added. That was something she had never admitted to anyone. Not even Margaret. "We were close."

Guy nodded at that, his dark hair glinting in the shafts of green-flecked light that filtered through the trees. He was watching the depths of the forest with half-closed eyes. Ghislaine considered the stern set of his mouth as she put the herbs in her pouch.

"So you have no one left?" His eyes had switched to her face and for some reason Ghislaine could not bring herself to look at him.

"Not now that Margaret is dead."

The words seemed to echo on the still air between them. She had not meant to say them, but something deep within her forced them out.

"Margaret? You knew her?" Guy's face was very still, his eyes boring deep into her.

"Of course. She was married to my brother before Peter Staveley. They had been wed only a few months before his death. Peter was a friend of my father's. That was how he met her." The words trailed off as Guy stood squarely before her.

"You did not know?" The words came out almost as a whisper. Then a thought struck her. "You are not in the least concerned about who you marry?"

His grim face lightened a little at the scandalised tone in her voice. "It was not quite that bad. Arnaud had looked into her background and found nothing amiss. I had planned to find out more from the lady herself."

His words were a little defensive and Ghislaine was intrigued. "Are you always so careless when you woo a lady?"

"It's not something I do every day," he admitted, a smile lurking on his lips. Her raised eyebrow told him what she thought of his methods.

"My lord, has anyone told you that offering your worldly goods to an unknown, or abducting an innocent and forcing them into marriage is not the usual way to go about these things?''

''Oh? Do you recommend a better method?'' Ghislaine saw the humour glinting in his eyes.

''Well I have not had much personal experience in these matters, of course, but ladies like to think that they have a certain attraction, of course.''

''Of course,'' came the grave response. ''I can see how badly I have erred.'' He smiled down at her, and Ghislaine held her breath. When he looked at her like that the man truly had no need for words. ''Have you any other advice?''

''Aye,'' she said tartly. ''Attempting to beat a woman is no way to curry their favour.''

As she bent down to pick up more herbs, his hand pulled her up again. His eyes roved over her face and she detected a gentleness that she had not seen before.

''I did not mean to hurt you, girl.''

She did not want his sympathy or his pity.

''My name is Ghislaine. That would be a start.''

Guy watched her flounce off, and he smiled to himself. Maybe he had been too hasty in his assessment of his wife.

By the time the party had reached the manor gates, they had been soaked in a sudden downpour. Despite her bedraggled appearance, Ghislaine's mood had lightened and the tension she had been feeling seemed to be slipping a little. Guy had ridden by her side and although he had not said much she sensed a thawing between them. At least he had not scowled. In fact, when he looked at her, Guy had this rather strange smile on his lips.

Looking down at her costume, Ghislaine realised rather belatedly that she did not appear in her best light. Her hair hung in sodden rats tails over her back and her cloak and gown resembled little more that dripping rags. A very feminine desire to look her best beset her. Preferring not to examine the cause of this desire, Ghislaine mentally went through the choice of gowns available to her. It was an exercise doomed from the start as Ghislaine knew deep down that there was nothing suitable.

"Ghislaine."

Shocked at hearing her own name from his lips, Ghislaine started. Her palfrey reacted in similar fashion and did not settle until Guy steadied her.

"I had no desire to startle you, lady." Back to normal, she thought wryly, but nothing could douse that small flame of cheer that began to burn when he spoke her name.

"Just deep in thought, Sir Guy."

Guy smiled at her use of his title. "I hope that you will join me this evening, lady. We have not supped together these past few nights and I believe that your company has been sorely missed."

He had not said that he had missed her company, but it was the next best thing. His eyes looked almost shyly into hers and what she saw there made her heart beat faster.

Warmth flooded through her as their horses drew to a halt alongside each other. Guy waved their escort through the manor gates and they were left alone. He picked up her wet hand and brought it to his lips. He pressed a gentle kiss on her frozen fingers and smiled at her. It was a smile that made her resistance to him weaken and her heart pound. It was a smile that promised much.

"My lord." One of Guy's men came running from within the gates. "We have visitors. They request your presence."

Ghislaine bit back the words of disappointment and turned her eyes to the gate. Whoever was there had very poor timing. She followed her husband across the moat.

"Walter!" He was the last person she had expected to see, although she had been willing him to come. And now he was here, she was suddenly very confused about her feelings. Ghislaine eyed her husband in a new light. She had witnessed a softer, more gentle man with humour and intelligence, but he was still her enemy. How could she have forgotten that? Divided feelings warred within her, for she belatedly realised that she had willingly let herself be won over by this enigmatic mercenary. What a fool she was.

Guy had dismounted at the same time as Ghislaine and had come to stand at her side. His cold expression told her that he knew the visitor's identity. Remembering his earlier threat, Ghislaine introduced the two men in as dutiful a voice as she could muster.

They eyed each other with dislike. Guy was a good head taller than Walter, his stormy blue eyes taking in every detail about the man his wife had confessed to loving. For a moment she saw him through Guy's eyes. Arrogant, disdainful and dressed like a peacock. But just for a moment. Those mutinous thoughts disappeared the minute Walter's gentle, friendly smile told her how relieved he was to find her still alive.

She felt contrition, for he was not to blame. Walter

de Belleme was as bound by convention as she. Defying the Earl could have been far worse for him than her marriage to Guy de Courcy. And she was pleased to see him. His short blond hair ruffled in the wind and his grey eyes told her what she wanted to know.

"I believe good wishes are due, Lady Ghislaine. Your marriage was most sudden. I came as soon as I was able."

Ghislaine ignored the snort that came from Guy's direction. She would have to be careful if Walter was to continue living. Despite his expertise with a sword, she did not doubt that her husband could overcome him should he put his mind to it.

"Greetings, Sir Walter. Your visit was most timely."

Walter's raised eyebrow and his rather pointed look at her sodden clothes told her what he thought of that. Flustered that she should be caught so out of looks, Ghislaine nervously suggested that he wait in the hall whilst Sir Guy and herself changed into more fitting attire.

She could feel Guy's eyes follow Walter's back as he made his way across the bailey. He had brought an escort of five men-at-arms and two knights she vaguely remembered seeing at the court. Had she been expecting a rescue party, Ghislaine thought wryly, she would have been sorely disappointed.

"I hope you remember my promise, lady." Guy's deep voice penetrated her thoughts. The charm and gentleness that he had displayed earlier were once again hidden beneath a black scowl, but Ghislaine was no longer fearful.

"I remember everything, my lord." Casting a disdainful look in his direction, Ghislaine lifted her chin and crossed the bailey, her dripping gown thrashing against her legs. She would not be gulled like a foolish child and at that moment she did not care what his reaction would be. That mercenary oaf had lumbered into her life and ruined her dreams. She had been the victim, not the other way round.

With such thoughts racing through her mind, Ghislaine flounced up the staircase to her chamber. It was not until she had peeled off the sopping gown that she belatedly remembered that Guy still had possession of her clothes. Her first reaction was to storm from the chamber and find him, to pour her anger over his shoulders. Her second was to remember to stay calm. It would benefit no one, least of all Walter, were she to stir her husband's temper. Irritated beyond all measure, Ghislaine threw herself onto the bed. She would have to ask Guy for suitable clothes.

Effie returned with her oldest, most threadbare gown of brown wool over her arm, her cheeks tinged pink with the humiliation her mistress would know. Ghislaine had spent her temper by rubbing her hair dry. As soon as she saw what Guy was giving her to wear, Ghislaine smiled to herself. Was he jealous? Was her oafish, scowling husband jealous of Walter? For a moment she wallowed in the delicious feeling of having two men fight for her attentions, before reality washed over her. Neither of them were interested in her for she had neither looks nor charm to recommend her. Hadn't she always known that?

Changed and coiffed, Ghislaine felt no less nervous than before, but her courage had returned. She would face her fate with bravery and she would save Walter.

A soft tapping at the door of her chamber did not cause her any concern. Thinking it was one of the servants, she bade them enter whilst she continued to adjust her braids.

"You are in better looks, Lady Ghislaine."

Ghislaine whirled round to see Walter standing before her, admiration beaming from his eyes. Or was it something else? The flicker of uncertainty must have registered, for Walter stepped forward in concern.

"Do not worry, lady. Your husband is in the stables still. I would not willingly cause you grief but I had to see you alone."

"Your concern does you much credit, my lord, but it is unfortunately a little tardy."

"You are upset," he began soothingly. "But I have come to rescue you, Ghislaine." Walter had closed the gap between them and his hands had risen to her arms. Gently he pulled her towards him.

Ghislaine stiffened. "And what makes you think I wish to be rescued, Sir Walter? I was married to Sir Guy before God. Naught can change that now."

There was no mistaking the accusing emphasis that Ghislaine had laid on that last word and Walter released her quickly. A look of acute distress flooded across his face.

"Aye. You are right to be angry, Ghislaine." His hand reached out to move a tendril of hair from her eyes, but she moved back to avoid his touch. Walter smiled wanly and pushed back his own perfect curls with a sigh. Why, she thought, did that movement look so contrived?

"I tried to stop the marriage," he murmured miserably, "but the Earl would not allow it."

Ghislaine eyed him uncertainly. She wanted to believe him, but so much had happened that she no longer knew whom to trust. At least Guy was open with his scorn and his anger.

"Why would you wish to anger the Earl with my rescue now?" Ghislaine almost held her breath as she waited for his reply.

Walter hesitated for a fraction of a second. "You would not need to be rescued," he began. "De Courcy is very likely to meet his end sooner rather than later. It is, after all, the price a mercenary pays. Dettingham and his men are sniffing round all the time. It won't be long before they catch up with him."

His words echoed in her head. She did not wish to be married to de Courcy, but nor did she wish him to die. "No."

Walter stared at her and for a moment, Ghislaine was sure she detected irritation in those soft grey eyes.

"Are you sure?" His hands covered her shoulders and began a gentle, rhythmic rubbing with his thumbs.

"Aye. He was not my choice, but I do not willingly wish his death, if I had understood you aright." She shook off his hands, her pleasure in seeing him again somewhat marred. "I thank you for your concern, Sir Walter, but I think it best you leave my chamber."

Tight-lipped, Walter nodded and left her without a sound. It was not until she heard his voice below that Ghislaine let out a sigh of relief. At least he was safe. But what of Guy? Was he safe? Somehow she did not think Walter would give up quite so easily, although she was sure that he was not interested in her any more. And if it was not her, then what was it?

Puzzled, Ghislaine left the chamber.

Chapter Eight

Ghislaine glared at the spindle and the mangled heap of raw wool in her lap with a malevolent eye and stood up. The distaff and wool swept to the floor as she retreated to the fire in the hall. Her patience and her temper had been much tried this past week since Walter's disastrous visit and Ghislaine was in no mood this morning for practising her limited skills in the art of spinning. Her ineptitude in such matters was widely lamented.

Several of Guy's churlish men were lounging noisily in the hall, gaming with dice or arm-wrestling and generally disturbing the peace and order that had always reigned in her home. Treating a particularly loud and discordant trio to one of her glacial stares, Ghislaine determined to tackle her husband about his men's general behaviour. She had continued to receive complaints from her women about their coarse language and lewd suggestions. Sighing with frustration, she turned back to the fire.

Talking to Guy de Courcy was another problem. Since Walter's mistimed appearance, she and her husband had barely exchanged more than a few words. Any rapprochement that might have existed between them had been well and truly shattered.

The meal that dreadful night had been a quiet, strained affair, with Walter and his knights attempting polite conversation whilst her husband had just scowled at them. Eventually his black mood had descended on the whole company and it had come as a relief when Walter had announced their immediate departure.

Ghislaine had retired to her chamber in silence, leaving her husband to pour his wrath on his own men. She had lain awake for hours, contemplating Walter's belief that Guy might be killed, and had finally come to the conclusion that as the de Courcy widow she would be richer than as John de Launay's heiress. Had that been the key to Walter's renewed interest in her? Ghislaine had grown stiff with cold and misery, torturing herself over her own naïvety. She had not wanted to believe it, but she had had to admit that Walter had not tried very hard to prevent her marriage to the mercenary.

And now? She was married to a man who was using her to clear his name, who scowled at the world, who was a murdering mercenary. But honest, voiced her inner conscience. He had always been truthful with her. He had never hidden his feelings or his reasoning in his dealings with her. No, she could not honestly wish for his death

"Lady Ghislaine?" Effie tapped her mistress gently on the shoulder.

"My pardon, Effie. I was woolgathering."

Effie cast a baleful eye in the direction of the spindle and the wool. "Aye," she said doubtfully. "And most of it on the rushes."

A loud guffaw from the direction of the noisy trio caused Effie's cheeks to flush a becoming shade of pink.

"There's a pedlar at the gates asking if we need aught. Can we allow him in?" Her eyes shone with eager anticipation.

They could do with the diversion and Ghislaine knew that many of the women would welcome the chance to purchase ribbon, needles and several other items so essential to the female mind. As Guy was out hunting, the responsibility lay on her shoulders. "Aye," she said finally. "Have him come to the hall."

The pedlar was unknown to them but not unwelcome for that. A small, thin man with straggly brown hair and one blind eye, he welcomed the bowl of pottage offered and drank a skin of ale with relish. Ghislaine noticed that as he ate and drank, his good eye was carefully observing the men and the surroundings.

"Have you come far?" she enquired. His observation was making her feel uneasy.

The man shook his head. "Not far," he responded pleasantly enough. "Spring is always a good time of year. You ladies is always keen to buy things to attract the eyes of the men."

His words were well meaning if a little crude. "Then we would not wish to delay you on your travels. Perhaps you would show us your wares?"

Correctly interpreting her desire for him to conclude his sales speedily, the pedlar quickly arranged his goods to advantage. Ghislaine had to admit that the array was enticing and soon found herself caught up in the excitement. She had need of a new comb and several new laces and took great pleasure in making her final choices. Her eye was also caught by the perfumed phials and trinkets which elicited such sighs of pleasure from the others. The hall was buzzing with the animated chatter of the women and their exclamations of delight over their purchases when in walked Guy de Courcy.

At first, Ghislaine did not notice his entry but a loud thumping on the table soon brought her attention to him.

"A word with you, lady," came his voice, loud and cold, across the hall. It seemed as if the entire crowd was holding its collective breath as Ghislaine headed towards the door. Flushed to her toes with the humiliation, Ghislaine faced her husband with tight lips.

"You wished to speak with me, my lord?"

Guy stood before her, his hands on his hips. It was not an encouraging posture, she decided.

"You are right, lady." His eyes had turned a dark blue and his skin was still pink from the chase. "I demand to know who gave permission to let the wretch in?"

Ghislaine stiffened. "I did. There seemed no harm…"

"No harm!" came the interruption. "Do you know him? Have you proof of his occupation?"

Ghislaine had to shake her head, and the suspicions she had initially harboured returned. The man had seemed unusually observant. "Perhaps you wish to share your concerns with me?" she suggested with as much dignity as she could muster.

"I had thought there would be little need to explain things to you, lady. But it seems I must. All Henry Dettingham needs is proof of my existence here and information about the number of men under my roof. The Earl's men have not yet materialised and we remain vulnerable to attack. Your lack of vigilance endangers every life within these walls. No stranger is to enter the gates of the manor without my express permission. Have I made myself clear?"

Had he spoken quietly, then Ghislaine might have been able to swallow her pride for what he said made sense. However, Guy de Courcy seemed unable to speak quietly and she was certain that everyone in the hall must have heard him, including the pedlar. Her humiliation was complete.

"You have made yourself perfectly clear, my lord. However, I would like to point out that the women, myself included, had need of several items offered by the pedlar and were glad of his presence. I take it we will be allowed to complete our purchases?" She eyed him with a mixture of humiliation and irritation.

"The other women may do so, but I am not aware that you have enough money to pay for your own items."

Ghislaine's cheeks burned at such treatment. "Sir Brian will…"

"Sir Brian will no longer be providing you with funds just to indulge your fancy whims, lady. I thought I had made it clear that I do not fritter hard-earned money on women's nonsense." His words left her speechless. Had she ever harboured any softer feelings towards the man, they were certainly destroyed now. Ghislaine lowered her eyes, determined not to let him see how much he had hurt her. Aye, the things were no more than indulgent fripperies, but he had deliberately made her look foolish.

"Very well, my lord. Sir Brian will send him on his way."

"See that he is gone by the time I return from the stables. I trust him not." So saying Guy stalked off towards the bailey leaving Ghislaine uncertain whether to cry or to attempt murder.

The pedlar left within the candle notch and Ghislaine retired to her room to lick her wounds. Her husband had been right; she had made a foolish error of judgement and it would not happen again. There had been no good reason why he should have upbraided her in such a high-handed manner, though, and the incident had upset her deeply. It would seem that she received less consideration than his squire. So much for his soft, gentle words of the week before.

A curt knock at the door caused her to stand quickly and wipe her eyes with her sleeve. So her husband had relented already! Well, if he thought her willing to take such treatment meekly, she was going to disabuse him right quickly.

When she yanked open the door to find Sir Arnaud d'Everard, however, her face must have betrayed her thoughts.

"I am sorry to disappoint you, my lady, but I have come to bring you some wine and company. I had thought you may have need of both." His smile was gentle and Ghislaine was not proof against it. She stood back to allow him entry. There would be no need of a chaperon with Sir Arnaud.

"Your charm is difficult to resist, Sir Arnaud," she returned. "'Tis more than a shame that so little seems to have rubbed off on Sir Guy."

He looked up at her sharply as he poured the wine into two goblets. "He has not had much charm in his life, lady. It is not surprising that he may seem harsh at times. He has much on his mind."

"He is often like a bear with a sore head," she retorted as she turned to look out of the window embrasure. "It is not at all easy to deal with him. My servants are terrified of him."

Sir Arnaud was silent as he handed her the wine.

"His temper can be sour, but he is a good man. It would be hard to find a more trustworthy friend."

"Aye. I'm sure that may be true for you, Sir Arnaud, but he does not view me in the same light," she replied doubtfully, turning back to look at him.

Arnaud laughed. "Now that, lady, seems most promising to me."

Ghislaine gave him a withering look. "He prefers not to view me at all," she continued. "Most of the time he avoids my company. When he does attempt conversation, more often than not it is to upbraid me in a most harsh manner."

The amusement had died from Sir Arnaud's eyes as he watched Ghislaine's spirit sink.

"Do not take it so badly, lady. It is just his way with ladies."

Ghislaine snorted her disgust before taking a soothing draught of sweet red wine. "He is naught but an oaf. It matters not to me that he lumps me with the rest of womankind, but I wish to be treated with more respect. He has control over my home, my servants, any money…everything. For the time that I have left here, I want…I want to be treated as if I mattered." She turned her back towards Sir Arnaud so that he would not notice the brightness of her eyes, nor the trembling of her chin.

"Lady, I am sorry for your distress, but mayhap I can relieve some of your troubles by way of explanation." He looked warily about but the room was empty.

Ghislaine turned to look at him, her mouth set in a hard line. "I will listen, Sir Arnaud, but I doubt you will change my mind."

Arnaud inclined his head and shrugged his shoulders. "Nay. But it might go some way to help you understand him better."

"Very well, but do not expect too much."

"He has never liked ladies much," he began hesitantly, and frowned at Ghislaine's responding sigh.

"His own mother left him at the age of three to run off with her lover. His father had some maggot in his head that the fault lay at Guy's feet and practically ignored him from then on."

"Guy?" she questioned. "How can a three-year-old be responsible for that?"

Arnaud shook his head. "Guy was a difficult child whose boisterous behaviour had caused disagreements between his parents. His mother was a gentle creature apparently who resisted her husband's attempts to discipline the child. It would seem his father was a harsh man who beat Guy and his three brothers frequently. When he was seven, Guy was sent to be fostered as squire under the wings of Lord Marigny, whose reputation as a brutal taskmaster was well deserved."

"And that was where you met him?" Ghislaine asked.

"Aye. We became friends. He had the brawn and I the art of diplomacy. Between us we managed to survive those early days."

"Most interesting, Sir Arnaud, but I fail to see how his treatment as a child is different to that of many other men. He has had time to get over a few beatings surely?"

"Perhaps a little more patience, lady? I am not yet done." Sir Arnaud paused to sip the wine. "Marigny always seemed to single him out for punishment if there was trouble of any kind. Guy didn't complain since he was determined to make his father proud of him. He was convinced that once knighted, his father would show him some respect and their differences buried. He finally won his spurs at eighteen and I swear that was the first time I had ever seen him smile."

"Well, that perhaps goes some way to explain his bad temper, but not his attitude towards myself?"

"Despite his scowls, Guy's looks drew much attention from women. He was ever a shy one, but felt most at ease with the simpler, serving wenches who demanded nothing more from him than an hour or two of his time." Even Sir Arnaud flushed a little at that! "The ladies of the keep wanted much the same, but would also mock him for his plain speaking and lack of pretty words. In the end he found that surliness answered the problem best. Until he went back home."

"Home?" she enquired, her curiosity piqued. "Where is that? Guy has never talked of it."

"His father owned a good-sized estate near Avranches, but that meant little to Guy since he was the fourth son. Still, a home is a home and Guy had hoped that in eleven years his father would have become more approachable." Arnaud paused to swirl the wine round in his cup.

"So he went back to the estate in the end?" she prompted.

"Aye. But it was not much of a home-coming. After having his first marriage annulled, his father had hopes of remarrying a younger, very pretty daughter of a neighbouring landowner. Guy welcomed the match but it would seem his new step-mother-to-be found it impossible to keep her hands off him. She followed him everywhere and finally, when she could not get him to bed her, she went to his father accusing Guy of trying to do exactly that."

Ghislaine frowned. "He must have denied it?"

"Of course. It did no good, though. His father wished to hang him on the spot, but his elder brother, well aware of the lady's predilections, helped him escape."

"So he became a mercenary," she surmised.

"Aye, and never had anything to do with women of rank since then."

"Until Margaret Staveley, thinking she would be a good wife?"

Arnaud sighed. "Luck was not with him there either."

"Margaret would have made a good wife." Ghislaine pointed out sadly. "She was good, kind and loyal. And very pretty," she added.

"Perhaps," said Arnaud distractedly, sniffing the wine.

"You do not think she would have made a good wife?" Ghislaine was fascinated by the very idea.

He hesitated. "I am not sure Margaret Staveley would have made Guy a good wife."

"Margaret would have made any man a good wife. Except she would not have liked his black scowls."

"You do not seem to mind them so much," he replied flatly.

Ghislaine shrugged her shoulders. "They are rarely based on substance of any sort. Besides, I have noticed that he shouts and threatens a lot, but rarely acts."

"Do not let the men know that, lady, or his reputation will be worth naught."

They laughed together at that unlikely thought.

"Are you suggesting that the next time he shouts at me I cover myself in bruises?" Ghislaine smiled at him.

"Lady, the fact that he shouts at you at all is what interests me."

"How so?" Ghislaine demanded, fascinated at this line of thought.

"He has never shown so much interest in any other woman."

Ghislaine frowned. "I can assure you the experience is one most women would gladly avoid."

"I meant that he finds it hard to stay away from you."

Ghislaine shook her head. "You are wrong, Sir Arnaud. He avoids me at all costs. I would even go so far as to say that he plans it like a military campaign."

Arnaud laughed. "You might find a little gentle persuasion works wonders."

Ghislaine received this suggestion with a contemptuous expression. "I am not at all convinced of the wisdom of encouraging his attentions, Sir Arnaud. My husband has made it clear on several occasions that he will be pleased to rid himself of me and my accursed tongue."

Arnaud d'Everard regarded Ghislaine with a thoughtful expression on his face. "He is a proud man who has had to fight for everything. There has been no kindness in his life, no warmth and no love. Were he to be shown a different way, lady, he might learn to change." He paused to place his goblet on the floor. "I believe you to be a good woman, lady. Be patient with him and you may find Guy a worthy husband."

"You ask much, Sir Arnaud. He has caused me hurt and humiliation." Her dark eyes challenged him. "Give me one good reason why I should. The convent seems a more acceptable solution."

Sir Arnaud pushed his blond locks back from his face in frustration. "I cannot believe you have a vocation," he offered hopefully. "Nor would your life ever be dull."

"A most unoriginal thought, Sir Arnaud," she replied waspishly. "But if it makes you feel better, I shall consider what you said." Inwardly Ghislaine chided herself for such weakness. She had absolutely no intention whatsoever of considering a proper marriage to such a man. None at all.

Elfrieda stood in the middle of her warm kitchen with her arms across her ample chest and glared with intense dislike at the huge man stood before her.

"This brute thinks that just because he catches most of the meat, it entitles him to take liberties." The woman's voice was indignant and somewhat too self-righteous for one well-known to enjoy the pleasures of the flesh. Ghislaine stood between the warring pair in an attempt to prevent mayhem from destroying the evening meal.

Whatever Elfrieda's morals, the woman had proved herself an excellent cook since the previous incumbent had died suddenly from a lung fever last Yuletide. Although most head cooks were men, Ghislaine had seen no point in replacing her. Her quick temper, however, was legendary.

Despite being no more than twenty-four summers in age, Elfrieda ruled the kitchen with strict authority and had no time for idle loafers and scroungers. Anyone found to be overstepping the mark was subjected to a tongue lashing of great volume and thrown from the kitchen under a hail of pans and bones. Mindful of her husband's admitted parsimony, Ghislaine felt it was an extra expense they could do without.

Tall for a woman, and plump as a well-fed chicken, Elfrieda's size and stubborn expression would have been more than offputting for most men. Her clear blue eyes flashed mutinously and her generous mouth compressed in a tight line as she prepared to do battle with Guy de Courcy's giant sergeant.

Joachim, however, seemed not one whit dismayed by Elfrieda's aggression. A Frank with a sullen disposition and thick, greasy blond braids, he ruled the de Courcy mercenaries with little more than a few growls and snarls. None of those louts had ever shown any desire to pit their strength against Joachim's huge bulk. Elfrieda knew no such apprehension, and Ghislaine was almost certain she saw a responding glint in the sergeant's dull blue eyes.

Feeling somewhat like an insect caught between two huge rocks, Ghislaine held up her hands. "I will not have any disruption in my kitchens," she began in a firm tone. "Go to the bailey and get about your duties. If you have any complaints, address them to Sir Arnaud and we shall deal with them in a civilised fashion."

"Oh, aye," responded Elfrieda with a sly glance at Ghislaine. "Like you and Sir Guy, you mean?"

"Hush, woman." Joachim's two words practically boomed around the kitchen and even Elfrieda seemed a bit taken aback. "Show respect to your mistress or I will beat you." He stared intently at Elfrieda, his sullen face almost carved in granite. After a moment or two of silence, he nodded curtly at Ghislaine and turned to leave.

Ghislaine exhaled in relief as he thudded down the stone-flagged corridor to the bailey. Elfrieda appeared to be rooted to the spot, completely taken aback at having been spoken to so roughly. It was certainly a novel experience.

Just as she was about to upbraid Elfrieda, a sudden outburst of frantic shouting in the bailey distracted their attention. Hurrying outside, Ghislaine found her bailey swarming with Guy's mercenaries and her own soldiers charging to their posts. Joachim stood in the middle of it all, like an immovable tree, dispensing orders in his slow, gruff voice. There was no sign of her husband or Sir Arnaud.

Catching sight of Edwin, relief flooded through her. At last, a friendly face! Her pleasure was to be short lived. "Get inside the keep, my lady, and stay there. That's an order!"

"I will not move until I know what's happening," she retorted defiantly. Edwin had certainly changed over the last few weeks. Gone was the gentleness and the familiar resignation, replaced by a light in his eyes which she fancied was a sort of excitement. Her husband had taken her childhood friend and brought him to manhood. Edwin had left her behind. Maybe it was time for her to take the same path.

Crossing her arms over her chest, Ghislaine faced Edwin in much the same way Elfrieda had faced Joachim. Edwin pulled an iron helm over his head as he spoke. "Dettingham has arrived with his men and he is likely to cause trouble. Now go inside and deal with the women and servants." His narrowed eyes were watching the men beyond her shoulder.

"Where is my husband?" That brought Edwin's eyes to hers.

"Putting on his hauberk and expecting obedience from you." He reached to touch an auburn braid in a familiar gesture, his expression softened. "Do as he says, Ghislaine. I need to know you are safe."

A pang of fear shot through her. Edwin was genuinely worried. "Aye," she grinned at him reluctantly. "I'll go, but if you get yourself hurt because of Guy de Courcy's quarrel, I shall be most vexed. Take care."

Reluctantly, she returned to the keep. Was Dettingham's presence a result of her foolishness? Chastened by the very thought, Ghislaine set to sorting out the supplies in case of battle. Much as she wanted to put him from her mind, Guy de Courcy was at the forefront of her thoughts. Had she signed his death warrant by her actions?

When the water was boiling in the huge cauldrons and enough cloth had been gathered to make binding for wounds, Ghislaine made her way to the top of the keep.

"What do you think you are doing here, lady?"

Guy de Courcy's angry voice boomed across the battlements. He was standing at the south side with Sir Arnaud and three of his men. Flushed with the effort of climbing the steep staircase, Ghislaine had to wait a few moments to catch her breath. Biting back a scathing retort, she advanced on the group of men.

The view from the battlements was most informative. Beyond the palisade gathered a large group of mounted soldiers headed by a smaller group of more elaborately attired knights. Swords, rivets and helms glinted in the last rays of the late afternoon sun.

"I wondered if I might be of help, my lord." Ghislaine stood before her husband, her eyes drinking in the sight of his sword and helm.

"You would be of more use within than up here," he barked irritably. "Obey me in this."

Ghislaine schooled her temper. "I have met with Henry Dettingham, my lord. He came to my brother's wedding and is...was a kinsman in a way. I thought perhaps if I could talk with him..."

Her voice trailed off as her husband's scowl grew

even blacker, if that was possible. "You have done more than enough..."

"Wait, Guy," interrupted d'Everard quickly. "The lady has a good point. If he trusts her, he may agree to talk. It's worth a try, don't you think?"

Ghislaine offered Sir Arnaud a grateful smile. Her husband continued to frown, but rubbed his chin in thought. "Aye," he conceded eventually, "but I am not sure that I trust her."

Ghislaine flushed to the roots of her hair. "You are most insulting my lord. My concern lies more with the safety of my people than your own skin, I admit. However, I am not so foolish to think that, by delivering you to Henry Dettingham, my people will be spared. You have threatened their lives often enough and I am sure that Sir Arnaud will not hesitate to carry out your orders in such an event."

Both men gaped at her for the space of several minutes. Guy de Courcy was the first to find his tongue. "Honesty was always your strong point, lady," he ground out. "But you are right. In the event of your treachery, your manor would be wasted and your people killed."

Ghislaine noted the look exchanged between the three-men-at-arms behind them. She was beginning to realise that those orders were merely a threat to keep her in check. She had no wish to put it to the test, though. "I give you my word that I shall commit no treachery."

Guy sighed heavily, his eyes distracted by a movement in the formation of soldiers below. Ghislaine recognised the small, rotund figure of Henry Dettingham detach himself from the main body and position himself before the manor gates. His grey destrier pawed at the ground restlessly as if he sensed the tension in the air.

"Come out, de Courcy. You cannot hide forever and the Earl's men are not here to protect you. I have no wish to destroy the manor so I offer you a duel. A fight to the death and that will be an end to it."

Henry Dettingham's bluff voice carried to the battlements.

Guy shook his head resolutely. "You know what to say, Arnaud. Take my wife. He may harbour some liking for her, at least."

Arnaud d'Everard inclined his head. "As you say." His lips had twitched slightly at his friend's last words.

As the huge gates were opened, Ghislaine felt a frisson of fear shoot through her. Perhaps Henry Dettingham had changed and he would not listen to her? He had been a mild-mannered, rather diffident man who had a penchant for pompous speeches and ale. Not even Henry could allow his sister's murder to go unchallenged, though. Her heart went out to him.

"Courage, Lady Ghislaine." Arnaud smiled at her as they urged their horses forward. Ghislaine could do naught but swallow as they came to a halt before their doughty foe.

Henry wore a bright red tunic over his hauberk which made his pale, round face look sallow and washed out. Small green eyes stared out below bushy brown brows. His body, ever broad and thick, was now portly and his plain, kindly face flabby. The man did not cut an imposing figure.

"Sir Henry," she began rather nervously, "I bid you greetings."

"My Lady de Launay," he exclaimed with sincere pleasure. "It is some years since I have seen you."

"De Courcy now, my lord. I am recently married to Sir Guy." Ghislaine gazed at him with steady eyes. No, she doubted if Henry had changed.

"Aye, I had heard rumours of that monstrous agreement." His gaze transferred to the man beside her. "You are not de Courcy, I take it?"

Ghislaine shook her head. "Sir Arnaud d'Everard is come to speak on my husband's behalf."

Henry Dettingham drew his small figure to his most imposing height and stared pointedly at the handsome d'Everard.

"The man is as great a coward as ever. He takes refuge within, I see."

Sir Arnaud's grey eyes glittered and Ghislaine knew he was reining in his anger. "My Lord de Courcy bids you greetings, Sir Henry, and begs you to reconsider your position."

"The man's a coward," came the pompous reply and Henry turned to his band of knights and shook his head.

"Guy de Courcy is innocent of the crime of murder. He is hopeful of clearing his name and in doing so may discover the true criminal. He regrets your loss deeply, Dettingham, and was heartsore when your sister was killed. You must have heard he offered her marriage."

Henry snorted rudely. "If he was keen to marry Margaret, then he should have come to me first before skulking around her skirts like the brigand he is."

"Sir Henry, I beg you to think again," broke in Ghislaine. Raking over old insults would get them nowhere. "My husband swears he committed no crime against Margaret and over the past few weeks I have come to believe he speaks the truth." Sir Henry's expression was not encouraging, but she decided to continue. "He has never denied his rough ways nor his ability to kill adeptly, but I have come to know him as an honest man. Guy de Courcy would gain so little from her death that it would make no sense."

"We waste time, Lady de Courcy. Your husband is a mercenary with a liking for money. Margaret's keep was sacked of its wealth. There is reason enough." Dettingham brushed aside her reasoning with a wave of his gauntleted hand. "It grieves me to see you so trapped, but I offer you my protection. Come with me to safety." Henry's green eyes watched her carefully.

"You mistake the matter, sir. I gave my husband my word that I would remain loyal to him for all the right reasons. I stay here with my people and my husband." Ghislaine lifted her chin proudly.

Sir Arnaud inclined his head in her direction. "My lady speaks well. Guy de Courcy refuses to come out because he will not waste blood needlessly. Go home, Sir Henry. The man responsible will be found sooner or later and then we can all live in peace. You do yourself no favours with the Earl here."

"Think you to gull me so simply?" Dettingham hissed sharply. "The Earl cares not whether a crime has been committed. His only concern is to keep de Courcy alive so that he can receive his silver marks. I'll wager that no one is brought to justice under such a system."

Ghislaine stared at him, a thought striking her. "How did you know where to find my husband?"

Henry Dettingham shrugged his shoulders. "Walter de Belleme sent word."

So Walter had tried to engineer this fight after all. Shocked at such underhand manipulation, Ghislaine searched the ranks of his men. "He is not here, though?" she enquired carefully.

"No. This is between me and de Courcy."

It was clear to Ghislaine that Henry was not going to go away. He wanted a fight. Just as she was about to signal to Arnaud, there was a shout from Dettingham's camp. "The Earl's men!"

All eyes turned south, scouring the line of the forest. Ghislaine counted at least thirty soldiers standing amongst the trees. She breathed a sigh of relief. They had been saved.

Henry Dettingham jerked his horse's head round and turned back to his knights. Following several minutes of heated discussion, he returned to Ghislaine and Sir Arnaud. "Do not think for one moment that this is the end. You may have the Earl's men to help you now, but I shall kill de Courcy for what he has done." He nodded briefly at Ghislaine. "My compliments, Lady de Courcy."

So saying, he wheeled round and joined his army. Wordlessly they departed, leaving Ghislaine to stare at the reinforcements. "They do not wear the Earl's colours." She squinted her eyes to peer more carefully.

"They are not the Earl's men. They belong to Lady du Beauregard from Omberleigh," came the curt reply.

Ghislaine looked at Arnaud in surprise. The man seemed not at all grateful for Lady Helene's timely intervention. Confused, she turned back to the palisade. She, for one, would welcome the lady with pleasure.

Chapter Nine

"Why did my husband not meet with Henry Dettingham himself?" she asked Sir Arnaud. "It would have been much simpler."

"Aye," allowed her companion as he helped her dismount. "But Guy de Courcy places little trust in a man demanding vengeance at any price. Nor," he added grimly, "has he any wish to kill him. Sir Henry is no swordsman."

Once more on firm ground, Ghislaine turned to face her husband's friend. "True, but I had no idea that Sir Guy would be willing to sacrifice his reputation to compassion."

"Make no mistake, lady," warned Sir Arnaud. "If his life was in danger, Guy would not hesitate to fight. However, he believes that Dettingham's death would neither clear his name nor allow him the return of his old manor." He flickered her a look of reproach. "His name is all he has and the manor he lost was the first step to making a real home for himself. He will not rest until they are restored."

Their attention was claimed by a rider approaching

the gates. He bore a request from Lady du Beauregard
for permission to enter the manor gates and Ghislaine
gave her assent.

"Do you not stay to bid Lady du Beauregard welcome?" she chided, as Arnaud turned towards the
keep.

Arnaud's grey eyes bore into her before smiling
lightly. "No doubt you ladies have much to discuss
without my interference."

Ghislaine drew in her breath sharply at the inferred
insult. "I had thought you might wish to thank her for
her timely appearance."

His grey eyes turned steely and seemed about to say
something, but thought better of it. "I have no doubt
that the lady will be more than satisfied with your
gratitude," he murmured finally, tossing the reins to
the stable boy.

Lifting her chin, Ghislaine regarded him coldly. "I
had not thought you the sort of man to continue a petty
disagreement. Surely you can forgive the Lady du
Beauregard for her concerns over my health before the
marriage."

A frown marred his brow. "You are too trusting,
Lady Ghislaine. People are not always as they seem."
With those enigmatic words, Sir Arnaud turned on his
heels and picked his way across the mud-churned bailey.

His words were most confusing, but Ghislaine had
no time to ponder them as Helene du Beauregard
passed beneath the manor gates atop a magnificent bay
gelding.

"Greetings, Lady du Beauregard, and welcome."
Ghislaine smiled as she rushed towards the older

woman. The stable lad aided Helene to dismount and she brushed the dust from her riding cloak.

"I am pleased my appearance was timely," Helene remarked, her cheeks flushed with the fresh air. "I had feared I might be too late."

"You knew?" Ghislaine slipped her arm through Helene's and guided her towards the hall. She was glad to see her friend appeared in better health.

"Aye," came the guarded reply. "I admit to being concerned for you and had some men watch over the manor." She stopped and turned towards Ghislaine, taking the girl's hands in hers. "I hope you will forgive me for such an intrusion, but there was every possibility of a reprisal against your husband. I believe my men saved your life with a good shot in the forest."

At last an explanation for the mystery. It was a relief to know that the other men had been friendly. Ghislaine still remained somewhat surprised by Helene's unexpected intervention, though, and thought back to Arnaud's odd words of parting. Clearly he knew more about Lady du Beauregard than she had at first thought. Smiling, Ghislaine placed her arm around the woman's shoulders and led her inside the keep. "I can only be grateful for your vigilance since we remain safe."

When the du Beauregard troops were organised with ale, Ghislaine returned to Helene. She was sitting comfortably by the fire in the hall with her head tilted back and her eyes closed.

"You are tired, Helene? Perhaps you would prefer to lie on my bed for a while?" Ghislaine regarded her anxiously.

Helene smiled and opened her eyes. "Not at all, my dear. I have simply learnt to take advantage of every opportunity to rest. A short nap can be most restorative." She sat up and leaned closer to Ghislaine, gesturing her to sit by her side.

"And how have you fared, Lady de Courcy? Has marriage to the mercenary been as bad as you feared?" Her expression showed concern rather than a desire for gossip and Ghislaine did not take offence at the question.

Shrugging her shoulders, she smiled wanly. "He is not an easy man to live with. Sometimes I think I have made some progress and then he does something which causes me much vexation." Placing her head on her hand, Ghislaine sighed heavily. "He will be pleased to put me in the convent, I believe."

Effie bustled up with some wine and a bowl of nuts. Helene smiled her thanks and remained silent until she had moved out of earshot. "Do you still think him guilty of the murder?" Helene regarded her with searching eyes.

Something in her expression struck a familiar chord in Ghislaine, but the memory remained just out of touch. She lowered her eyes and plucked absently at a loose thread on her mantle. "No, and for all his brutish ways he has always been straightforward in his dealings with me."

Pursing her lips thoughtfully, she edged a little closer to Helene. "I do not think him all bad," she admitted reluctantly. "And once he was even quite…gentle." Her cheeks heated, but somehow she did not mind talking to Helene. It had been a long time since she had confided in another woman.

Helene folded her hands in her lap and stared into the fire as if deep in thought. "Would you perhaps reconsider your decision to retire to the convent if your husband was more…amenable towards you?"

It was a question Ghislaine had pondered several times over the past week. Today she had learnt quite a lot more about her husband thanks to Sir Arnaud and, despite her protestations to the contrary, his words had given her pause for thought.

That day in the forest, Guy had admitted he found it hard to speak gently. In truth, pretty words were not what she wanted. She liked his honesty and straight-forward speech. Over the weeks he had proved hard-working, responsible and astute. His authority over his men was absolute and in return they offered him their loyalty—aye, he had even won over Edwin. He lacked manners, but of late these had shown some improvement in her company. His temper, of course, left much to be desired and yet that was really so much hot air.

Nor had he ever forced himself upon her, she reminded herself. Many women of her station would no doubt welcome such a paragon! "I think I find it hard knowing what he expects of me," she murmured softly. "Sometimes he glares at me as if he hates me."

Helene shot her a sideways glance. "Would you really prefer the convent?"

"I am not what he wants in a wife." Ghislaine's voice had taken on a weary tone. "He frequently tells me how much trouble I am."

At that, Helene laughed. "And what sort of a wife would you think a man like Guy de Courcy needs? A sweet, meek creature such as Margaret Staveley?" She raised her dark brows in question.

"W-well…" stammered Ghislaine, searching for the right words. Suddenly she stopped and looked at Helene. "How do you know what sort of wife he needs?"

"I know far more than you about Guy de Gourcy, my dear." She reached down to smooth her gown over her knees. "More to the point, I think you would make him a good wife." Her face was expressionless as she watched her words sink in. "Don't you?"

Ghislaine eyed her warily, confused by the way Helene had managed to twist things round. She was reminded of Arnaud's parting words. "I'm not sure."

"Well, perhaps you should find out."

Raising her hands in confusion, Ghislaine shook her head. "I understand none of this. Why are you so concerned about this marriage? Neither of us wanted it and we have agreed to go our own ways once Guy's name is cleared."

Helene smiled, her eyes resting on Ghislaine. "I made mistakes in my marriage that I now regret and I do not wish you to tread the same path."

It was quiet in the hall for a change with just the crackle and hiss of the wood in the fire to disturb the peace. The shutters at the windows had been closed and the only light within came from the torches on the walls. Now that the danger from Henry Dettingham had gone, temporarily at least, the tension that had been building up had suddenly eased.

"I still don't see how…"

Helene held up her hands. "Enough talking, young lady. Since your mother is not here, I think I knew her well enough to know she would approve of me giving you some maternal advice. Come. Let us go to your room. I believe it is time you were taken in hand.''

Submitting herself reluctantly at first to Helene's lamentations over her gowns, her hair and her freckles, Ghislaine eventually began to relax. Effie's presence was requested, and between them they experimented with several suitable styles for her hair. Privately Ghislaine doubted whether Guy would notice any difference in her appearance, but it was an enjoyable experience nevertheless. She had never spent time on such feminine frivolity, lacking both an attentive audience and a teacher, but it was certainly a change from hunting down the Earl's game!

Once Effie was dispatched to concoct a salve for roughened hands, Helene turned her attention to Ghislaine's clothes.

Casting a baleful eye over the contents of her wooden chest, she shook her head. ''I cannot believe you manage with such rags. Has your husband said nothing?'' Helene picked up the tattered hem of Ghislaine's current gown and let it fall in disgust.

''No. He seems to regard my gowns more as a method of restricting my activities.'' Ghislaine hesitated and then added more quietly, ''Nor is he overly keen to spend his money. He does not seem to rate gowns very highly.'' Feeling somewhat guilty for being disloyal, Ghislaine continued, ''But then, if I'm to enter the convent, there really seems little point.''

Treating that remark to a dismissive gesture, Helene stared thoughtfully at Ghislaine who was perched on the edge of her pallet. ''I have one or two gowns that might be suitable.'' She rubbed a long finger over her chin. ''They might answer for now.''

Neither of them had heard the door open. ''I'll thank you to leave the question of my wife's attire to me.'' Guy de Courcy stood in the doorway, his hands placed somewhat aggressively on his hips. Although he had at least removed his helm, Guy still wore his battered leather hauberk and looked every inch the mercenary of his ill repute.

Helene jerked her head in his direction. As the silence lengthened, the tension between them increased. ''Then the blame for such rags can be placed at your feet, my lord.'' The lines around her mouth deepened in disapproval. ''Does it give you pleasure to see your wife shamed like this?''

Colouring furiously, Ghislaine jumped to her feet. ''Please, Lady du Beauregard. This is a matter between my husband and myself.''

Her words were ignored as Guy and Helene faced each other. ''I thought I had made it clear in Chester, lady. Your presence is not welcome in my home.'' Guy's handsome face was bloodless as he eyed the woman with contempt.

Ghislaine felt as if she was a spectator in a scene she had only half understood. She was certain now they knew each other. ''Guy! After Lady du Beauregard gave us aid against Henry Dettingham, the least we can offer is our hospitality.''

Her rebuke earned Ghislaine nothing more than a scornful glance before he advanced menacingly on Helene. ''Lady du Beauregard has sampled enough of our hospitality. I am sure she has pressing business in her own manor.''

Ghislaine's cheeks burned with embarrassment at such a pointed remark. ''Lady du Beauregard is welcome to remain here as long as she wishes,'' she hissed, glaring at her husband. "This is also my home, Guy de Courcy, and I have greatly enjoyed Lady du Beauregard's company. I have had little opportunity to indulge in feminine company over the past few years, and I confess to having missed it greatly."

Boosted by the warm smile she received from Helene, Ghislaine watched him cross the room. Carefully he placed his gleaming sword on the rushes and then unfurled his great length on the bed. She was reminded very much of a disgruntled child.

"It sorrows me to tell you this, wife, but I cannot permit your acquaintance with...Lady...du Beauregard to continue.'' He stared at her boldly, almost daring her to gainsay him.

"Give me one good reason for such an order,'' Ghislaine answered, her hands almost shaking in anger. How dared he presume so much? They were not man and wife in fact, after all.

His eyes glinted dangerously. "Because she is a brazen whore.'' Guy raised Ghislaine's goblet of unfinished wine to his lips and drained it in one movement.

Wheeling round to face Helene, Ghislaine was confronted with a raised hand. Helene was more than ready to deal with such lies.

"I have paid for my mistakes, in many different ways,'' she replied wearily. Her dark eyes were centred on the man laid out so nonchalantly on the bed. "And I see in Ghislaine and you much of myself and my husband. I have no wish for you both to end up the same way."

Guy's frown deepened. "I have no fear that you and Ghislaine are made of the same cloth, my lady."

Helene stooped to pick up her cloak and threw it about her shoulders with a proud flourish. "Then you must tread warily, my lord, for your wife does not seem very content to me."

"No," she assured Ghislaine, turning to her quickly. "This quarrel has naught to do with you, it is between me and Guy alone. I have no wish to come between you and so I shall leave without further ado." She squeezed Ghislaine's shoulders and headed for the door. "If you need me, please send word."

With a quick nod towards them both, Helene left silently, Ghislaine felt almost bereft. "How could you say such things to her?"

"They were true." He looked up in surprise "I do not expect you to further your acquaintance with the woman, or the consequences will be dire."

Chapter Ten

"If I am to dress, I need something to put on." Ghislaine's voice rose in frustration. Her husband had sent Effie to wake her at dawn and her mistress had not appreciated the early call. Sleep had been long in coming the night before, with visions of Guy and Helene walking in her dreams.

"He said you could wear this, my lady." Effie held up an old blue gown that had been well-mended and that was definitely on the small side. She looked at it dubiously. "I did tell him that it didn't fit now, but he didn't seem to hear."

Ghislaine stared at the dress. "So be it." She was too tired to argue and her head was aching.

Sighing heavily, Ghislaine donned the dress and allowed Effie to pull her hair into a more becoming braid than usual.

"It doesn't seem as tight as it was," offered Effie as she surveyed the fruits of her work.

Ghislaine smiled wanly. "Aye. Sir Guy seems to have kept me hungry of late. Perhaps he had this gown in mind?"

Seeing naught to smile at, Effie shot Ghislaine a look of exasperation. "Well, not all of you has succumbed to his methods, it seems."

Ghislaine followed the direction of her eyes and admitted that the gown was strained across her chest. She shrugged her shoulders. "It would appear not."

The hall was quiet when she descended. Torches spluttered on the walls for the morning light was not yet advanced enough, but in the gloom she could make out the lone figure of Guy de Courcy. He was standing with his back to her, watching the bailey from one of the side windows. At a sound he turned, his hand on his sword. It was not his instinctive reaction that caused Ghislaine to draw her breath so suddenly.

Her eyes widened as they took in the magnificent sight before her. Never could she have imagined how handsome he could be. His long hair had been trimmed and washed and his tunic of midnight blue gave Guy a most elegant appearance. Yet it was his face that was transformed. The weeks of thick, stubbly growth had been barbered to reveal a face that was strong, masculine and devastatingly attractive.

Realising that she was gaping at him, Ghislaine gathered her wits.

"I see you took my advice," she began tersely. "But I do not consider your first bath as cause enough to rouse me from my bed."

If he had expected a humble and contrite wife, he was sadly mistaken. Ghislaine's tongue was as sharp as ever. A wry smile formed on his lips.

"No?" he countered. "I had thought you most eager to share the moment with me."

In an effort to dispel the effect of this vision of

masculine beauty before her, Ghislaine retreated to a facial expression of complete disdain.

"Why am I here?"

Guy offered her a seat at the table. A servant emerged from the gloom to provide her with a dollop of grey porridge. If he noticed her gown was tight, he made no mention of it, although Ghislaine was aware of his eyes on her.

"I have to leave for a few days." The statement was short and to the point.

Ghislaine felt herself go cold. Already he could not bear her company. "I still do not see why it necessitates my presence at this hour. Sir Brian is perfectly capable of protecting the manor in your absence." Her tone was cool and stiff, belying the turmoil within her.

His dark brows raised at this evident inaccuracy but he shrugged his shoulders rather than voice his thoughts. "Sir Brian could not tell me whether you wished to accompany me."

Her eyes flew to his. This was no jest.

"Where do you go?" The words were almost a whisper.

"Chester. On business with the Earl."

Ghislaine stared at him a moment, trying desperately to stop herself from flinging her arms around him.

"And he wishes to see me?" Ghislaine certainly had no desire to see him.

Guy shook his head. "I thought you might wish to purchase more spices and cloth. You have spent the past few weeks pointing out how needy the kitchens are and I have seen for myself that you are lacking in gowns."

"Aye," she replied as dutifully as she could. "The kitchens are in sore need of stocks." Her eyes remained fixed to the porridge, not risking a glance in his direction. Did the man think this was some sort of chore?

"Then we leave in five minutes. I leave d'Everard to aid the worthy Sir Brian." Guy strode from the hall before she could utter a word. Ghislaine sat there another full minute savouring the elation before finishing the porridge and hurrying for her cloak. Life was certainly not dull these days.

The sun was at its highest before the walls of Chester came into view. The turquoise banner of Hugh d'Avranches could be seen fluttering in the March wind from the keep of the castle. Halting on a ridge some distance to the south of the city, the party was able to view the comings and goings at leisure.

Ghislaine watched the great River Dee flow and curve around the city walls and then off north towards the sea. A large trading galley was moored in the port on the west side amid a hubbub of activity. Below them, to the south of the Bridge gate, the wheels of the flour mills paddled steadily through the water. Beyond them stood the outline of the Lupus's castle. Proud and impenetrable, its walls were heavily fortified against any Welsh attack.

Pulling her cloak close to, Ghislaine could not conceal a shiver against the cold wind that blew in from the coast. Morwenna stomped and whinnied, keen to find a warm shelter and bag of oats. Ghislaine had other reasons for wishing the journey ended. Her nerves had been stretched to the limits by her endless

expectation of an attack, either from Walter de Belleme, Henry Dettingham or outlaws. Each noise had
caused her to jump and to look about carefully, her
eyes locking on to anything that moved. She had ridden alongside her husband, too nervous to offer more
than desultory conversation.

Guy, sensing her reluctance to talk to him, honoured
her silence and was pleased to sink into his own
thoughts. He needed all his wits about him to deal with
the wily Earl of Chester.

It was with great relief that the party was allowed
entrance to the city. The de Courcy colours had been
identified long before they had reached the bridge and
the guards allowed them passage with little attention.
Quite carelessly, Ghislaine decided. Had her men done
as much, she would have had them whipped.

Inside the walls, the noise was almost deafening.
The sounds of people and animals echoed through the
narrow, muddy streets that led off the main way to the
Cross. Ghislaine stared about her at the cramped,
wooden buildings that crowded inside the walls. The
smell of human life washed around her and Ghislaine
thought she was like to choke with the stench. Her
mother had been right about the place. It would be
easy to die here.

Her palfrey picked the way carefully through a
filthy passage, her ears twitching nervously when a
screaming child came too close. Ghislaine's eyes
drank in the scenes as if seeing them for the first time.
When she had visited with her father, he had insisted
on taking her directly to the castle, and she had barely
a glimpse of the colour and the life that existed within
the city walls. The streets were teeming with noisy

people who paid scant attention to the danger of Guy's huge horse. Pedlars idled against the walls of the narrow dwellings, their eyes darting hither and thither, hoping to catch the attention of a passing maid. Street-sellers mixed with bewildered farmers, journey-men with tavern wenches. Ghislaine stared wordlessly at the stalls that sold fine silks and linens, furs, cheese, soaps and pots.

As the cross came into view, Guy turned to the left, and Ghislaine was able to see another gate at the end of the street. Beyond the top of the gate fluttered the flags of the large galley they had seen earlier in the harbour. Hardly able to contain her excitement, Ghislaine could not help her gasp of delight.

"We head for the harbour?"

Guy turned at her words, and watched her unguarded face for a moment.

"Aye. I have business with the captain of the *Isabella*. You will wish to view the wares in the storehouses along the quayside. Joachim will accompany you."

Ghislaine nodded. Joachim was Guy's second-in-command when Arnaud d'Everard was elsewhere. Few men were willing to gainsay him; for those that were, his menacing war-axe proved a mighty deterrent.

The party halted in the shadows of the old wooden gate whilst Joachim dealt with the guards. A steady stream of merchants and purchasers made their way in and out of the gate, but it was a sorry line of dark-haired men shuffling towards the harbour that caught Ghislaine's eye. They were dressed in tattered leather and wool, chained at the ankle to the man in front and behind. None looked anywhere except the ground before them, their lips tight, backs straight.

"Where do they go?" Her eyes followed the men until they had passed between the gates.

"They are slaves for trading." Guy's voice was toneless in reply. "They will board the *Isabella* and be sold en route."

Ghislaine stared at his harsh profile. "But they are Welshmen."

"And are a valuable commodity to Hugh Lupus."

Sickened by the knowledge that these warriors would leave their homelands, families, friends, to be sold to the highest bidder in a foreign port, Ghislaine closed her eyes. "Where is the *Isabella* bound?"

"She heads south to Normandy and then on east through the Mediterranean to Genoa and Venice."

The day had suddenly turned sour. The dealings of men were sordid indeed. Ghislaine turned to look at her husband. "You have business with the captain, you said?"

Guy nodded, his blue eyes following the silent line of warriors. "Personal business." The flat tone of his voice and the set of his lips brooked no further discussion, but Ghislaine could not help herself.

"Do you trade in slaves?" She regarded him steadily, her mouth equally set. Whether she realised it or no, her breath held until he gave his reply.

"Nay. I trade information only." His black frown dissuaded any further discussion.

Ghislaine followed as Guy progressed slowly amongst the throng, her mind busy with the latest piece of information he had given her. Why would Guy de Courcy wish to buy information from a pedlar of human flesh? He had denied trading, and she knew him so far to be honest. Mayhap it had to do with the murder. She would have to keep her ears open.

The ship was a truly breathtaking sight. From a distance it was beautiful, but from close to she was magnificent. She bobbed gently with the lapping waves, gulls flapping near her masts. The giant sail was furled carefully away, leaving the rich wooden skeleton to rise and fall majestically. Unable to tear her eyes from the *Isabella*, Ghislaine watched the cargo being loaded by strangely garbed men of indeterminate origins.

Guy de Courcy stood at her side, an eyebrow lifted in question.

"I'm sorry?" she said. "Did you say aught?"

Guy viewed her distracted gaze with irritation. "I said that I would join you in the warehouse later. This purse contains more than you need for your purchases." He had her full attention now, he noted wryly. "Joachim knows what to do."

The leather pouch felt surprisingly heavy at her waist as she dismounted outside a large wooden trading house. Guarding her money as best she could, Ghislaine took grateful refuge behind Joachim as he cut a swathe through the crowds. Ignoring the urgent requests of the traders to sample their goods, he made his way silently to the far end of the building. The noise and the colours were beginning to press painfully in her head and Ghislaine longed to be out in the fresh air once more.

At the far end of the warehouse Joachim gestured Ghislaine to stop whilst he disappeared behind a heavy arras. A moment later he emerged once more and beckoned her to follow him. The arras hid another world from the hubbub of the warehouse. Ghislaine's head echoed with the noise and the colours, but gratefully entered into a small, low chamber that at first seemed empty save Joachim and herself. A cool breeze gently breathed air into her throbbing head and Ghislaine closed her eyes momentarily with relief.

"Would you sit, lady? I will bring refreshments for you."

A small pair of faded blue eyes blinked up at her before uttering words in a strange tongue into the gloom at the far end of the chamber. Gratefully Ghislaine sank into the comfortable seat offered her. It was like nothing she had ever encountered in her sheltered life. It was more like a small, narrow bed but draped with cloth and padding that allowed her to lie back and rest her weary shoulders.

"My thanks, sir. I would be most grateful for a little wine for we have travelled far today."

The tiny man nodded his grey head and gestured towards the shadows. He was dressed most oddly in a voluminous surcoat of blue and grey stripes, his thin hair pulled into a braid at the back of his large head.

"I would suggest, my lady, that you may wish to try a tisane? A hot drink that is both reviving and refreshing."

The merchant, for Ghislaine was now convinced that was his business, stood before her, his hands clasped before him in the manner of a willing trader. And yet there was nothing humble about him. The man was of indeterminate age, tiny but well-formed, and stood assessing her with eyes that spoke volumes. Intelligence, shrewdness and compassion were visible in their pale blue depths. Despite his lack of humility and his proud air, Ghislaine felt at ease.

"That would be most welcome, sir." She smiled at him, a little unsure for all the boldness of her words. "I am sure that Joachim would also wish to try this…tisane."

The merchant smiled faintly. "Joachim's tastes will be catered for. As you wish." A gnarled hand snapped in the air and a bronze flagon was placed before the Frankish warrior by a small boy that Ghislaine would have sworn came from thin air. At her nod, Joachim grabbed the flagon and retreated to a gloomy corner where he proceeded to down its contents with obvious relish.

The same boy brought another seat for his master and a small wooden table. Upon the latter he placed a steaming bronze vessel and two tiny blue and white bowls. Quite the most exquisite Ghislaine had ever seen. Her fingers reached out to touch them. They were smooth and very delicate. The merchant proceeded to pour a light brown liquid into each bowl, the pungent aroma that met Ghislaine's senses quite unlike anything she had encountered before. He then picked up one of the bowls and sipped lightly from the rim. Not wishing to seem ill-mannered, Ghislaine followed suit. The tisane was strong and so hot that it burnt her lips. She replaced the bowl firmly on the table.

The merchant's eyebrows raised in question. "And what may the house of Kalim offer you, lady?" He sat perfectly still as he awaited her reply.

"My husband sent me in your direction for I have need of cloth and spices." For some reason she could not fathom, Ghislaine was aware of an undercurrent between them, as if he were expecting her to say more.

After a brief pause, Kalim smiled slowly to reveal perfectly white teeth. "When you have finished your tisane, lady, I shall be glad to show you my wares."

Ghislaine sipped at the drink again more slowly, but found after a short while that the taste was becoming less unpleasant. In fact, she certainly felt less tired and dusty.

"You know my husband?"

"Guy de Courcy has been known to me for many years, lady. I have always found him to be a fair man. And an honest one."

Had the merchant added those last words for her benefit? She took another sip of the tisane, allowing the strange flavour to fill her senses before swallowing. The man was right, for she was beginning to revive a little.

"You are not from this land?"

The merchant shook his head, causing his silver earrings to jingle. "I am a merchant, lady, travelling from land to land. My home is where I choose it to be." Ghislaine watched in fascination as his long, beringed fingers raised the bowl to his lips. As he did so, their eyes collided and held. Kalim put the bowl down slowly.

"May I ask you a question, lady?"

Ghislaine flushed at her implied gaucheness and inclined her head in assent.

"Do you trust Guy de Courcy?" Those faded blue eyes bore into her, compelling her to answer truthfully. After no more than a few seconds, the words came.

"I, too, believe him to be an honest, proud man who

does not give his word lightly. Although we have not dealt long together, I find myself increasingly willing to trust him.'' Where had those words come from? Ghislaine flushed at her garrulous tongue. How could she be so bold with such a stranger?

''Then he chose well.''

Ghislaine felt the blood rush to her cheeks, but her innate honesty compelled her to explain. ''He did not choose me, I was forced upon him.''

All her shame and misery were expressed in those few words. The merchant watched her for a moment as if deep in thought. ''It is often so that the burdens we find the hardest to bear may bring us the richest rewards.'' Kalim sighed before rising gracefully to his feet. ''I will show you some of my wares now, lady. Maybe you will find something that takes your eye?''

His gentle smile chased away some of the gloom she was feeling at being reminded of her predicament. Ghislaine rose, her limbs stiff from the long ride, but grateful to avoid further conversation of such a personal nature. It was indeed painful to be reminded of her shortcomings.

Kalim's chamber was filled with beautiful cloth which Ghislaine eyed longingly. Bolts of gorgeous materials were paraded before her and Ghislaine found the choice almost impossible. Practicality, however, reasserted itself and she decided finally on soft grey and blue wool for herself, and serviceable browns and greens for the servants. Two bolts of linen were added to her list. A rich red brocade, chased with gold caught her eye, and in a fit of extravagance, Ghislaine decided that Guy would look particularly fine in a tunic of such attractive hue. Realising that her husband was also probably in need of further garments, she purchased some green and blue wool which could always be used for others if need be.

The food spices were more easily purchased. Ginger, cinnamon, nutmeg, mace, cloves and cardomoms were placed in a small chest, together with galingale, cubebs and grains of paradise to flavour the salted-down winter meats. Kalim also persuaded her to try currants, figs and dates as well as a generous portion of almonds to use on fast days and Lenten stews. Reminded that her husband had a sweet tooth, Ghislaine added some dried fruits to try in the custard confections he seemed partial to.

As she was deliberating over the wines, the arras was pulled back and Guy de Courcy stalked into the chamber. One look at his grim countenance told Ghislaine that she had probably purchased far more than she had licence to do and his disapproval told its own story. With a curt nod to Kalim, who bowed quietly and retreated to the shadows, Guy stopped before Ghislaine.

"I see you have nigh on exhausted my funds, lady." As the expression on his face did not change, Ghislaine gulped quietly before mentally discarding those items not absolutely essential. She cursed her own greed and childlike excitement in having such great choices. Pulling at her fingers, she murmured that she had indeed gone beyond her limits.

There was a momentary pause before Guy spoke in a more gentle tone. "Perhaps you would show me what you intended to take." Ghislaine nodded and commenced an item by item account of her purchases, but it was not long before Guy interrupted with amusement in his voice.

"Wife, your choices are most creditable. But," he added softly, "I had hoped that you would buy yourself some more...ah...some finer cloth."

Ghislaine looked up at him sharply. Gone was the grim frown that he had entered the chamber with. Mayhap she had misinterpreted his look.

"I thought only to dress appropriately, in the circumstances, my lord." Her tone had returned to its usual waspishness and that brought a faint smile to his lips.

"Aye. And your choice of cloth is most...worthy." His large hand raked his black locks as he surveyed the assortment of cloths. "Kalim. It would seem I have need of your excellent advice." The merchant stepped forward. "My wife requires some finery. Have you aught that would do?"

Seizing his opportunity, Kalim smiled broadly and pulled down bolt after bolt of jewel-bright emeralds and blues, golds and creams, chased and plain.

"With your lady's unusual hair colour, perhaps some brighter hues that would enhance and complement?"

Ghislaine held her breath as her husband and the merchant selected three. Ghislaine could hardly believe that she needed anything near so fine and yet found her protests sounded weak even to her own ears. The idea of her possessing such beautiful gowns was an exhilarating one. Together the merchant and Guy had decided upon the emerald-green and the peacock-blue with little difficulty. It was the final choice that had Ghislaine feeling no more than a fine object.

When they had finally plumped for a gold brocade chased with midnight-blue, Ghislaine had retreated to a dark corner in high dudgeon. No one had consulted her about the choice, and much as she approved of the material, she remained inexplicably angry nevertheless.

Ignoring her protests, Guy then went on to examine the brooches and belts. His largesse was making her feel most uncomfortable and she had no idea how to stem the tide of such uncalled-for generosity. At no time in her life had anyone bestowed such gifts upon her and, in truth, it was hard to accept them so. She was used to very little, and realised how vulnerable that made her.

"Are you purchasing my goodwill, sir?" she demanded finally.

Her rudeness took him by surprise for he had genuinely not realised how offended his wife was becoming.

"I did not know you offered it for sale. Had I done so, I feel certain it would have cost me less dear."

His bantering tone only aggravated Ghislaine more and he knew it. "You are most insulting. If you wish something of me, you have only to ask, although that is not within your nature since you took the rest of my possessions without my leave." So saying, Ghislaine flounced towards the arras and would have pulled it aside had Joachim not forestalled her with his huge bulk. Not relishing the prospect of an undignified scuffle that she would undoubtedly lose, Ghislaine sat on the comfortable seat.

"Perhaps my lady would now like to take some wine whilst Sir Guy completes his purchases?" Kalim stood before her, his cool eyes informing her of his disapproval.

Aye, her behaviour had been less than ladylike and she flushed with shame that she could have let her feelings show. Since Guy de Gourcy had entered her quiet life, Ghislaine had found her emotions difficult to contain. And there was no good explanation for her bad temper. She would enter the convent as soon as he cleared his name. That was what she had demanded and he had agreed. Why she found it so difficult to behave normally when she was with the man, Ghislaine was at a loss to explain. Mayhap her wits had gone begging after all.

"I do not deserve such consideration, Kalim, but you may be right. The wine might help to restore my temper, if not my wits."

Kalim bowed gracefully before the repentant Ghislaine before summoning the boy once more. "Your husband is not a man used to sharing, lady. But he acts with no ill will."

"I know it," Ghislaine murmured. "I, too, have much to learn."

Kalim smiled. "It is not my place to suggest it, but perhaps he has much on his mind."

The merchant retreated to a gloomy corner and involved himself in searching amongst his wares for something that was no doubt vital. Joachim, apparently satisfied that she was not about to escape the clutches of her husband, sidled rather self-consciously towards Kalim and muttered a few words under his breath. Ghislaine picked up the two goblets of fruity red wine that the boy offered and made her way towards Guy. Her husband was frowning at the pile of cloth and did not change his expression when he saw her approach.

She gritted her teeth. "It is not usually my way to be so ill-mannered." Ghislaine ignored the raising of his eyebrow. "Well, perhaps it is. But you did not deserve such treatment."

Guy took the wine stiffly, not in the least mollified by his wife's words. "If the cloth was not to your liking, you only had to say," he said finally.

Ghislaine's cheeks flushed. "I like your choice well enough. It's just..." her sentence trailed off as his blue eyes pinned her mercilessly. She tried again. "It is pointless to waste such finery when I am bound for the convent." The words were spoken but still she held her breath.

Guy knocked back the wine before slamming the goblet down on the table. "Maybe so. But I have no need to be laughed at further by having a wife who looks like a serf. Until you take your vows, lady, you will dress with more care and not besport yourself in gowns that do little to hide your ample...charms."

Her face burned with the indignity and the implication. "You chose this gown yourself," she hissed in fury.

"It was the only one that hid your ankles," he retorted heatedly.

"No one else seems to have noticed that before.

"Walter de Belleme's eyes were hot on you last week?" he growled. His hand raked back his black hair as his temper rose.

"So that's it!" Ghislaine's outburst was one of complete disbelief. "You do not want me, but you will not allow anyone else to have me either. There is no dealing with you, Guy de Courcy."

So saying, Ghislaine would have pushed her way past him, but her husband was quick to react. Her arm was caught in a hard grip that brought tears to her eyes. Looking up at him with fury, Ghislaine got a perverse pleasure from seeing that he was equally as wroth.

"I am no uncouth soldier to be ordered around as you see fit, my lord. I will not be treated as less than a member of your family."

Those words earned a humourless laugh. "If you wish to be treated like a lady, then you needs act more like one. If you do not, then I give you fair warning that your people will suffer harder than you."

Chapter Eleven

Ghislaine glared at Guy as she waited for him. He had taken his time over the final transactions knowing that the delay would irritate her. The chamber seemed much smaller since his arrival and she longed to be in the fresh air and sunlight—or what remained of it. She had no idea how long she had spent with the merchant, but she was certain that it was longer than Guy had intended. And more expensive.

The thought that she had spent more than was absolutely necessary did not give her any pleasure and Ghislaine felt irritated with herself that she had allowed Guy to purchase the extra cloth. And yet his jealousy had given her a warm glow that had not died in their clash. It was completely unexpected and all the more surprising since he had given her no indication that he took any notice of her or how people treated her.

As she watched him now, Ghislaine no longer knew what to think. His countenance remained as grim and dour as ever, but from the way he stood and talked with the merchant, it was clear they had dealt with each other oftimes before, as the merchant had said. The purses of silver marks that Guy handed over were far in excess of the amount due, as Ghislaine was aware. What possible reason would he have for giving Kalim so much? The answer was not likely to come easily. It could be an old debt, but knowing her husband's insistence on paying for goods with silver in the hand, Ghislaine doubted that was the reason. More likely it had more to do with the murmured words than aught else.

When he joined her, Guy was frowning darkly. "'Tis time we left. I have business with the Earl." His voice reflected his irritation.

"I...I wish to apologise for my behaviour," Ghislaine began. "It was uncalled for." She peeped at his face shyly, but her heart plummeted when she saw his expression unchanged. "My father...I..." Why were the words so difficult? She tried again.

"I am not used to receiving gifts and have not learned to be graceful in my thanks." Her eyes held his steadily. "If it makes you happy to bestow such finery upon so unworthy a recipient, then I will gladly accept."

"'Tis lucky that I did not return the cloth then," came his curt reply. Despite the coolness of his words, Ghislaine was sure she detected a slight thawing in his manner. Well, at least the man was predictable in his grouchiness and she would have to be content with that. Except that those moments in the forest when he showed such gentleness kept intruding in her dark thoughts. Aye, the man had a softer side to him, and perhaps it was best hidden.

* * *

It was the smell of roasting pig that set her mouth watering as they walked up the wooden steps of the castle bailey. The castle guests had been called to dinner almost as soon as they entered the gates, and Ghislaine had been sore pressed to wash, brush her hair and shake the dust from her gown. Aware of how dowdy she appeared, especially as her husband looked so fine, Ghislaine quaked inwardly at having to face the court of Hugh d'Avranches. Unable to quell the trembling of her hands she hoped that Guy would not notice it through his thick surcoat.

"I had not thought you feared me, lady." They drew to a halt beneath a flickering torch. The dark frown was ominous but not threatening for all his great size. It was on the tip of her tongue to tell him that, aye, she feared him, to hurt him just a little for his grudging acceptance of her apology, but the words would not come. Anger and frustration played far more on her emotions than fear, and she doubted that lying would help much.

"I do not fear you, my lord."

"Then why does your hand shake so?"

Ghislaine glared at her husband. Did the man really not know how she must feel about entering a room full of spiteful tongues, especially dressed as she was? Truly the man was lacking in wits.

"Have you really no idea?"

He shook his head in confusion. "I would not have asked if I did, but as you have pointed out before, my wits are clearly lacking."

Mercy! Could the man read her mind now? Ghislaine's cheeks burned a little at his perception. After a glance about the bailey to ensure that they were alone, her eyes returned to his. "I have no wish to make a fool of myself before the Earl's court."

Guy just stopped himself from raising his eyebrows. This was probably not the moment to remind her that she had made a fool of herself there before without any help from him. "How so?"

Ghislaine gave him a withering look that was rewarded with a quizzical shrug. Sighing irritably, she decided that she would have to tell him.

"I look like a serving wench in this gown," she hissed. "And you look so fine. They will laugh at me and pity you." Folding her arms firmly across her chest, Ghislaine turned away from Guy, embarrassment stamped across her burning cheeks.

Guy cursed his own stupidity. Were women not well-known for their foolishness over their gowns? And there was also that tiny feeling of relief to know that the woman did not fear him. Where had that come from? And those other words?

"Fine? You think I look fine?"

"Have I not already said so?" came the disgruntled reply.

"My finery is an improvement, then?"

Ghislaine shrugged her shoulders, reluctant to commit any more words and knowing that her actions were childish but unable to react any other way.

"Mayhap this will help? I had thought to give it to you later…"

Ghislaine turned round slowly to face her husband. The man was really infuriatingly unpredictable in this strange mood, and she was not at all sure that she preferred it. At least when he was frowning she knew where she stood.

In his outstretched hand was a small bundle wrapped in blue cloth which she took with a rather bemused smile. What on earth had come over him? Carefully she undid the thin cord and unwrapped the gift.

"'Tis beautiful, my lord." Never had she seen a more magnificent belt. Three fine strands of gold were interwoven with a delicate pattern of filigree. An opal gleamed prettily from the clasp. Guy took it from her shaking fingers and placed it around her waist. His closeness had an immediate effect on her heart which suddenly began to pound. If he noticed, Guy gave no sign of it.

"It would please me were you to wear it this night." He was standing so close to her that she was forced to look up directly into his eyes.

"I have never seen so pretty a belt—" she began, but her words were halted by a finger on her lips.

Whatever he was about to say was interrupted by a loud gurgling. Guy grinned down at her burning cheeks. "Perhaps the clinking of the belt will disguise the noise from your stomach, lady. But unless you eat soon, I will be accused of your starvation."

The great hall was alive with light and music when they arrived. Scented beeswax candles lit up the rich colours of the tapestry hangings on the walls and the huge fire at the top end of the hall was stoked with the more pungent wood from the orchards. New rushes had been recently laid on the floor, although the hounds that fouled them were still in residence, Ghislaine noted with a sniff.

Drawing a long, steadying breath, Ghislaine stepped into the light. For a few heartbeats she was plunged into dazed confusion by the sight that greeted her. There must have been close on fifty people sitting at the long table, ranged on either side of the hall. Others remained standing, talking or watching a dazzling performance of acrobats and jugglers. Above the noise and hilarity Ghislaine could hear the music of the troubadours.

Hugh d'Avranches surveyed his court from the raised dais in front of the fire. Lounging back in his chair with his thick arms stretched across the back of his neighbour's, his eyes surveyed the scene with regal satisfaction. Feeling his eyes on them, Ghislaine was almost tempted to retreat to the shadows of the ladies' bower, but she knew that she would have to face these people sometime and she would not be called a coward.

A large hand covered hers and placed it gently on his sleeve, reminding her of his presence. Ghislaine darted a look of grateful relief into Guy's glittering blue eyes and then lifted her chin as she tried to walk gracefully to their places on one of the lower tables.

It was as if they were walking through a sea of eyes. With her stomach churning, Ghislaine tried to shut out the scorn directed towards her and concentrate on each step at a time. If only she had taken more notice of her mother's strictures on dress and behaviour, she would not be feeling so gauche.

The open admiration she witnessed as the women caught sight of her handsome husband only made her misery greater. That Guy de Gourcy was feeling as uncomfortable as she only served to fuel her frustration. Had he not kidnapped her, none of this would be happening. As they took their seats, her stiff, tight-lipped expression caused Guy to frown in confusion.

That Hugh d'Avranches always provided an excellent feast was the only reason for which Ghislaine had to be grateful. Roast pork, venison and lamb were served to the lower tables, either plain or cooked with garlic and honey. The emergence from the pantry of an elaborately stuffed peacock earned a buzz of excitement amongst the guests, although Ghislaine found the flavour not at all to her taste. Fortified at last by strong wine, well-spiced food and de Launay courage, Ghislaine scanned the crowd for a glimpse of a familiar face.

She spotted Walter easily as he stood near the fire talking to a tiny woman with thick blonde tresses and an older man, presumably her father. Walter had a silver goblet in his hand and his head was bent low as he listened attentively to the smiling girl. He laughed at something she said and Ghislaine flushed as she remembered only too well the way he had laughed with her.

Oblivious to the din around her, Ghislaine watched him and realised how little she really knew of the man. Here, in the great castle, Walter de Belleme was in his element. He revelled in the power and the glamour, the hubbub and the excitement. All the things she hated and would have despised him for in time. Part of her girlish dreams dissipated with the laughter and the noise and a veil came down over her heart. Never again, she vowed silently, would she be so naïve.

Abruptly, Ghislaine forced her wandering wits back to reality as she realised belatedly that she had continued to stare at Walter, and that he had suddenly looked up to catch her in the act. Flushed with embarrassment over being caught staring, Ghislaine hurriedly reached out for the goblet of wine before her, knocking it over.

"I suppose you think that was my fault as well?" The words sounded harsh but Ghislaine was sure that she detected teasing. She turned sharply to look at Guy.

About to open her mouth in retort, the meaning of his words suddenly sank in. It was impossible to stop her lips from forming into a quirky smile. "Whatever made you think that?" she replied airily.

"Hah! It is any immense fortune that your eyes are not weapons, else I would be long dead, lady." Guy tossed another goblet of the wine down.

"Most fortunate indeed, my lord. However, I do have other weapons at my disposal that could achieve the same end." Was this really Guy de Gourcy she was talking to? Nay, flirting with? He was surely not the same man?

That seemed to strike a chord within and Guy burst out laughing. Ghislaine looked on amazed. Without the grim frown, the man was positively beautiful. She did not doubt it for almost every woman in the vicinity had turned to look at him.

"Ah, yes. The ale."

"Ale?" She looked at him quizzically. Perhaps his wits had gone a-begging after all. "Nay, I was talking about my arrows." A quick glance round at the rest of the hall told her that they were no longer the focus of attention. "I have a good aim." The pride in her voice shone through.

Guy turned the full force of his blue eyes upon her. "There are times, lady, when you miss the target."

His eyes strayed momentarily towards Walter and
Ghislaine flushed as she realised that he had witnessed
her humiliation. Had he been watching her then? Her
eyes searched his face but she detected no sign of pity.
And she did not wish to see that from him, she realised. His teasing, however, was most unsettling. To
cover her discomfort, Ghislaine took another sip of the
wine. It burnt a path to her stomach and boosted her
courage.

"I thought you had business with the Earl?" she
enquired coolly.

"Aye, but I had not reckoned with this." His large
hand gestured to the gathering before them. In doing
so, he clipped his goblet and the red wine seeped
across the table.

A mortified sigh from the page behind them caused
the two of them to twitch their lips conspiratorially.

"It would seem that we have a problem, the two of
us."

Ghislaine could not prevent an involuntary chuckle
over his double meaning and she looked at him with
a warm sparkle in her eyes.

"Just the one, my lord?" she enquired conversa-
tionally.

Guy gave her a withering look and raked his hair
back. The familiar gesture sent a smile fluttering
across Ghislaine's face, but the frown on de Courcy's
deepened.

"Do not waste your pretty smiles on me, lady. I am
not de Belleme."

The icy tone of his voice doused the warmth of her
feelings most effectively and Ghislaine was left wondering why on earth she had ever thought the man was

human. Her thoughts were interrupted by a large hand grasping Guy's shoulder.

"So, de Gourcy. It pleases me that you came with such speed. I was mightily concerned that you might have fallen foul of Dettingham after all."

Hugh d'Avranches' blue eyes bored into Guy with piercing shrewdness. Ghislaine noticed that her husband's black frown had turned into one of icy politeness and for some inexplicable reason, it pleased her. At least she had not been subject to his cool distance.

"I was given to believe that you desired my presence immediately."

The Earl's fat jowls quivered as he nodded, the hooded eyes not leaving Guy de Courcy for a moment. A slow smile crept over the fleshy lips but it did not reach his eyes. "Your directness is most commendable, de Courcy, as one would expect from a mercenary."

The intentional sneer in the Earl's voice caused Ghislaine to hold her breath: but her husband surveyed him with an expression devoid of feeling. "I take it that you are in need of my skills, sire?" His voice was as cold as ice.

Hugh d'Avranches returned the cool stare and then transferred his gaze to Ghislaine who had remained silently seated, praying to God that he would forget about her. Unfortunately, God was not listening this night.

"My lady. A pleasant surprise."

Ghislaine inclined her head stiffly, murmuring her words of acknowledgement.

"Marriage seems to suit you, my lady."

Ghislaine shot him a quizzical look. "I had not noticed any appreciable difference, my lord."

"My foresters have reported no lack of game near your manor since your wedding and for that I must extend my thanks to your husband." The Earl smiled lazily at her and Ghislaine could feel the heat rush to her cheeks. She noticed that several of the couples seated near them were watching avidly and seemed to be enjoying her discomfort.

Before she could reply in kind, Guy interrupted. "I can take no credit for the increase in your game, sire, but it may be that the poachers have stayed away since the arrival of my men." Ghislaine shot him a grateful smile.

The Earl briefly inclined his head. "Then I may be doubly in your debt, de Courcy. Not only have you curtailed your wife's less endearing habits but you seem to have the manpower I need at the moment."

Guy's expression did not alter. "The men I have, sire, but I cannot admit to aught else. In truth, I have found my wife's behaviour most…refreshing. Marriage is far more diverting than I had imagined."

Ghislaine could hardly believe her ears. Guy de Courcy was defending her before half the court. No doubt he had a reason, came the voice of conscience. Aye, but it felt good to hear none the less.

"Most gratifying, de Courcy. Then mayhap we can examine the extent of your gratitude privately." This was not a question. Hugh d'Avranches nodded to his two nearest companions. One she recognised as William FitzNigel, whose lands stretched far beyond the rest in the county. The other was a smaller, younger man who had a look of the Earl. Ghislaine decided he was probably one of the Earl's bastards.

Guy rose to follow the three men without even a glance at her, but his words had been enough. She did not trust the Earl and whatever business he had with her husband would no doubt be dangerous. Ghislaine's eyes searched once more for Walter. She had to find out whether Walter was still entertaining hopes to kill Guy and the only way she could do that was to talk to him. Fortifying herself with another goblet of the soft wine, Ghislaine determined to find him.

She did not have to search far. A gentle hand grabbed her wrist as she made her way towards the acrobats.

"Well met, my lady!" Walter's soft grey eyes roved over Ghislaine's face. Whatever his feelings, they were well hidden. Did he trust her still?

"I had not thought to see you here, Sir Walter." Her voice was deliberately prim and cool since their last parting had been less than cordial.

"Nay?" His blond hair curled perfectly around his handsome face and Ghislaine suddenly wondered why she had found him so trustworthy. Everything about him, from his delicate hands to his handsome boots, seemed so perfect. She noticed his lips twitch as he took in her drab attire. Had he always been so? "Then a happy coincidence, my lady."

Ghislaine smiled at him wanly. "It would appear that this is not your only happy coincidence, Sir Walter. You seem to make a habit of talking to ladies."

She hoped fervently that his vanity would take control and think her suffering no more than jealousy. His grey eyes brightened considerably at her words.

"Blanche?" His eyes surveyed her speculatively. "She was a close friend of my wife. I had not seen her since Anne-Marie's death." His demeanour suddenly took on a much more sombre appearance. It was strange that she had not noticed that chameleon-like ability before.

A rather cheerful conversation under the circumstances, thought Ghislaine suspiciously. And if the name rang true, Blanche Cholmondston was one of the wealthiest widows in the county. How simple he must think her. And yet, if he thought her so gullible, it might not be too difficult to allay any suspicions he might have about her.

"Forgive me, Sir Walter, but I have not been myself of late." She peered up at him shyly, her mouth making a brave attempt at a cheerful smile. "My marriage was not of my making and I fear that I need some time to…adjust." Her fingers twisted nervously at the gold belt draped low over her hips. "My husband is not…the man I would have chosen."

Ghislaine took a chance and turned her eyes back to her companion. "I hope you will not think ill of my manners, Sir Walter?"

Sympathetic grey eyes pierced into her and Ghislaine wondered, just for a second, whether she had truly misunderstood him and Walter was still the man she had dreamed he was. Ruthlessly Ghislaine quashed the thought. She had not dreamed up his plan to kill Guy de Courcy.

"I think I have already told you how I feel, Ghislaine." The words were murmured softly so that only she could hear. "Mayhap I expressed myself too strongly at the time."

"I had not expected it," she replied quietly.

"Had you not?" His voice inflected a little so that she would hear the amusement in his words. "For all your simple appearance, I have never underestimated you."

Was that a warning? Ghislaine raised an eyebrow. She would have to brave it out. Around them the acrobats flared into action, encouraged by the appreciative shouts of their audience. They watched a tiny woman draped in green and gold fly through the air to be caught by her burly companion. Ghislaine looked towards the dais but was denied sight of Guy by the crowd that had gathered around the acrobats.

Ghislaine turned back towards Walter and watched him as he laughed at the players before him. His skin was soft and lightly tanned. Strange that she had never noticed that about him. "You spoke of a plan. Have you thought any more of it?"

Walter's eyes remained glued on the shapely form of the woman. "Nay. Not as yet." His eyes darted quickly in Ghislaine's direction.

For a sick moment, Ghislaine wondered if Walter de Belleme had seen through her after all, but judging by his slight smile, she decided he hadn't. Across from them the woman acrobat smiled invitingly at Walter. Slowly he turned his head towards Ghislaine. "I was waiting for your assent."

Ghislaine's heart froze as she heard the soft words. "My assent?" she whispered hoarsely. "What had you in mind?"

"Oh, nothing terrible. A simple riding accident in the forest. Or an ambush." The words seemed to Ghislaine to have been plucked out of thin air, but they

had not. She knew that deep within her. Walter de
Belleme wanted her husband dead.

"When?" came her quiet reply. She had to know.
Her heart was racing as she waited.

"Not yet." Walter turned the full blast of his soft
eyes upon her as he gently pulled her fingers to his
lips. "Not yet, sweet Ghislaine." The feel of his lips
made her jump back in surprise. Walter smiled. "I will
come for you soon."

They parted before crowds of people as if they had
done no more that speak of the weather or of hunting.
His bow was perfect even if hers was rather clumsy.
Ghislaine made her way back to her seat in a whirl of
thoughts.

The gentle flickering of the torch in the ladies'
bower drew Ghislaine's eyes. Sleep had eluded her for
some time and she could tell from the lightening shadows that dawn was well underway. And yet it had not
been the coughs nor the snores from the other ladies
that had kept her awake, even though the noise from
them would have been loud enough to waken deaf
Leowulf, the village smith. Nay. It had been Guy de
Courcy that had caused her puzzlement.

The moment Ghislaine had left Walter to resume
her seat, Guy had swooped down on her. Without a
word, her husband had led her from the hall, smiling
coolly at passing courtiers and their ladies, until they
had reached the other side of the heavy doors. He had
gripped her arm so tightly that she could feel the
bruise even now. Tight-lipped, he had propelled her
without a word to the door of the ladies' bower. His
face was dark and angry, and instinct warned her not

to say a word. Whatever the cause of his anger, she was sure she would find out.

"If you take an assignation with de Belleme," he had whispered in her ear with such disgust, "then I promise you, lady, your people will find out the truth of my reputation. Do you understand me?" He underlined the question by shaking her.

"Yes!" As the answer had been wrenched from her, Guy had pushed her roughly from him and stalked away into the shadows, leaving Ghislaine to recover her breath and her senses.

That had been hours past and Ghislaine was no nearer the answer than she had been then. Seeking respite from her jumbled thoughts, she finally closed her eyes and sank into a wild turmoil of shattered pictures and voices.

Chapter Twelve

Ghislaine stared gloomily at the hunched shoulders of Guy de Courcy, his whole body radiating anger and irritation. Light rain was blowing in gusts from the north-west and dusk was already sweeping across the darkening sky as the band moved steadily onwards. Relief began to seep through her bones as Ghislaine recognised familiar landmarks. Home was not far now.

The journey back to Chapmonswiche had been a long one. Guy had hardly addressed one civil word to her and had treated her like a leper. Indignantly she had remained behind Guy's destrier, resenting her petulant reaction but wishing to provoke a reaction all the same.

As they headed towards the forest, Ghislaine's preoccupation with their safety grew. The outlaws operated almost with impunity in the area, especially in the darkening half-light. It would, she decided, be very easy for Walter to do the same. A cold shudder ran through her.

Ghislaine eyed the forbidding back of her husband with increasing uncertainty. Guy de Courcy had been acting like a jealous lover ever since he had seen her talk with Walter. He had asked her no questions nor, more oddly, had he offered any opinions on her behaviour. He had just taken her away without a word. If she told him why she had been talking to Walter, she doubted very much that he would even listen.

A rustling of the leaves to the side of the track made her jerk her head round, but nothing was there. Ghislaine's heart slowed down and she wiped her palms on her dusty cloak. Guy had barely spared a glance in the direction of the noise and she silently cursed his ignorance. Of all the people she knew, he was the only one who was capable of resisting any attack of force. It was his living and he would be defending his own property. Resolving at least to try to talk to him, Ghislaine gently spurred her horse on to catch up with her husband.

"Why have you left Joachim in Chester?" she asked as pleasantly as the gusting wind would allow. Guy's cold silence echoed about them whilst the guards stared doggedly on ahead. Ghislaine shot him a dark look that fell on very stony ground.

Angered by his continued refusal to talk to her, Ghislaine tried another tack. "Surely you did not forget Joachim, my lord?" Her mocking exclamation earned her at least a hardening of the jaw, a sure sign that he was listening. "Poor Joachim," she continued unabashed. "But yes, you have the right of it, Sir Guy. Joachim is not really a man you would notice, and although his skills are certainly..."

"Cease this prattle, girl. Joachim remains in Chester to oversee the supplies. To my mind 'tis your wits that have gone awandering."

Guy settled back into disgruntled silence, his eyes fixed on the path ahead. Ghislaine sighed. At least she had earned his attention if nothing else.

"My wits?" she continued in shock horror. Cocking her head to one side as if contemplating the thought, Ghislaine then smiled broadly. "You are right, of course. It was my foolish wits that allowed me to be taken hostage by a desperate mercenary, to be married off as part of some deal and then treated as if I didn't exist. And," she continued with inspiration, "if that weren't enough, as a reward I have been allowed to spend the rest of my days in a convent, to forgo children and all those other domestic chores that seem to give the rest of womankind such pleasure."

Ghislaine slid her eyes over Guy's face and decided she was about to get a reaction.

"Your mindless chatter is doing naught but testing my temper, girl. If you had any wits about you, you would be contemplating how best to avoid my hand on your backside when we reach home." Guy spurred his horse a little faster as if to place himself beyond her reach.

Ghislaine was momentarily diverted by his use of the word "home" to think about what else he had said. It seemed strange to hear anyone other than her family call the manor home. When she finally realised what the man had said, her irritation with his pigheaded, obstinate truculence provoked her into more drastic action.

Kicking her horse forward, Ghislaine suddenly galloped ahead. With the wind and the rain pelting into her face it was hard to see where she was going, but she ploughed on. Behind her, Ghislaine could hear the shouts of men and on another level a heavy thud that could only be her husband's horse. Determined to put as much distance between them as she could, Ghislaine pushed on.

The track they were following to the side of the forest was awash with mud and rainwater, and Ghislaine's horse was finding a steady pace increasingly difficult. Slowing a little to negotiate a hanging branch was her undoing, for Ghislaine found her reins ripped from her frozen fingers and pulled hard towards the black destrier. There was no sign of the other men.

Remembering her provocative attitude just moments before, Ghislaine paled. Guy had clearly taken exception to it and was planning to chastise her here and now. She had not honestly believed he would lay a hand to her, for he had often made that threat without ever following it up. But he had seemed to be far angrier than normal. Leaning forward, Ghislaine tried to grab the reins back, but Guy's grip was too firm. As the horses came to a halt, she held her breath, watching her husband dismount. Running did not seem to be a sensible option.

As his strong hands gripped her waist, she finally found her voice.

"What do you plan to do?"

"You were warned, lady." The fierce look in his eyes was not something she could ignore. When her feet finally sank into the mud, Ghislaine's eyes searched for the safety of his men. In vain.

"Now? Here?" For some reason she seemed unable to utter any more and watched in disbelief as he tied the horses to a nearby branch and then yanked her towards the undergrowth. They stopped behind a large hawthorn clump.

Ghislaine was roughly turned towards him and slammed into his hard chest. It was difficult breathing but she was determined that he would not see how alarmed she was.

"Do not forget that I am your wife, Guy de Courcy," she uttered with a defiant gleam in her eye.

"I do not forget it for a moment, lady," Guy cut in sharply. "But it would seem that you do."

Her mouth opened and then abruptly shut. Mayhap defiance was not the answer either. "Nay, I do not forget it," she replied quietly. Her head was level with the middle of his chest and she closed her eyes as his hand slid under her chin and forced her to look upwards.

"So you have no longing for the convent after all?" Guy's voice was harsh and uncompromising.

"I did not say that exactly." Surprised at the question, her eyes snapped open.

"I distinctly recall you regretting the pleasures of domestic life. Was I wrong?" He shook her slightly and caused her to gasp. Her continued silence wrought another shake.

"This marriage was not of our choosing and I have no wish to remain a burden on anyone." Her decision to remain calm forgotten, Ghislaine's eyes spat fire at him.

Guy watched her with narrowed eyes as the cold wind blustered about them. "You have no vocation, that much I do know," he countered.

"You know no such thing," she retorted her lips tight. "In fact, you know very little about me at all."

Guy continued to stare at her for a moment before the merest hint of a smile broke his icy expression. "Then I shall put it to the test."

Before Ghislaine realised what was happening, Guy's lips had taken possession of hers in a kiss that seemed to go on forever. The more she resisted, the more insistent he became until finally her lips parted. As his tongue explored the softness of her mouth, Ghislaine felt all thoughts of resistance flutter away. As the kiss deepened, Ghislaine's hands slid up his arms to tangle her fingers in his thick hair.

Guy's mouth became more demanding whilst his hand slid from her waist to caress the full curves of her hips. Ghislaine gave herself up to such unfamiliar, erotic sensations as his tongue began to move in a forbidden rhythm that set her nerves dancing.

Startled by the strength of her response, Guy lifted his mouth from hers and gazed down at her flushed face. Slowly he put her from him and drew a steadying breath as Ghislaine's scattered senses returned.

In a daze of confusion, Ghislaine forced herself to focus her thoughts. Shame roared through her as she realised just how willingly she had yielded to him. Frantically she tried to think of something witty or defiant to say, or anything at all, but no words formed in her mind. Her cheeks burned hotly and she felt like a child who had just been taught a lesson.

"Take your reins, Ghislaine. The men are waiting back up the track."

Her eyes shot to his, but whatever her husband was thinking was masked by a cool veneer of apparent indifference. It had meant nothing to him, this kiss, after all.

Wordlessly Ghislaine turned to mount her horse.

The dark was swirling about them as the group finally entered the manor gates. Guards scattered in all directions as Guy slid wearily from the saddle and Ghislaine noted that there were more men in evidence than usual. Guy helped her from her palfrey and she warily placed her hands on his shoulders. She need not have worried for Guy did not linger. He turned on his heels and strode towards the hall issuing orders as he went.

"Sir Guy! Lady Ghislaine!" Sir Brian's loud voice carried across the bailey, halting both mid-step. This was not his usual method of greeting and the tone of his voice did not bode well.

"Is aught amiss, Sir Brian?" Ghislaine was pleased to hear her voice sound confident.

The hapless knight looked drawn and pale in the flickering torchlight as he stammered another greeting and bowed low before them. "Grave news," he began. "D'Everard is badly wounded and I fear for his life."

Guy stared at him for a moment in disbelief before he turned back to where Sir Brian was hovering. "How did it happen?" His voice was toneless but Ghislaine was beginning to realise that he always spoke this way when he wished to hide his feelings.

"Only a short time ago, in the forest. D'Everard was searching for the outlaws as you ordered when they were set upon. He has a bad wound in the thigh."

"Was there any other damage?"

"One dead and two minor wounds. Three of the horses have cuts." Sir Brian's hand gripped and ungripped his sword as he spoke.

"How many of them?"

The older man raked back his grey hair in imitation of the new lord. "About twelve to our eight, Sir Guy. It was a surprise ambush, although the guards say they were not soldiers. Like as not it was the outlaws."

There was not a sound in the bailey as Guy rubbed his chin with his gauntlet. "Where is d'Everard?"

"In the hall."

Without a word, Guy turned quickly and headed towards the hall. Ghislaine put her hand on Sir Brian's arm. "Could you send Effie with my medicaments and get Edwin to fetch Hulda from the village?"

Sir Brian nodded curtly and rushed off, grateful no doubt to be out of Sir Guy's way.

Even before she had reached the hall, Ghislaine could hear Guy blasting the men and she quickened her pace. They had no need of further injuries as a result of his anger.

The two wounded men possessed bad sword gashes on their arms and legs but Ghislaine quickly assessed their condition as curable. D'Everard was a different matter. His tunic and chausses were soaked in blood and he was very pale from loss of blood and exhaustion.

"How long has he been bleeding like this?" She addressed the question to the man hovering about Sir Arnaud.

"Since he was hit, my lady." The soldier frowned as he attempted to guess the time. "Nigh on two notches of the candle. We brought him home as gently as we could, but there was not much else we could do aside from removing his chain mail. Your maid did what she could." Silently he handed her an iron-tipped arrow. "He pulled it out himself. The tip's missing, my lady." Casting a pitying glance at Arnaud, the soldier shuffled to the far side of the hall.

It was far worse than she thought. Quickly Ghislaine directed a torch to above Sir Arnaud's leg and eased away the blood-soaked pad. In his muscular left thigh was a large, jagged hole that oozed blood.

Ghislaine had treated many such wounds before and was used to the sight of blood, but it was the sight of her husband that moved her most. Their eyes met as she assessed the extent of the damage. The arrow had torn the flesh badly but she was not certain whether a piece of his chain mail as well as the arrow tip was still within. If that was the case, then infection would set in quickly and Sir Arnaud would not linger long. Guy's face was white.

"Tell me the worst, lady."

Her eyes dropped to the wan face of his friend and decided honesty was the best she could do.

"I do not yet know how bad he will be. If the fever sets in, there is no telling whether he will pull through or not. I must clean the wound properly first but it will be a day or two before we know." She stared at her husband steadily. It would be no use promising life if she could not save him. It was in the hands of the Lord.

"Whatever you need, lady, just ask. The man is like a brother to me." The gruffness in his voice was heart-rending but Ghislaine put all tender feelings aside. Sympathy was not what he needed.

"I have sent for Hulda. She will save him if she can."

Guy opened his mouth as if to protest, but Sir Arnaud groaned most eloquently and he took two steps back. Nodding gravely, he retreated to the back of the hall, ushering out the rest of the men and sending for servants to provide whatever she deemed necessary.

The arrow had indeed caused much damage and d'Everard had lost a great deal of blood. The man was weak and in poor shape to fight for his life; Ghislaine decided he had best take a sleeping draught to gain some strength. First she set about forcing some poppy juice down his throat, and then, when satisfied it had taken effect, she had him moved to a smaller chamber where Ghislaine could examine the wound more carefully.

Her fears were justified. The tip of the arrow was lodged deep within although there was no sign of any chain mail. It was some time before she was satisfied that the wound was clean and could heal safely. Hulda, arriving soon after, was not hopeful of success. Every so often the old woman would stare at Arnaud's face and shake her head gravely, before examining the colour of the blood still seeping from the wound. Finally she placed a vile concoction of mallow, holly bark and elder over the clean hole to reduce the swelling.

At last she sat back and looked at Ghislaine. ''The Norman is in God's hands now. There is no more I can do.''

Ghislaine nodded as she took the pot of herbs from Hulda and searched the man's face for any sign of improvement. D'Everard looked very grey and ill.

Hours later, the fever took hold of him and Ghislaine truly feared for his life.

Through the night and all the next day she changed his bandages and forced various of Hulda's concoctions down his throat, but the heat from his body would not abate. As his thrashing continued and delirium took hold of his tongue, Ghislaine sent to the Abbey for a priest. No matter how ungodly the man, she would not let him die unshriven.

As the last rites were being said over his friend, Guy stared impassively at the group but made no attempt to join them. He had remained in the chamber the whole time but had not approached the pallet, carefully heeding Ghislaine's warning about not disturbing Arnaud. He had ordered fires, wallhangings and clean bedlinen as required. When the priest had finished, Guy quit the room.

Ghislaine watched him leave with a heavy heart. There was naught she could do to ease his suffering but maybe capturing the men responsible would go some way to help. She wished him luck.

"Lady Ghislaine, I have a message for you." The priest's reedy voice was close in her ear and Ghislaine whirled round, somewhat flustered at being caught watching her husband.

"Aye. There is a purse for the abbey, Father. I will send Effie for it."

Father Gregory was a small, thin man with a thin, foxy face that missed nothing. "My thanks, good sister. That would be most appreciated." He hesitated a moment and Ghislaine watched him dart a quick look around the room to see if anyone was listening. She drew closer. "I have a message. Father John wishes to speak to you concerning Margaret Staveley. He…is most anxious to see you."

Arnaud's groan captured Ghislaine's attention.

"Aye," she replied distractedly. "I'll come when I can." It was an odd request, but then priests were not of the same world. "Please take food and drink, Father."

She had the impression that the priest would have said more, but finally nodded his thanks and disappeared into the kitchens. Dismissing her fancies, Ghislaine hurried to Arnaud's side.

The fever finally broke the next morning, much to her relief. Had the man died, there was no knowing how her husband would have taken the news. She sent silent thanks up to heaven and a messenger to Guy. It was late in the afternoon when he finally returned and d'Everard had improved greatly.

His search for the bandits had proved fruitless so far, but he burst through the chamber doors with a hopeful smile on his face.

The smile wavered when he witnessed how pale and ill his friend looked, but he sat down at his side none the less. D'Everard blinked up at him, his eyes dull and sullen. He offered Guy a clammy hand to clasp.

"So, d'Everard. You go far to find a way to stay in bed." His blue eyes looked suspiciously bright.

Arnaud managed a faint grimace and plucked at Guy's arm. "If you need my services, best get me some food. Your lady would starve me on gruel."

Guy grinned up at Ghislaine as d'Everard sank back into exhausted silence. "My thanks, Ghislaine. Arnaud sounds almost himself again."

The smile he turned on her was dazzling and she was quite flustered by the sincerity she saw there.

"Thank me not, Sir Guy. It is merely my duty as lady of the house."

"None the less, you have watched over him tirelessly. Name whatever you wish, lady."

Her smile began to fade. He had called her Ghislaine before, and she had no wish to be paid for her services.

"There is no debt, husband," she replied stiffly. As she turned, her arm was gripped tightly.

"I did not mean to offend you, girl. My thanks are most heartfelt."

Ghislaine looked up into grave, blue eyes and her huffiness melted. She nodded, disturbed somewhat by his closeness. "Have you caught the outlaws?" They needed a distraction.

Guy sighed heavily. He looked very tired. "Nay, not yet. But I will."

Ghislaine had no doubt that he meant it and that cold gleam in his eye did not bode well for the men he finally caught. "Go eat and sleep, my lord, or else I'll have two patients on my hands." She watched her husband glance at d'Everard. "If there is any change, I'll wake you myself," she assured calmly. As she spoke, Ghislaine had placed one hand on his arm to add reassurance.

Guy placed his callused hand over hers and patted it gently, almost as if they had been married for years. "You are right," he grimaced. "I'm bone tired and stink like the devil. We'll speak on the morrow, Ghislaine." With a parting glance at d'Everard, Guy left the room.

A good night's sleep had worked wonders for her patient and Guy had left the manor with a much lighter heart that morning.

"So, my lady. Am I well enough now to eat like a man or must I persevere with this…slop?" Sir Arnaud's querulous tone brought a smile to Ghislaine's lips.

Rising quietly from the embrasure where she had been watching the forest, Ghislaine made her way to her patient's pallet. "If you are well enough to grumble, I am sure that you are well enough to eat something more substantial, Sir Arnaud." Bending over him, she placed her hand on his forehead. It felt cool to touch, although she did not like the grey tinge that lingered around his mouth.

Noticing her frown, Sir Arnaud sighed heavily, expecting Ghislaine to change her mind. "Hulda's gruel would be enough to make even your husband ill, lady. Perhaps we ought to try a little meat, as an experiment?" His voice was so plaintive and desperate that Ghislaine was not proof against it.

Raising her hands in defeat, Ghislaine smiled. "So be it, my lord. I'll send for a little chicken and bread."

Sir Arnaud tossed a surly look at her. "Chicken and bread! I think you and that hard task-master of a husband of yours have more in common than you think."

Ghislaine smiled broadly at the petulant tone. "You may be sure that I am not about to waste days of care by allowing you to eat yourself into death. Sir Guy would no doubt agree, were he but here." Her expression was implacable.

Sir Arnaud flushed somewhat guiltily. "Aye, that was most churlish of me. I am grateful for your care, lady."

"Think nothing of it, Sir Arnaud." Ghislaine rose to add some more fragrant wood to the fire. "I am well aware that my husband would be most disappointed were he to find you dead. Since you have managed to consume a goodly part of his wealth over the years, I am certain Guy de Courcy would view you as a poor bargain."

A reluctant smile played on his lips. "In truth, lady, it is not just myself who finds your domestic comforts attractive." He raised his hands in mock defence as Ghislaine shot him a withering glance. "Guy has lost a little of that bad-tempered surliness you complained of. See, lady! I warned you that with patience and a little comfort the man could be changed."

Staring into the flames as she raked over the embers, Ghislaine thought more of the man she had married. He had been a loyal friend to Arnaud and he had shown her how much he cared about him. Were he to feel the same about her some day! "Maybe," she replied distractedly.

"I have seen him watch you as you tended me; he looked much like a jealous man, lady." Arnaud slid her a covert glance as he settled himself comfortably against the bolster. "Perhaps if you lavished more care on him he might respond more...er...amicably?"

Ghislaine frowned, not at all certain that Guy wanted her attentions. "Why do you tell me all this? I would have thought it would suit you far better to have me sent to the convent so that you could return to the old life." She jabbed the stick deep into the fire.

"He is lonely and I think you do him good, Lady Ghislaine. Our friendship runs in both directions." He looked over at her, his smile gone. "Try it, lady. You have nothing to lose."

The light was fading fast by the time that Guy returned from his outlaw hunting. The cold, blustery wind of the day had turned bone-perishing and Ghislaine had made sure that extra wood was burning in the grate. She had also taken the trouble of ordering roast beef and Guy's favourite sweet tartlets. Whatever she had said to Arnaud d'Everard, Guy's story had played on her mind and touched a soft spot deep within. For some unfathomable reason she felt sympathy. It was her duty to try to give him some comfort, she told herself.

Guy's face was etched with lines of tiredness and the sullen expression he wore told its own story. Ghislaine rose to greet him as he entered the hall. Self-conscious that she had changed her gown and brushed her hair, her hands twisted the edge of her cuff as he approached. He was not only tired but very wet.

"Come, take off your cloak and rest by the fire to warm whilst I get you some wine."

Guy looked as if he would say something but obviously changed his mind. An expressive grunt was the most he could manage before he threw himself gratefully into the chair. Ghislaine carried away the discarded cloak and brought him a goblet of spiced wine.

"To what do I owe this?" he enquired with eyes closed as he stretched his long legs before him.

"I had thought you might appreciate it. If I was wrong, you have only to say," she replied stiffly. Had she really felt sympathy for this oaf?

Guy let out a low groan. "I did not mean to offend you, Ghislaine. This is...most welcome."

Thawing a little, she nodded. "I did not mean to be irritable either. There is a bath in...our room if you want it."

She stood up only to be stopped by his hand on her wrist. "Is aught wrong with Arnaud?" His eyes were grave and anxious.

"Nay. He is full of complaints. At this moment he is resting, but I am sure that he will be giving you a complete list of my crimes first thing in the morning."

His answering grin was one of relief, but he did not let go of her wrist. Instead he stood up.

"You have earned my deepest thanks, Ghislaine. I repeat that whatever you wish will be yours."

He raised her hand to his lips and gently placed a kiss on her fingers.

"Well, there is one thing," she remembered hesitantly. "Father John has asked to see me at the abbey and I would like to go."

Guy looked down at her, his eyes holding hers. For once his closeness did not distress her nor make her uncomfortable. "You have my word, if you promise to return the same day. My men will accompany you to ensure your safety."

A soft glow lit deep within her as Ghislaine nodded her agreement. Maybe Sir Arnaud had spoken some sense.

Chapter Thirteen

From the dark recesses of the bedchamber Ghislaine sat watching the sleeping form of her husband. The weak light of the dawn filtered through the shutters but did not reach the bed. He had not moved since he had collapsed on the bed the night before and she had not had the heart to wake him. There was always room amongst the women servants and Ghislaine had found a quiet pallet where she would not be disturbed by the gossiping and snoring. Normally she fell asleep immediately, but last night her mind had continued to think about her husband.

Eventually she must have dozed for she was awakened by the clattering of the women around her who were rising to begin the chores. So that the servants would not wake him, Ghislaine had laid the fire in the bedchamber herself to ensure that the room would be less chilly when he awoke. She had also placed a pitcher of the ale he liked and a small, freshly baked loaf of bread near the bed.

Pulling her knees to her chest, Ghislaine continued to stare at him. The man did not even snore, she realised suddenly and decided that he would be far easier to sleep with than the women. A deep flush stole across her cheeks at that daring thought and she was grateful that Guy was not awake to witness it.

His dark hair was tousled in a boyish way and made the harsh planes of Guy's face much softer. Long, dark lashes fanned his cheeks and his lips looked very gentle in the firelight. She wondered what he would have looked like as a boy and decided he would probably have been rather endearing. Maybe, as Arnaud had suggested, it was the harsh treatment he had received that had made him the man he was. Yet he did have a softer side and he had shown it to her on occasions. Guiltily, Ghislaine remembered how badly she had behaved towards him when he did try to show some consideration towards her. Resolving to act with more grace, Ghislaine uncurled her cold, stiff limbs and moved closer to the fire.

Mesmerised by the dancing flames, she sat back in the seat and let the warmth seep through her body. At length her mind began to slow down until sleep finally claimed her.

A sharp crack from a log on the fire made Ghislaine shoot up in surprise. The shock had numbed her brain for it took a minute to realise where she was or what she was doing there. The light was much brighter and Ghislaine surmised that she had been asleep for at least a candle notch. Looking quickly over in the direction of her husband, she was taken aback to see him sitting up and staring at her, a frown creasing his forehead.

"Good morning," she offered.

"Did you sleep there all night?" he demanded, the frown deepening to a scowl.

Ghislaine rose as gracefully as her stiff legs would allow. He was always grouchy in the morning. Smiling pleasantly, she shook her head. "I slept with the other women. You were so tired that I would not wake you."

"Most thoughtful, lady." If anything the scowl had grown blacker.

Growing uncomfortable with the increasing tension, Ghislaine decided perhaps honesty would clear the air. "Have I done aught to displease you? If that is the case, please tell me so that I can rectify the problem. I do not wish to worry about your scowls all day."

"I did not think you worried about my scowls," Guy countered.

"At times they have been justified," she allowed, "but I can think of no reason this morning."

"You have a clear conscience then?" His eyes regarded her suspiciously.

Ghislaine stared at him, her mouth agape. His arrogance knew no bounds. Resolutions forgotten, she advanced on him with a fierce gleam in her eyes. "If I were a man, Guy de Courcy, I would run you through. As I am not, I shall have to resort to other means. It grieves me to think that I laid the fire and brought you some ale and bread. My wits must certainly have gone awandering if I thought you might be grateful for a little care."

Angrily, she turned on her heels and stormed towards the door, but just as her hand touched the latch his voice reached across the room.

"I am grateful for your care."

Her fingers stilled mid-air. "You do not sound very grateful," she responded dryly.

"Then come back here and let me try again." His voice was no longer harsh, but soft and compelling.

Sir Arnaud's words echoed in her mind and Ghislaine sighed heavily. Why did she want to believe what he said? She turned slowly. "If you shout at me once more or give me another black look, I will leave," she muttered.

Guy nodded curtly. "Perhaps you could warn me when my looks start to get too offensive?"

That little play on words caused the barest twitch of her lips as she sat down gingerly at the foot of the bed. "Rest assured, Sir Guy, I will inform you."

"I prefer it when you call me Guy."

Ghislaine inclined her head. "Very well."

There was a momentary pause when neither of them seemed to know what to say, and Ghislaine was finding her proximity to the man rather nerve-racking. She was determined to sound as casual as she could. "Perhaps you would explain why you were so angry with me."

Guy looked at her with a wry smile on his lips. "I remembered nothing after I fell on the bed last night other than you had been insisting I ate and bathed. It...er...bothered me that had you stayed here, I knew naught about it." Guy shifted uncomfortably. "I...er...wondered why you had looked after me so well." He had the grace to blush under her curious gaze.

"But I did little."

"Aye. Well, that is the reason," he replied gruffly. "My apologies if I upset you."

"You are very easy to please," she teased gently.

Reaching for the ale, Ghislaine poured a small amount into the silver goblet and handed it to him.

Guy eyed the goblet with an odd expression on his face. "Did you brew this yourself, lady?"

Ghislaine could have sworn that his voice was laden with suspicion, but that was too far-fetched. "Aye. A good batch, I am given to believe."

"You have not tried it yourself?"

What was wrong with the man? "If you do not want the ale, Sir Guy, you have only to say."

Guy frowned at the stiff tone of her voice. "Nay. 'Tis not that," he added quickly. "I have a definite preference for ale brewed by you." So saying, he closed his eyes and tossed back the ale in one.

"My thanks for the compliment, Sir…er…Guy." Why did she feel so tongue-tied and awkward? "I shall remember it."

Guy was still staring at the goblet, sniffing tentatively at the residual aroma.

"Do you wish for more?"

Finally he looked up at her and smiled his boyish smile. "Not at the moment, but I admit that a man could set used to this personal attention."

That brought a flush to her cheeks. "If you continue to be so charming, I might be persuaded to try more often."

Guy leaned forward so that she could smell the lavender he had used in the bath. The sheets slipped and she realised that he was naked beneath it. The squire must have undressed him after she had left. His finger touched her cheek lightly and he smiled into her eyes.

"And what sort of persuasion would it take, lady, to stop you from going to the abbey?"

It was not just the question that caused the heat to flood through her body. His face was close to hers and she could see the stubble on his chin and the softness of his lips. The other hand had wandered to her braid and was gently pulling it towards him.

Ghislaine knew he was going to kiss her but she could think of no good reason to stop him. Slowly, so slowly he lowered his mouth to hers, but she did not pull away. His lips were soft and sensuous, caressing hers gently and without demands. It was over before she could respond.

"Why should I not go to the abbey?" she breathed, her eyes watching his lips.

His fingers slipped down to her arms and pulled her towards him once more. The blue eyes were turning darker as he kissed her with more force.

"I told you. You have no vocation," came the rasping reply.

Ghislaine tried to make sense of his words whilst her wits were scattered far and wide by the sensations swirling within her. Whatever his kisses contained, they had a seriously debilitating effect on her.

"What? Nay," she murmured breathlessly. "You misunderstand. I received a message to visit one of the priests there, no more." Watching the look of relief on his face, her mind began to act. Placing her hands on his chest, she pushed him back and gave him a look of much displeasure. So this was just a ruse to keep her here.

His hands snaked back around her arms again and

he looked at her almost fiercely. "So you do not stay there, then? This was no plan to escape?"

"Nay, it was not. I would not do anything so faint-hearted, When I leave for the convent, I will tell you."

His fingers relaxed their tight grip on her a little but did not let her go. "What message did you receive?" His voice was suspicious.

Ghislaine shrugged. "It was from Father John. He wished to talk to me about Margaret Staveley. There is naught odd about it," she continued as she saw his frown. "He would often stay with her. Margaret was most devout."

Guy thought for a few minutes and then sighed heavily. "It seems I must apologise once again, lady. I admit to thinking it merely a cover for an assignment with your lover."

Ghislaine stared at him aghast. "My lover?" she repeated. "Who is my lover?"

Guy gave her a withering look. "Walter de Belleme, lady. Do not play games with me."

Ghislaine folded her hands across her chest. "So that was why you behaved so jealously in Chester?" she demanded crossly. "You thought he was my lover."

"You deny it?"

"Aye."

"Then why were you talking to him for so long, looking at him just so, smiling?" His lips were set tight in an angry line and he imitated Ghislaine by folding his arms across his chest.

Ghislaine hesitated and lowered her eyes. Now was the time to tell him. "When he was here last," she began slowly, her fingers pulling at the sheet nervously, "he told me he had a plan to—"

"What plan?" Guy broke in. "Why did you not tell me afore this?"

"If you interrupt me again, I will not explain." Two bright spots of red burned on her cheeks and Ghislaine closed her lips tightly.

Guy gave a snort of disgust and fell back onto the bolster in frustration. "Go on," he murmured through gritted teeth. "I shall endeavour to keep my tongue and my hands in check."

Ghislaine raised an eyebrow at the threat, but she trusted him to keep it. "He planned for you to have an accident."

"So he would marry you and inherit not only your land but mine too. The Earl has not been slow to tell his knights of the details in our marriage contract," he finished bitterly.

She frowned at this further interruption but nodded. "Aye, I believed that his plan stemmed more from greed than for a desire to marry me." She gave a rueful, self-deprecating smile. "I could not agree to it, but I had to find out what the plan was so that I could warn you."

"And were you successful?" There was a disbelieving tone in his voice that Ghislaine did not like.

She shrugged her shoulders and shook her head. "He only said that he would arrange for a riding accident or an ambush, but not yet."

"Why did you wait until now to tell me?" Guy's eyes had turned flinty blue and she found it hard to look at him. Shamed by her lack of courage, Ghislaine turned her head away.

"You were so angry, you would not listen. I did try, but then Sir Arnaud…" Her voice trailed off. "I am sorry," she whispered.

"And why were you not tempted to be rid of me? It would seem that de Belleme was offering you a simple escape."

Ghislaine looked at him sharply. "I have no wish to see you dead. You may be a bad-tempered, ignorant oaf at times, but that is not deserving of death."

"And why should I believe that?" His voice was gruff and the expression on his face unreadable.

"It seemed sensible at the time," she retorted waspishly. "My wits must have left me."

Guy smiled at her huffy expression. He reached a hand out to gently brush back an errant curl and Ghislaine did not move back. "And how might you prove to me that you mean what you say?"

"I…I have no idea."

The soft smile returned to his lips and Ghislaine found her eyes drawn to them once again. His fingers had trailed gently down her arm and were tracing circles on the sensitive part of her palm. Confused by his actions, she looked up into his darkening eyes.

"Come here, wife."

A curious lethargy had taken hold of her body and Ghislaine knew she should move right away from Guy de Courcy. But she did what he had commanded without even realising it.

Hesitantly, she placed her hand in his and found the warmth there oddly reassuring. His fingers pulled her gently down to him so that she lay alongside his body, her lips practically touching his. There was nothing gentle about his kisses this time.

His hard body rolled half across her so that their
legs became tangled amongst the sheets. For a brief
moment Guy hesitated, drinking in her flushed cheeks
and huge brown eyes that seemed suddenly so childlike. And then she raised her fingers to his face, gently
tracing the outline of his lips. That was his undoing.
With a soft groan Guy closed his eyes and pulled her
tight against him so that she could feel every inch of
his body. How much he desired her. The knowledge
filled her with a feeling of elation, of power, and
something else she was not sure of.

When his mouth covered hers, Ghislaine responded
instinctively. Her lips parted and her tongue tentatively
touched his. As their kiss deepened, his hands glided
over her body possessively. His touch felt so good, so
deliciously exciting that she no longer wanted to think
at all. She felt herself falling slowly into a whirling
sensation of sensuality and awakening passion that she
was powerless to stop. Did not want to stop.

In some distant part of her mind, she felt his hands
fumble with the front of her gown and then the shock
of his lips on the delicate skin. His hands rose to
gently cup her breasts and Ghislaine gave a gasp of
delight. When at last Guy lifted his mouth from hers,
his breathing was harsh and rapid and he looked as if
he wanted to devour her.

As he gazed down at her white skin and soft,
rounded breasts, Guy placed a finger under her chin
and lifted her face to look at him. His eyes were
smouldering with desire.

"I want you, Ghislaine," he whispered.

Her fingers gently touched his face and pushed back
the locks of black hairs. Slowly her hand crept around

the back of his neck and pulled him back to her again. It was all the answer he needed.

The urgent banging at the door shocked them into a tense stillness. Guy lifted himself, his body alert.

When the banging came again, Guy was already on his feet, pulling on his braies.

"News of the outlaws, Sir Guy. Edwin is outside and would have words with you."

"A moment," he answered as the tunic went over his head. Turning back to the bed, Guy bent over Ghislaine who was still dazed and confused. His features were no longer soft and lover-like but harsh and implacable.

"We will speak when I get back, Ghislaine."

She watched him stride through the door without a backward glance, her mind in a whirl and her body still yearning for his touch.

Chapter Fourteen

The abbey lay but a short ride to the south of the forest and Ghislaine was heartily glad of the fresh air and the chance to think. Arnaud was recovering well and she had left him to Effie's enthusiastic care.

Surrounded by six guards, Ghislaine felt embarrassingly overprotected but Sir Guy had insisted. She had no wish to argue with him. As they made their way through the valley, she kept thinking about her husband. Nay, that was not right. She wanted to put him from her mind completely, but memories of his face, his voice, his frown kept crowding in. Finally, she simply gave up trying.

It was most odd that he had thought her likely to escape to the abbey. Stranger still that he had not wanted her to go. There was no good reason for that either—at least, none that he had given. Her lack of vocation would not normally be a barrier for a husband wishing to rid himself of his wife.

Other, more erotic memories kept dancing through her mind causing her to blush suddenly. None of the guards seemed to have noticed this unfortunate afflic-

tion, however, but none the less she kept darting covert
glances at the men nearest her.

Perhaps, she decided restlessly, time spent with the
priest would douse the fire that seemed to burn within
her still.

She ought to have been grateful for the timely interruption, but what she had felt was cheated. It was
so good lying with him, touching him, kissing his soft
skin, being caressed. Her control had long gone and
he knew it. She would have done whatever he had
wanted her to, willingly. He had made a wanton of
her and it hadn't mattered.

But what then? He had always insisted he did not
want marriage to her. It was his freedom he wanted.
A gawky wanton was not part of his plans. Would she
then have gone to the convent willingly? And if there
were a child? A wry smile played around her lips at
that thought. What a monster they would produce between them! No, she could never give up his child.

As the abbey gates came into view, Ghislaine resolved to put all thoughts of Guy de Courcy from her
mind and concentrate on pure love. But it was hard.

The guards remained outside as the young nun at
the gate led her across the muddy courtyard. The abbess's rooms were located beneath the low stone
arches at the far side, next to the heavy oak doors of
the chapel. Ghislaine waited outside, as bidden, watching the peaceful lives of the nuns trickle by. It was
curious that the faces of those women seemed remark-
ably smooth and unlined, as if, by missing the great
joys and sorrows of womanhood, time did not leave
its mark. Was that what she wanted? To be untouched
by life?

"Lady Ghislaine, please enter." The abbess's stern face was full of foreboding, and Ghislaine followed the tiny, thin figure into her room. The cold seemed to echo around the stone floor and walls and then seep into her very bones. There was but a meagre fire in the large grate that seemed to Ghislaine to have no effect at all. She shivered.

Ghislaine sat on the simple wooden stool offered by the abbess. Declining a goblet of wine, Ghislaine pulled her cloak closer.

"Father John sent a message to you. Is that the reason for your visit?" Her voice was surprisingly low, but Ghislaine detected the tension in it.

"Aye," she replied. "He wished to speak to me of Margaret Staveley, I believe."

"That is so, but I must ask first if your husband is close by?" The round, grey eyes of the older woman watched her steadily.

It was an odd question. "Nay. He is searching for the outlaws in the forest."

"Good. You will understand in a minute, Lady Ghislaine." For the first time, a thin smile banished her joyless expression. "Father John." Her voice was raised no more than a fraction, but a heavy curtain to the right of the fire stirred. "Come, come," she urged the tall, nervous figure who emerged to step closer towards Ghislaine.

Father John gave the abbess a quick nod which was the signal for her to leave the room. Once alone, he turned to Ghislaine. He was not so old as she had at first thought. Thin brown hair blossomed out from his tonsure and covered a broad forehead. He had a boyish air, although she reckoned him to be in his late thirties. Myopic brown eyes peered down at her.

"I am most anxious to restore the peace to my soul, Lady Ghislaine, but the information I must give you to do so could be dangerous for us both. Margaret Staveley always spoke highly of you, of her regard for your friendship, so I place my trust in you." His voice was high, nervous, and the words delivered in a staccato fashion that was at odds with the normally quiet, slow pace of the priests.

Ghislaine inclined her head, not quite understanding what he meant. He must have sensed her confusion.

"I was present when she was murdered."

Ghislaine paled at his words, a wave of ice cold flooding through her body. "Why are you telling me?" she demanded in a fierce whisper. "You must know the name of my husband and why he demands protection from the Earl."

"I do, but I also know that the marriage was forced upon you. You did not choose to do so. Your first loyalty is to God. Am I right?" He watched her with nervous eyes.

"Aye. But I must first tell you that I believe him to be innocent of the crime." Ghislaine rubbed her freezing hands together to warm them a little, her eyes not leaving the man pacing backwards and forwards before her. She took a shallow breath at his continued silence. "Do you know who killed Margaret?" Her wavering voice betrayed the tension that was building deep within.

"Yes…and no." The priest's eyes darted about the room as if he feared attack at any moment.

"I do not understand," she replied. "Did you not recognize who murdered her?"

"I did not see him, Lady Ghislaine. I was hidden behind an arras in an alcove. It was his voice I heard."

"You heard what happened? You survived?" she breathed.

"Aye," came the bitter reply. "And I never wish to hear such sounds again. My faith…has been sorely tried these last few weeks." He stopped before the fire to watch the tiny flames. "In the end, God prevailed over my fear." He turned to face her, a weary, haggard expression on his face. "But I need your help."

"My help? How?" Ghislaine stared at him.

Father John looked at her unblinkingly. "Your husband is accused of the murder. If I heard his voice, I would be able to recognise it."

A cold hand seemed to squeeze her heart. She had wanted to believe his protests of innocence and now she was being given the chance to put it to the test and clear his name. Or prove him guilty.

"I will do what I can, Father. My husband wishes to clear his name and I am certain, despite his…violent profession, he would not kill an innocent woman for refusing him marriage." And if he was found innocent, he would have no further use for her. She lifted her chin. "I am certain you will have no cause for alarm."

The man looked rather doubtful but smiled hesitantly. "Your husband is not known for his gentle nature, Lady Ghislaine, and after what I…heard, you must understand my hesitation."

Ghislaine returned his smile, but it did not reach her eyes. "Aye. I understand. Surely, though, it would be better if Sir Guy did not know the reason for your presence. There are some amongst us who would be grateful for your advice, although I doubt my husband is one of them.''

Father John nodded his head. ''As you wish, Lady Ghislaine.''

He lapsed into silence, his thoughts elsewhere.

''What did you hear?'' She had to know what had taken place, to know what Guy was accused of.

Closing his eyes as if picturing what had happened, the priest sighed wearily. ''I had been preparing to pray with Lady Margaret in a small chamber off the hall. It is hidden from view by a heavy curtain to ensure privacy. She preferred to pray without an audience,'' he added softly. ''As a truly good woman would.''

''Strange, loud noises caught my attention as I prayed, and I went to the curtain. Lady Margaret was shouting. She was very angry.''

''What did she shout?'' demanded Ghislaine.

The priest raised his hands in a despairing gesture. ''I could not hear everything, you understand, but she told him he was a despicable man, a murderer, a betrayer whose life depended on the misfortunes of others.''

Ghislaine blenched at the words and her fingers rose to her throat. Could Guy have lied to her? Aye, he could. Very easily, came the voice in her head. The man killed for his living. Lying well must be a bonus in his profession.

''Was there aught else?'' she asked quietly. Surely this could not be the man who had threatened her loudly on several occasions with a beating but had never carried any out, despite severe provocation? She could not believe it was, no matter how damning the evidence.

"When Lady Margaret repeatedly refused his offers, he threatened to kill her. Even then..." His voice trailed off. The priest turned to the window and stared up at the sky as if exhorting God to give him strength. "Even then...I did not go to her aid. I cannot forgive myself for being such a coward. She needed me and I stayed behind the curtain."

Ghislaine stared at his shuddering back, hearing his agony but unable to help him. "She would not have wanted your death, Father John. Margaret would have called for you had she thought you might have been able to help." The words sounded empty and trite to her own ears.

He raised his hand to stop her words. "This is between me and God now, Lady Ghislaine. The only way I can help her now is to name her murderer. Although...it was not at his hands that she died."

Ghislaine raised her head to look at him. "How did she die?" She waited as the man gained control of his voice, dreading his words.

"She jumped from the window to her own death," he whispered. "The others were killed by the knife," he added with a shudder. "They knew what they were doing. None survived. When they had gone, all I found was blood, bodies and a mess. They had taken the silver, her jewels...even the gold and pearl cross from around Margaret's neck had gone."

The priest turned towards her, his face white and old in the light. "I could not tell them she died by her own hand. She did not deserve that. I wished her to

be buried like a good, honest woman, in the church-
yard next to Sir Peter.''

Ghislaine rose from the stool and stood before him.
''Thank you, Father John. You are a kind man.''

Their eyes held for a moment before he looked
away and Ghislaine saw there the torment and the agony that the man was suffering.

''If you are ready, we should go now.''

When they eventually rode back across the moat,
they were greeted by confusion. Carts and unknown
men littered the bailey. A wild profusion of colours,
provisions and tongues assaulted their eyes and ears.
Kalim and Joachim had arrived.

The priest's nerves had increased with every step
that took them closer to Chapmonswiche and now that
they had arrived, the man jumped at the slightest noise.
The fact that Guy had not yet returned did little to
relieve the escalating tension in his mind. Seeing his
trembling hands and the anxiety in his face, Ghislaine
dismounted and showed him the way to the private
chapel. As far as she knew, she had been the only
visitor there for some time. Father John retired gratefully to his gloomy seclusion. Food and drink would
be sent to him as soon as she saw the kitchen staff.

When Ghislaine entered the hall, she found Kalim
and Arnaud sitting comfortably before the fire, sipping
some of the wine that had just arrived. A small chest
lay next to Kalim's feet.

''My lady.'' He rose gracefully and took her hand.
''I am most pleased to see you in good health.''

Ghislaine smiled warmly. ''My thanks, Kalim. I

was not aware that you would be bringing our supplies personally.''

The old man held her questioning eyes for a moment and then looked around the hall. ''I have much to discuss with your husband.'' His cold hand squeezed hers gently. ''Perhaps you would sit with me awhile, if you have the time?''

Something in his eyes warned her that this was not going to be as casual as it sounded. ''Gladly,'' she responded quietly. Kalim pulled a chair for her next to his and handed her the wine when she had made herself comfortable.

''I shall make myself useful in the bailey,'' Sir Arnaud began tactfully as he pulled himself to his feet. ''But before you say aught, Lady Ghislaine, I am not about to undo your good care. Rest easy.'' The merry grey eyes twinkled down at her.

As Sir Arnaud was not noted for his love of hard work, Ghislaine smiled her agreement. ''Be sure to return to the fire the moment you are fatigued,'' she replied sternly. Her eyes followed him as he limped heavily from the hall.

''Sir Arnaud has been most impressed by your healing skills, Lady Ghislaine. I am interested in how you acquired them.'' That was not what he was here to discuss at all, but he wished to do so and Ghislaine complied. Her mind was racing on ahead to the moment when Father John heard Guy's voice. To the moment when Guy realised he had no need of her.

''If you twist the belt much more, Lady Ghislaine, it will fall to pieces.''

Ghislaine looked up at him, startled and then down at her own fingers. She had not been listening. Flushing with shame at her lack of manners, she began to apologise.

Kalim held up his hands. ''You have many concerns at the moment and have no need to explain.'' The old man's nut brown face creased into a smile. ''I have a gift for you.'' Bending down to open the chest, Kalim gently took out a small pot. ''My tisane?'' he announced gravely. ''It will help your nerves.''

''I think I will need more than a tisane, Kalim. But your gift is very kind.''

Kalim nodded slowly. ''Then perhaps the information I have will assist in some small way.''

''What information?'' Ghislaine's interest was piqued.

''About Walter de Belleme.'' He took a long draught of the wine before taking a sidelong glance at her. ''He has been frequenting the harbour more and more of late, recruiting the scum of the waterfront to his employment.''

Ghislaine did not really know why that was so important, but hesitated to say so.

''It is also well-known that he has been borrowing money in the expectation of receiving a large sum shortly.''

That caught her attention. ''How do you know all this?'' she asked, a frown creasing her smooth brow.

Kalim shrugged. ''I have my sources and they are always reliable.''

A welter of thoughts collided around her mind at once. Walter must be planning the attack soon, but why should he be expecting money? If he was going to marry her, then he would not receive any large dowry. That was well-known. Unless... A thought

suddenly struck her. Guy had said something odd
about the Earl not being slow to tell all his knights
about their marriage contract. At the time she had ignored it, but perhaps there was something most sig-
nificant in it.

"I know he plans to ambush my husband," she began slowly, "and I have warned Guy. But as for the
money, I know nothing about that."

Kalim continued to stare at the fire. "He is a man
who loves only himself," he said eventually. "The
greed in his heart shines in his eyes."

"Whereas it is the anger in my husband's heart that
shines in his eyes," she added quietly. Ghislaine
looked up at Kalim, her eyes mirroring her worry.
"Arnaud told me much of Guy's life and how wary
he is of women." For a moment she watched her fingers fiddle with her belt. "I have found that I have
grown to care for him, despite his temper and his oafish ways," she admitted. "But it is very hard to show
him when I doubt he is concerned at all."

Kalim watched her clenched jaw and tightened lips,
knowing how hard it had been for her to admit to such
feelings. "Perhaps it would interest you to know that
Guy is not completely lost to feeling," he said
thoughtfully. "I have heard him say he knows nothing
of his family, but he still gets information about his
brothers in Normandy."

"He does?" she questioned.

Kalim nodded his head. "He usually buys it from
one of the captains on the trading ships at the harbour.
At a price, of course."

For some reason, that piece of information cheered
her up. So he had been trading information with the

captain of the *Isabella* about his brothers. The thought of him paying for the information made her smile. "He said he never thought of them," she murmured.

"It is hard for Guy de Courcy to admit to caring for anyone, but he is just a man."

Ghislaine raised her eyebrows in wry disbelief at that statement. "'Just a man'," she repeated in a voice loaded with sarcasm, "does not apply to my husband."

Kalim laughed, his white teeth flashing in the firelight. "You are wrong, Lady Ghislaine. I have no doubt that should you wish to put it to the test, he will not be proof against your pretty smile and a warm welcome."

Ghislaine felt the blush steal over her cheeks. Did she wish to put it to the test?

The pale sun was low in the sky before Guy's arrival home was announced in a flurry of movement and excited calls. The trestle tables were already laid in preparation for the feast Ghislaine had ordered.

A cow had been killed in honour of their guest and a fat pig was roasting on the spit. Several mouthwatering pies and pasties, chicken boiled in wine and mushrooms and pike served with galentyne sauce were being enthusiastically prepared in the kitchens. Sweet cheese tarts and coloured custards were kept for dessert. Elfrieda had excelled herself and Ghislaine wondered greatly at her cooperation. Whenever a feast had been ordered in the past, Elfrieda's temper was predictably explosive. Now, not even Joachim's inexplicable presence in the kitchen appeared to upset her. She decided to think on the matter later.

Effie had brushed Ghislaine's long hair until it shone like coppered blonde. Despite her drab green gown, Ghislaine's eyes told her that she looked much better than usual. Perhaps she was growing up?

Guy strode through the door of the hall, a broad grin on his face.

"My lady. Good news indeed." His smile was infectious.

"You have found them?" she guessed excitedly, his good humour lightening her heart.

"Aye, we did. No small thanks to your man, Edwin."

As all eyes turned to the tall figure behind Guy, Ghislaine watched as a slow smile began to form on the Englishman's face. Guy clapped his large hand on Edwin's shoulder and shouted for ale.

"A good day's work. It pleases me greatly to see you anticipated our success," he noted with an amused smile on his face. The grin broadened as Ghislaine blushed in embarrassment.

"I...er...Kalim has arrived with the supplies and the cloth, my lord. We...thought you would appreciate a...celebration."

Guy gave her another crooked grin and then, to her complete shock, he pulled her close and kissed her full on the lips.

"My lord," she gasped, as soon as he let her go, "what are you thinking of?"

"What I have been thinking of all day," he whispered into her ear, before giving her a playful peck on her burning cheeks. Ghislaine looked around quickly, relieved to see that no one else seemed to have heard. The fire within was ignited.

Elizabeth Henshall 231

The night was spent celebrating the capture of
Thomas Bollyngton and four of his men, with each
knight giving their own competing account of their
bravado and skill. There was much laughter and good-
natured pulling of legs as each tried to outdo the other.

Guy was like a different man. The frown was banished for the moment and Ghislaine was able to see
him for what he was. Young, handsome, strong and
brave. He was also astute and the men respected him.
Not perhaps very god-fearing…her thoughts suddenly
flew to Father John. She had not seen him since she
had slipped into the chapel earlier to tell him that Guy
had arrived. He had declined her invitation to eat with
them, saying that his presence might not be too welcome this evening.

Deciding to see him in the morning, Ghislaine
slipped away from the feast. Guy was deep in conversation with Kalim and the rest of the men were
doing their best to exhaust their new supplies. She had
ordered Effie to pack the beautiful material away in a
lined chest, since she was sure that Guy would send
it back when his wits returned.

The fire was burning brightly when she entered the
bedchamber. Below, she could hear the shouts and
raucous laughter of the men. Guy had not spared her
a glance as she left, and her heart was heavy with
disappointment. Slumping down on the stool before
the fire, Ghislaine slowly unbraided her hair and began
to comb it carefully, her thoughts lost with the flames.

The door latch clicked back firmly into place and
Ghislaine whirled round.

"Escaping, lady?" Guy leaned back against the

door, his eyebrows raised in question. His hands remained behind his back.

"Not at all, my lord."

"Guy," he supplied gently.

Her heart began racing. His voice was soft and compelling.

"Guy," she repeated nervously as he sauntered towards her stool. "I thought you wished to celebrate with your men."

"I had other plans for this night, Ghislaine."

She gulped hard as his hand reached to take the comb from her hand. Gently he pulled her to her feet.

"Kalim's arrival was most timely, though."

"It was?" Her voice was almost inaudible.

"He bought me a special order. For you." He held out a small parcel.

Ghislaine looked at him as if he were mad and then nervously set about unwrapping the gift.

"They are beautiful," she whispered, as she held up the delicate linen for inspection. Two of the loveliest chemises she had ever seen. They were made of the softest linen and embroidered with exquisite patterns. A deep blush flooded her from top to toe. He had paid someone to make them for her.

"I had thought," he whispered back huskily, "that you would wish to express your gratitude more fully."

Her eyes raised slowly to his and saw the leap of desire there. Her finger pushed back an errant lock of his hair. She smiled.

"What had you in mind?" Ghislaine peeped up at him coyly.

"A kiss, perhaps?"

Standing on tiptoes, Ghislaine gave him a gentle peck on the cheek. "Like this?"

"That would be most...worthy, had I given you a...horse comb," came the dry retort.

"I see," she replied, catching her lower lip between her teeth. A frown completed her puzzled expression. "Perhaps you could give me a hint as to the worth of these chemises then, Sir Guy?"

His lips twitched with amusement before claiming hers in a soft kiss that completely took her breath away. Ghislaine stepped back, her chest still rising quickly.

"That was most clear." She smiled up at him, drowning in the desire she saw there. "But I really believe that I would find it...easier to express my thanks...if there was perhaps less light."

The spots of red on her cheeks were proof enough of her shyness and they tempered Guy's growing impatience a little. With a heavy sigh, he doused the wall sconces so that the only light came from the fire. Standing before him, watching his face glow in the flickering light, Ghislaine gave him the answer she knew he was waiting for.

Slowly her fingers pulled at the ties at the neck of her gown until they came free.

Unable to tear her gaze from his, Ghislaine watched as Guy's fingers reached out to touch her unbraided hair. "Have I told you how lovely you are, Ghislaine?" he whispered fiercely, pulling her gently towards him.

She shook her head, denying the thought as well as the words. "You have called me many things over the last few weeks, most of them less than flattering,'' she teased gently.

This time it was Guy's cheeks that flushed. ''Each one well deserved, no doubt,'' he countered grimly. ''Have I also told you that you are a most troublesome baggage?''

Ghislaine laughed at the ominous frown. ''I think I feel less nervous when you scowl at me.''

The frown deepened as his fingers lifted her chin so that her eyes looked into his.

''You are nervous?'' he asked uncertainly. He could feel her trembling and did not need the slight nod she gave to tell him she was very nervous. His finger slid over her cheek in the briefest of caresses before lowering to catch her hand and place it palm down on his chest.

Ghislaine could feel his heart hammering beneath his touch. He had shown her what he found so hard to tell her. Did she really have that effect on him? Sliding her hands slowly around his neck, she pulled his lips down to hers and kissed him as gently as he had done to her.

As she watched him breathlessly, her cheeks flushed, Guy stood back to remove his tunic and chemise. At the sight of his sun-darkened chest, Ghislaine's throat contracted. He was so beautiful, she just wanted to reach out and run her fingers over his soft skin. Hesitantly, Ghislaine placed her palm over his heart once again and she felt it race at her touch. Had she made him do that? At her look of surprise, Guy took her other hand and placed that one on his chest too. When his arms encircled her, pulling her body flat against his, and his lips touched hers, Ghislaine stopped thinking.

His mouth did not stop at hers. It trailed gently over a soft cheek to just below her ear, nuzzling wickedly at the tender skin beyond. Strange feelings she had never known shot through her body, causing it to arch against his. Her skin prickled with the velvet roughness of his tongue as it circled upwards towards the nape of her neck. Unable to bear the sensuality, her head fell back, thrusting her breasts into his chest. His lips moved to the creamy skin exposed just above her breasts. A gasp of delight escaped from Ghislaine at such sinful behaviour.

Just as she thought her knees would give way under this assault, his mouth returned to hers for a scorching kiss that ignited the fire within her. This kiss was completely different from any others. It was full of passion and longing, but there was tenderness and reassurance there too. He wanted her tonight. And she wanted him.

Guy's hands moved up and down her body possessively, sliding over her hips, pulling her deeper into him, showing her how much he desired her. Ghislaine felt herself slipping into the unknown world of passion, surrendering her aching body to the touch of his hands.

It was not until she felt the cool air on her breasts that Ghislaine realised that her gown no longer covered her, but as his hands gently cupped her swelling flesh she no longer cared. Her back arched into his erotic caress, her hips pressing into his. Softly his thumbs circled her hardened nipples as his mouth nibbled its way down her neck.

Weak with pleasure, Ghislaine was no longer able to support herself and wound her arms around Guy's neck. Her fingers tangled in his thick hair as his strong arms pulled her upwards until her breasts were within reach of his mouth. Her body exploded with sensation as each nipple was gently licked and then sucked until Ghislaine thought she would die with the pleasure. Slowly, she felt herself being lowered the full length of his hardened body until her feet touched the floor. Her gown and chemise fell at the same time.

She felt no shame standing before him naked. His eyes were dark with passion and told her that she was beautiful. His hands told her how much he desired her. Without taking his eyes from her, Guy removed the rest of his clothes. There were no more barriers between them and Ghislaine made no protest when he swept her up and carried her effortlessly to the bed.

They sank down together, Guy stretching out at her side. The firelight was not so bright on this side of the room, but she was able to see his eyes glittering with passion as he gazed down at her.

"Touch me," he commanded gently.

It was all the encouragement she needed. Hesitantly her fingers trailed a path across his chest, exploring the deep cuts of war and swordplay, the muscles of his arms. His soft groans of pleasure made her bolder still as her hands lowered to caress his back and his hips. She revelled in the soft feel of his beautiful body, of his hard muscles, of the dark hair that grew where hers did not.

Unable to endure her exploration any longer, Guy's hands cupped her face gently. "Kiss me," he ordered huskily before pushing her onto her back. His fingers tangled with her hair as his tongue parted her lips and kissed her with an intensity which left both of them gasping for breath.

Shudders of delight raced through her as Guy pushed his naked body hard against her. It was a raw, primitive act which served only to enflame her. A throbbing began somewhere deep within her with a rhythm that matched the thrusting of his tongue in her mouth.

Ghislaine responded instinctively by lifting her knees and winding her legs around his hips. His tongue plunged deeper into her mouth as his fingers explored her slender thighs. As they reached higher, Ghislaine tensed, uncertain suddenly.

"Don't," he whispered hotly. "It will make it better for you, Ghislaine." His voice was deep and husky with desire. She could not stop now. With a conscious effort, Ghislaine forced herself to relax as his fingers touched her in her secret place. His mouth trailed hot, wet kisses over her face, her eyes, her neck as his finger slipped inside her, exploring, rubbing, pleasuring.

Her eyes opened wide at the sensations he was creating in her, her breathing jerky and strained. Suddenly, a feeling so exciting, so erotic, fluttered deep within her and she pushed against him harder, knowing that he would be able to help her find it again. Raising her body, she buried her face in his neck, flattening her breasts against him.

"Show me," she whispered "Show me what to do."

Guy paused, his handsome face dark with passion. "It will hurt for a moment," he groaned, desperately wishing he could lessen the pain he would cause her. "Only for a moment."

Ghislaine wrapped her arms around his neck, her eyes full of trust. Guy placed his hands beneath her, lifting her hips. As he pushed gently towards her, his mouth covered hers in a tender kiss.

At first there was no pain, just the unfamiliar sensation of feeling him inside her. But as he pushed again, each time going deeper, Ghislaine realised he was just easing himself in as gently as he could. He waited until she was used to him before he started to move again.

Suddenly he plunged deep within her, deep into the tight, hot core of her, hating the pain she would feel. He waited a moment for her pain to subside and then slowly, as slowly as his aching body would allow him, Guy rocked backwards and forwards until he felt her push against him. As her body began moving with his, he thrust deeper and deeper, trying to give her the pleasure she was instinctively chasing.

Ghislaine felt the thrusts quicken as she pushed against him. The pleasure she was feeling was indescribable. Nothing had prepared her for this. Nothing. Desire leapt within her as the throbbing increased. Suddenly she stilled as his thrusts took her right to the brink of a sensation she could not name. Sensing she was almost there, Guy drove full length into her, again and again until he heard her gasps of pleasure as the spasms racked her body. When she stilled, floating dreamily in the aftermath, Guy surged to his own release, spilling his seed deep within her.

As sleep claimed her, Ghislaine snuggled up against her husband's warm body. There could be no sin in such pleasure. But how could she ever live in the convent now?

Chapter Fifteen

Dawn was spilling into the bedchamber as Ghislaine's eyes flickered open. Slowly, she turned to look at Guy sleeping soundly at her side, his arm possessively draped over her shoulders. A sense of well-being filled every inch of her body and she stretched languorously, revelling in the unfamiliar sensation.

Disturbed by her movements, Guy shifted position in his sleep. His hand slipped from her shoulder to cover her breast and his mouth began to nuzzle the delicate skin of her neck.

Ghislaine shivered with the sheer ecstasy of having his body touch hers. Sighing softly to herself, she snuggled closer. His smell pervaded her senses and she breathed deeply, drinking in his male essence.

She could not have known how it would feel to be made a wife, not in a million years. She was certain that she would look very different, that everyone would somehow be able to tell. Her cheeks flushed at the thought of having to face them at breakfast.

Her eyes swept over her sleeping husband and she

knew without a doubt that she wanted to be with him,
to find out about love with this man, to bear his child.

Gently she moved a lock of his hair that had fallen
over his eyes. He was so beautiful, this scowling husband of hers, but he had not been deterred by her plain
looks last night. He had even called her lovely. There
had been no trace of a frown then. The desire in his
eyes had made her feel delicate and pretty, and he had
urged her to touch him and love him with warm, encouraging whispers. Remembering the things he had
done to her sent hot and cold arrows shooting through
her body. The pleasure he had given her so generously
had seemed to last for hours, and she wondered if he
had found as much pleasure in her touch.

A deep, contented sigh reached her ears and a gentle
squeeze from the large hand at her breast brought a
smile to her lips. He looked so innocent.

Innocent? Her thoughts halted. A chill enveloped
her as she remembered Father John's story of Margaret's terrible death. Could the Guy de Courcy she
knew really have caused Margaret to take her own
life? She looked at his hand, the hand that had given
her such pleasure, the hand that had never carried out
his loud threats.

Nay, Ghislaine was certain he could not. He may
have been a cool mercenary with a reputation for ex-
celling in that vile profession but he had never displayed any violence towards innocent people. But if
he were innocent, and it could be proven, he had
wanted to return to his old life. A life without her. He
had only married her as part of his deal with the Earl.
It had been one of the few things that they had agreed
on that she was to go to the convent and their marriage

was to be annulled. He would then be free to look for someone more suitable. She grimaced. If Margaret Staveley was his first choice, then she didn't even come close. His desire for her was all the more inexplicable.

A frown creased her brow. Was it really so odd? She was not so innocent as to the nature of young men and Guy was young and lusty with the same desires as any other. Lust, she decided. It was simply lust.

The germ of hope that had flickered into life died then. All he had felt for her was lust, and if that was all it was, it would haunt them both for a lifetime if she let it. Watching his desire wither and die, seeing the indifference in his eyes would be a living death.

Idly she began to stroke the sun-coloured skin on his back as she tried to imagine how it would be between them. Cold, perfunctory and joyless. Nay, she could never want that.

Ghislaine gazed at him with loving eyes. Did she love him enough to let him go? A cold band squeezed her heart. How could she not? A strange calm descended as she came to a decision. She would make it easy for him, she resolved firmly. The convent would provide peace of sorts for her. A vision of the smooth-skinned nuns danced before her and Ghislaine suddenly felt a rush of tears.

Sensing a change in her breathing pattern, Guy opened one drowsy eye. Her tears were the first thing he noticed about the passionate wife who had loved him so joyfully the night before, and the smile in his heart faded.

So she regretted it? Had he really been so mistaken about her? He felt her long fingers slide up and down

his back in an unconsciously seductive movement that
stirred his pulse and his body. Covertly, he watched
the expression of pain on her face as she touched his
hair. Nay, he did not think he was mistaken, despite
his mistrust of women. She was an innocent who was
playing no game. He had known that instinctively last
night.

Hot blood fired through his body as memories of
the night before flooded him. She had been so sweet
and unexpectedly passionate. Whatever the problem,
he wanted her to trust him. Ruefully he reminded himself of all the criticisms she had launched at him. Oafish, brutish, scowling, stinking. Aye, he had been all
of those things in his dealings with her, and she had
not hesitated to let him know it. He had learned to
expect the truth from her lips. Ghislaine was always
prepared to tell him what she expected of him, and he
recalled that he had made several attempts of late to
do what she had asked. It was quite amazing that he
should even consider it, but her lovely smile had
somehow made him feel very pleased with himself.
He liked to please her, and he certainly enjoyed her
attempts at pleasing him!

His hand brushed gently down over her hips and
thighs and he could feel the tremors it evoked in that
wonderful body. He had not realised just how beautiful
she was beneath those hideous gowns. Her skin was
white and smooth, covering curves which were deliciously soft and generous. She was not an obvious
temptress and that pleased him greatly, although not
nearly as much as her wanton behaviour in private. He
should have known as soon as he saw her flashing eyes

and that first seductive toss of her fiery hair. No convent would take her in, he smiled confidently.

Experimentally his thumb flicked over a pink tipped nipple that puckered instantly and he ached to take it in his mouth.

"What are you doing?" Ghislaine gasped, heat flooding through her body.

"Taking advantage of your body," he murmured softly as his tongue trailed around one hardening nipple.

"You want to do this again?" she whispered faintly, not daring to believe it. As passion ignited at his touch, Ghislaine told herself that this would be the last time. She would love him once more. Just once more. As his mouth tugged gently at her breast, Ghislaine captured his head in her hands and pulled him closer.

"Again and again," came the muffled reply, before his hands gently caressed and explored the rest of her body.

They were both wordlessly caught in the mounting passion between them and surrendered without resistance. This time there was no pain, just sweet, almost unbearable sensation as Guy thrust slowly and languorously. Ghislaine was swept away by a wave of throbbing pleasure, and as she floated back, Guy followed her into blissful oblivion, groaning loudly as he reached his own release.

Bright sunshine was filtering into the bedchamber when Ghislaine woke again. Judging by the noises without, it was close to midday and it was the latest she had ever slept in her life.

Her mouth was suddenly caught in a soft kiss that made her heart shudder.

"How do you feel?" Guy asked quietly, pulling himself up onto his elbow.

Smiling up into his concerned eyes, Ghislaine pushed back the ever-drooping lock of his hair. "Like a wife," she replied firmly, before realising what she had said.

Guy looked at her, his eyes shining a deep blue. "Is that good?" he asked doubtfully, his interest kindling nevertheless.

"I feel very...peaceful," Ghislaine amended. Desired. Cherished. Those had been the words she had wanted to say.

"Peaceful," he repeated with a lazy smile. "You have never accused me of having that effect on you before." Idly, his finger began to trace patterns on her arm.

"No-o-o..." she allowed, distracted by the feelings the finger was creating within her. "But then you have never called me lovely before either."

Guy flushed. "I said that?" he questioned in mock disbelief.

Ghislaine sighed and gazed at him steadily. "You do not have to say those things."

Guy's eyes snapped open at the serious tone in her voice. "What do you mean by that?" His voice had lost its gentle teasing and his brows began to wrinkle into the beginning of a frown.

Ghislaine shifted uncomfortably. If she was going to save them both, she would have to be strong. Stronger than she felt. Her fingers twisted the sheet into convoluted knots, unconsciously baring her breasts.

"I mean," she began hesitantly, "that you should not make more of this than it is."

Guy continued to stare at his wife, watching her fingers and finding it very hard to take his eyes off the luscious curves exposed before him.

"You think I am making too much of it?" He questioned slowly, his mind trying to work out what she was leading to.

"A-aye," she stammered. "And I am not pretty at all, as you were pleased to remind me on several occasions." She held up her hand as Guy opened his mouth to reply. "But that is not really what I meant."

"Then perhaps you would explain exactly what you are getting at."

Ghislaine looked up at his darkening frown and almost smiled. Schooling her expression carefully, she hauled herself to a sitting position. "Last night has changed nothing," she explained carefully. "It was simply the result of a surfeit of drink and lust."

Nonplussed, Guy continued to stare at her. Perhaps he had best hear her reasoning. It was well-known that women had strange ideas about men. "Drink and lust," he murmured. She could not seriously believe that.

"It should not have happened," she continued. "But I have decided that the convent is where I still intend to go."

Guy eyed her in disbelief. "The convent," he said flatly, "would not have you."

"Oh?" she enquired, her eyes narrowing. "And why not?"

"Because you are an unruly wanton with a shrewish tongue, a huge appetite and a penchant for drink." The words were delivered with total resignation as he folded his arms across his chest. His disgruntled tone almost made her laugh. He was not making this easy for her.

"Since when have those particular traits barred entry to the convent?" she retorted haughtily.

"When they are accompanied by an angry bloodthirsty mercenary with twenty armed men threatening to attack if they did not," came the instant reply.

Ghislaine glared at him, irritation welling up inside her. "You," she accused angrily, "are naught but an oafish tyrant. We agreed I was to go to the convent."

"Things have changed," he snapped, his patience beginning to fray. "You are now my wife in body as well as in name and there may be a child."

Ghislaine stared at him open-mouthed. "You have frequently stated your desire to be rid of me. If I go to the convent, I will take the child with me."

"The child stays with me," he stated without hesitation. "Or is this part of some bizarre plot to deprive me of heirs?"

"What? What nonsense is this?"

His statement was as idiotic as her words, but it was the only thing he could think of in the heat of the moment. He forged on with the argument. "It is clear that you seduced me so that you became my true wife. If you disappear to the convent I would be unable to marry again and so produce no more legitimate de Courcy heirs." Guy had rounded on her, placing his arms either side of hers, his mouth just inches from hers.

Ghislaine pushed herself back as far as she could. "Why should I want to do that?" she asked weakly. "It makes no sense."

"Why indeed, lady? But rest assured I intend to discover the truth," he growled, trapping her legs within his.

A hot flush shot through her body as Ghislaine reacted to his nearness. "You would torture me?" she asked faintly.

"Whatever I need to do," came the soft reply. His lips moved over hers, gently seducing a response from her.

"Do not," she gasped, dismayed at her own weakness. "This is not fair."

"I fight for what is mine by any means I can." His lips moved to the tender spot at the base of her throat.

Ghislaine knew her will-power was slipping and that if she was to succeed, this would be her last chance.

"Do you wish me to hate you for it? Could you live like that?" she demanded with enough emotion to halt Guy's lips.

He stared at her, not believing she meant a word of it, but angry that she could not trust him with the truth.

"So be it," he growled and pushed himself away from her. "You would choose the convent. But you go on one condition. You remain here to ensure there is no possibility of a child."

"And if there is?" Ghislaine demanded.

"Then you stay until the child is born."

"That is too cruel," she said hotly.

Guy stood up and walked naked across the room to retrieve his discarded clothes. Ghislaine found it hard

to take her eyes from his body. "You have the choice,
I am perfectly willing to accept you as wife."

Ghislaine glared at him. "You are a cold-hearted,
oafish brute. The convent will be a welcome relief."

The door slammed with finality as Guy stormed out
of the bedchamber. It was not until she heard him
thudding down the stairs that she allowed her tears to
fall.

Kalim had left the manor long before Ghislaine set
foot in the hall and, much to her relief, few people
seemed to notice anything different about her. She
busied herself with the new supplies, deciding what
was to be stored or used. The whole time, Ghislaine
found it hard to concentrate on any task and her fingers
seemed permanently beset with clumsiness. Finally, in
exasperation, Ghislaine sought peace in the chapel.

The cool simplicity of the white-washed walls had
a calming effect, as they always had at moments of
crisis. It was almost as if the world did not exist beyond the walls of this small room. Ghislaine knelt in
prayer before the altar, unsure still whether she had
committed a true sin.

"You are troubled, Lady Ghislaine?" Father John's
voice seemed calmer and more controlled.

She scrambled to her feet. "My mind is somewhat
distracted today," she admitted. That was no lie at
least.

Father John nodded. "If you wish to make your
confession, I will be glad to perform the duty." His
dark eyes regarded hers steadily, and Ghislaine knew
that he would not be harsh on her.

"I am not sure that what I have to tell you will be welcome," she explained hesitantly.

"We shall have to put our trust in God," he replied kindly.

Her story was quickly told, and despite her lack of certainty about telling this man how much she loved her husband and how convinced she was of his innocence, Ghislaine finally told him all she could.

Father John looked at her with pity in his eyes. "We do not always have easy choices to make, Lady Ghislaine. I am sure that if you have made the right one, you will find comfort in the convent."

Ghislaine sighed. "I know it but my husband is not making it easy for me."

"Have you told him why you wish to go?" asked the priest suddenly.

Ghislaine nodded. "At least, part of why I wish to go. For the rest, I doubt whether that would be of interest to him." She could never tell him how much she loved him for he would never believe her.

"Then I will pray for us both, Lady Ghislaine." Father John knelt at her side.

It was late afternoon by the time Guy returned from his hunting. Ghislaine had delayed the meal until the guards announced his arrival and she was certain that the toughened meat would put him in an even blacker mood. Well, so be it.

She had spent hours dreading his return, worrying, thinking, and all to little avail, whilst he had been enjoying the fresh air. When he stormed through the doors, however, Guy did not look as if he had spent a pleasant afternoon.

"So, wife. I must be grateful that you have made no attempt to escape." His bitter sarcasm grated on her wrangled nerves.

"I have been happy to do your bidding, my lord," she replied as demurely as she could, knowing her tone would irritate him.

His snort of disbelief told her what he thought of that. Picking up a goblet of wine, Guy was about to toss it down when he caught sight of Father John. "Plotting again, lady?" he demanded quietly before drinking deeply.

Ghislaine flushed guiltily. "Father John is here to offer help and advice to those who require it. Perhaps some could do with more than others?" she added pointedly.

"When I need advice from a priest I will seek it out. My concern lies with what he has been offering you, lady." His blue eyes were glittering with anger as he looked at Ghislaine.

"Father John will be staying but a short time, my lord. I am sure that a few hours here will be enough to convince him that his efforts here are futile."

Ghislaine knew that she was provoking him greatly, but was unable to stop. Guy glared at her and poured himself another goblet of wine in utter frustration. "Enough, woman," he growled. "But if the good father so much as utters a word in my presence, he will find out firsthand the price of staying in so brutish a household."

Ghislaine gasped at such terrible threats and turned, red-faced, to the priest to apologise for her husband's outrageous remarks. Father John, however, on hearing Guy's tone and the marked antagonism between husband and wife, had removed himself quietly to the far end of the table out of harm's way.

Throughout the meal, Ghislaine kept glancing nervously at him, trying to assess his reaction to Guy's voice. He had certainly witnessed an angry situation that would have embarrassed most of the clergy, but he had kept his head down throughout the following ordeal of angry silence and not looked once in her direction.

The food was hardly touched by either Ghislaine or Guy and Ghislaine noticed that Guy kept staring at the ale in a most peculiar fashion. Only Sir Arnaud seemed able to carry on a lively banter with some of the other men, still discussing the fate of Thomas Bollyngton. The outlaw languished in the keep, awaiting instructions from the messenger Guy had sent to Earl Hugh. News was expected hourly.

By all accounts Bollyngton was a dead man. The dreaded court of Eyrie would deal harshly with so active an outlaw, even in a county as lost to law as Cheshire. Ghislaine wondered if she would have the chance to see him, thinking he might throw some light on the death of her father. She doubted if anyone else would remember.

"My lord," called a guard from the door. "A messenger comes."

Ghislaine breathed a small sigh of relief as Guy ended the meal by standing and throwing the finger cloth to the table.

"Send him in as soon as he comes." Guy moved to stand casually before the huge fire.

The messenger brought with him the smell of night

air as he handed Guy a roll of parchment bearing the seal of d'Avranches. Guy hastily broke it and cast his eyes over the message it contained. The man drank deeply of the ale he was given.

For a few moments Guy said nothing. He just looked at the parchment and then rolled it back carefully. His black scowl returned as he stared into the flames.

Unable to contain her curiosity, Ghislaine went to stand by his side.

"Is there aught wrong, my lord?" she asked quietly.

Guy did not turn to look at her, but handed her the message. She unrolled it quickly and saw the seal was indeed the Earl's. The words made no meaning since she could not read, but it was easy to guess what was wanted of him.

"He wants your services now? I thought you had agreed to go after the harvesting."

"The Earl of Chester is able to change his mind," he stated dryly. "I am to take my men to Chester this night."

"But what is so urgent that he requires you without delay?" she demanded. "And what of the outlaws?"

Guy did not answer immediately but went back to staring at the flames, deep in thought.

Ghislaine turned to the messenger. If Guy was not going to ask questions, she would do it for him. "Did you see the Earl before you left?"

"No, lady." The messenger wiped his mouth on his cloak. "I was given the message by one of his squires. He said it was most urgent and I was to get it here before nightfall. The squire told me that an escort will come on the morrow for Bollyngton and his men."

"Why can you not take the outlaws yourself?" she asked her husband. This turn of events was most vexing.

"It would hold us up," came the mumbled reply. "We would travel faster without them." Guy rubbed his stubbly chin with his hand and then turned towards her. "I suspect the Earl is using us as a decoy of sorts and it would seem I have little choice, lady. The Earl demands my services and my men. Much as I would rather stay here and see to Bollyngton, my continued protection from the shire reeves depends on Hugh d'Avranches."

His blue eyes pierced her as he placed his hands on her shoulders. "We also have unfinished business, Ghislaine. I would ask you to await my return before acting rashly."

Ghislaine smiled at him wanly and nodded. "I give you my word."

Content with that, Guy pulled her close and brushed her forehead with his lips. He then strode from the hall issuing commands to all and sundry. Ghislaine watched him disappear through the doors before picking up a goblet of wine.

Within the hour, Guy and his men had set off for Chester, although not without a great deal of noise and upheaval. He had left Sir Brian and Sir Arnaud in charge of the manor and the outlaws. Ghislaine could tell he was not content with the command, but he could do nothing. The Earl was his liegelord and his protector, and his life depended upon his mercy. Their farewell was cool.

Returning to the hall, Ghislaine sat in front of the fire, her thoughts scattered.

"May I join you, Lady Ghislaine?" Father John stood before her.

Ghislaine jumped up, suddenly remembering why he was here. The priest held up his hand, a smile on his lips.

"Fear not, Lady Ghislaine. Your husband is not the man, for all his anger. Your confidence in him was not misplaced."

Relief flooded through her and Ghislaine breathed again. "His temper leaves much to be desired, though."

The priest smiled again. "He is much tried, by the looks of him." The smile faded. "However, it means that the killer is still at liberty and I must continue my search. It would be too much of a risk to clear your husband's name and reveal my knowledge until he is discovered and brought to trial. The truth might never come to light otherwise."

Ghislaine's joy at the news was short-lived. Her husband's honour depended on the survival of this one priest. She could not let that happen.

"It would ease my mind greatly if you were to write down what happened as well as clear Guy's name," she appealed to him. "If aught were to happen to you, then he would never be free of suspicion."

Father John nodded slowly. "I would be pleased to do that, but it would be best to return to the abbey. At least there there is no chance of the information falling into the wrong hands."

Ghislaine gave him a dazzling smile. "I shall make arrangements for you to leave in the morning."

The manor seemed strangely quiet without Guy and his men. The noise and the mess that had caused her such aggravation over the past few weeks were gone, and Ghislaine found herself staring at her tidy hall in despair. Somehow, it just did not look right.

She laughed to herself. Guy would be much amused to hear the woman who had given him such earache over the less domestic attributes of his men say she missed them. But it was true.

The only remedy for such foolishness, she admonished sternly, was to keep busy. But for how long? The Earl's message had apparently given no indication as to how much time Guy would spend in his service this time. It could be days, weeks or even months. Dispirited, Ghislaine remembered the prisoner in the keep. If the Earl's men came on the morrow, this would be her only chance to find out if Bollyngton knew anything about her father's death.

The light from the one torch gave the small room a shadowy glow that looked most eerie. Ghislaine hesitated at the door, but firmly quashed all her fears. No one else would find out about her father. A small stocky man lay casually on the pallet at the far end of the room, his head resting on his hands, his pale eyes staring at the ceiling. Ghislaine was grateful that his hands and ankles were chained securely to a post in the wall.

At her entrance, Thomas Bollyngton merely raised his head briefly and then resumed his former position. A little piqued by his casual dismissal of her, Ghislaine advanced towards the bed.

"You are Thomas Bollyngton?"

A round, pale face with a small bulbous nose turned towards her. As his pale eyes roved over her with complete indifference, the thin lips broke into a smile which revealed a row of discoloured, sharp teeth. He reminded Ghislaine of an arrogant pig.

"I assume you are here to feed me or pleasure me, woman. In either case you have no need of my name." His voice was as loathsome as his body. It had an odd strangled quality that grated. As he shifted to sit up and watch her, Ghislaine took a step back in alarm, but not before his smell assailed her nose.

"I am here to do neither," she retorted haughtily. "My interest in you is confined to your…activities in the forest." Her voice sounded calmer and more confident than she felt. Knowing that there were two guards outside the door was some comfort.

Disappointed, Bollyngton resumed his former position, his greasy thatch of sandy hair shadowing much of his face. "I have no reason to discuss anything with you, woman. Now leave me be." His voice had a hard, irritated edge to it that did not inspire confidence.

Nevertheless, decided Ghislaine, she would keep trying. "I suggest you make it your business or you will find yourself without food or water for as long as you are here."

Bollyngton continued to stare at the ceiling, completely unconcerned at her threat. It seemed most odd.

"Think you a lack of food or water will have any great effect on me?" he eventually replied.

Ghislaine shrugged, fascinated by his calm, almost relaxed behaviour.

"Would it not?" she enquired.

A slow smile spread over his ugly face as if he found her words amusing. "Not for long," came the quiet reply.

"We await the Earl's men in the morning. I have no doubt you will feel more co-operative then," she added with more than a tinge of satisfaction.

Bollyngton just continued his annoying little smile by way of reply.

Clearly she would get no information from him and Ghislaine glared at him in frustration. There was naught she could do. As she left the room with an angry swish of her skirts, she thought his attitude was most odd for a man facing certain death. He was calm, cool and very at ease. It was almost as if he did not think anything was going to happen to him at all.

Somehow, there was a nagging feeling that something was not right. Ghislaine left the keep with much on her mind.

Chapter Sixteen

"My lady?"

The guard's voice broke into her thoughts as Ghislaine sat before the fire in the great hall. In the few hours that Guy had been gone, she had been puzzling over Thomas Bollyngton. As night drew in, nothing made sense and the uneven stitches in the hem she was attempting to sew bore witness to her poor concentration. Even the patient priest had been driven by her lack of conversation to take refuge in an alcove off the hall for private reflection. And she felt very vulnerable at the manor. Guy had taken his best fighting men and had even had the gall to commandeer Edwin. A weakened Sir Arnaud and a nervous Sir Brian were not a great deal of comfort. She stabbed at the linen in frustration.

"Sir Walter de Belleme is here on the Earl's business and requests entry."

Ghislaine's hand froze at the mention of his name. Sweet mercy, the man was here. At least Guy was safely on his way to Chester.

"Is he alone?" she demanded, thankfully putting her sewing aside.

"There are five men with him bearing the arms of the Earl of Chester, my lady."

Ghislaine nodded. "Send him to me here and see that Sir Arnaud and Sir Brian are informed of his presence."

When Walter de Belleme strode through the hall doors, Ghislaine had managed to compose her thoughts. Her trembling fingers remained firmly behind her back.

Searching his handsome face for clues as to his thoughts or suspicions, Ghislaine saw nothing there to alarm her. His grey eyes shone warmly as he greeted her and his smile seemed truly genuine.

"Lady Ghislaine. I am pleased to find you at home."

The tone of his voice was friendly and confident.

"Sir Walter. You are always welcome here." She smiled back as sweetly as her fluttering stomach would allow. "But I believe you are here on behalf of Earl Hugh?"

Walter advanced to the fire, tossing his thick green cloak onto the table as he went. Ghislaine noticed the fur trim on his beautifully made tunic and the handsome leather boots he sported. Indeed, the man lavished large sums of money on himself, it seemed. He accepted the proffered goblet of wine with a smile.

"Indeed I am. We are to escort the captured outlaw to Chester whilst your husband forays north to settle a dispute with one of the Earl's more truculent vassals."

"North?" exclaimed Ghislaine. "Why, I had the

impression that Guy was destined for the Welsh hills."
As soon as she spoke the words, she wished them
undone.

"You must have been misinformed, Lady Ghislaine," he replied smoothly. But she did not miss the
nervous glance he shot around the room nor the slight
faltering of his smile. She must tread carefully if she
was to find out what scheme he had concocted. Nor
must she underestimate him.

"Aye. Most likely I paid little enough attention. I
find all this talk of keeps and strategy somewhat te-
dious." She smiled self-consciously and even managed a faint blush.

Walter relaxed a little and moved closer to Ghislaine. "Indeed, my lady. It must be a sore trial to you,
having so bloodthirsty an oaf as de Courcy for husband." His eyes held hers for a fleeting second.

Ghislaine sighed and shrugged her shoulders de-
spairingly. "I confess my life has changed greatly
since my marriage, Sir Walter. I had never envisaged
it so." No one could accuse her of falsehoods there.
"My husband and I do not always see eye to eye. It
has led to...misunderstandings and disagreements."
Ghislaine allowed her eyes to remain cast towards the
floor, giving the impression, she hoped, of trying to
hide something far more intolerable.

Walter took her hand. "My lady," he murmured.
"I have offered you help before. Are you minded to
accept it now?" His eyes looked into hers with concern.

Ghislaine took a deep breath. "You risk much, Sir
Walter," she whispered, a blush staining her cheeks.
"I have no desire to see you in danger for my sake."

Walter smiled seductively, his grey eyes warm with anticipation. "There is little danger for me, Ghislaine. But I would willingly take a risk to ensure your happiness."

Ghislaine widened her eyes in disbelief. "I could not ask it of you, Sir Walter. My husband is a jealous man who would stop at nothing to protect what is his, no matter whether he truly wants it or not."

"If your husband were to…disappear, Lady Ghislaine, what would you do?" Walter stepped closer so that she could smell the rosemary in his clothes.

Ghislaine turned to face the fire. "Why, I don't know for sure, Sir Walter." She hesitated in a coy gesture that she hoped would find its mark. "There is always the abbey for women such as I. It has long been my desire to do so."

Walter remained still for a few moments and did not speak until Ghislaine turned back to face him. His face betrayed nothing. "It can be arranged for now at least," he stated finally. "Aye, that's a good plan."

Ghislaine's whole body went rigid with fear. "How so?" she asked, her voice almost a whisper. "My husband has ordered me to remain here. I dare not disobey him for he can be so…brutal in his displeasure." She shuddered with great effect.

"Leave it to me," he replied, gazing at her worried face with an expression of studied calm. Had he always schooled his thoughts so, Ghislaine wondered? If he was going to be this cool, how on earth was she to find out his plan for Guy?

Her thoughts were interrupted by the arrival of Sir Arnaud.

"I apologise for the delay, Lady Ghislaine, but Sir Brian has just left to take care of a fire in the village."

"Is it serious?" she demanded, her voice full of alarm.

"We do not know. The guard reported seeing flames and the villagers do not appear to have put it out yet. Sir Brian rode out with some men to see what they can do."

Ghislaine nodded. "Keep me informed, Sir Arnaud. Have any homeless villagers housed in the keep for the night. We have plenty of food and blankets."

Sir Arnaud inclined his head in assent but continued to stare at Sir Walter with undisguised interest. "Sir Walter. Your presence here is most…reassuring." Did Ghislaine only imagine that second's hesitation? "You are here to escort the outlaws I assume? We did not expect you until the morrow."

Walter stiffened but when he replied, his voice was bland. "That is so, Sir Arnaud. The Earl decided we should arrive earlier in case of treachery." He paused a moment, as if suddenly struck by a suspicious thought. "If there is trouble, then I believe I must take them without delay."

Sir Arnaud pulled his brows together in a suspicious frown and glanced at the five men Walter had brought with him. They stood perfectly still at the far end of the hall, their hands at their sides, awaiting orders. He rubbed his hand over his chin thoughtfully before appearing to come to a decision. "You are right. I'll have the outlaws taken to the bailey and you will be escorted past the village."

So saying, Sir Arnaud turned on his heels and left

Ghislaine and Walter staring after him. The faint smile playing on his lips was most unnerving.

Ghislaine shot Walter an apprehensive look. "What now?" she asked quietly.

His gaze, which had rested on the worn tapestries adorning the hall, shifted back to Ghislaine. "I shall take you with me."

Ghislaine swallowed hard. "But I said I wished to go to the abbey, Sir Walter." Her voice sounded determined despite the seesawing of her stomach. "Is there a problem with that?"

His eyes flicked over her flushed face. "Not at all. I intend to return to Chester via the abbey. Your safety is paramount and I cannot leave you to such despicable treatment a moment longer." Walter's eyes roamed over her face almost tenderly. "You must know that I once entertained hope of your hand, Lady Ghislaine, and I would like to think that we could both be very happy, should your husband die." His gloved hand reached out and gently touched a red-gold braid. "You are different to most of the other women I know."

Ghislaine was so dazed by this unexpected confession that for a brief second she believed he was serious. "Is that good?" she asked, unconsciously echoing a question that Guy had put to her only hours before.

Walter's skin flushed a little as if he suddenly realised what he had been saying. "I wish to be more than a friend to you, if you would allow it." His hands started to delve into a leather pouch hanging from his belt. "Perhaps you would wear this as a testimony to our friendship? It would give me great pleasure to think of you wearing it.''

Ghislaine stared at the delicately pretty gold crucifix decorated with pearls. It shone with a red glow in the firelight and Ghislaine took it from him to examine it more closely. Something about the crucifix looked familiar, but she could not place where she had seen it before.

"It is beautiful," she murmured as she placed it round her neck. "But you had no need to give me so valuable a gift. My friendship is freely given."

Walter smiled in the warm glow of his generosity. "It has been in my family for some time. Keep it close, Lady Ghislaine."

"You have my word."

"Good. Then I suggest we leave now."

His tone of voice did not brook dissension, but Ghislaine still had no idea as to what his plans were nor how to alert Sir Arnaud. Suddenly, from the corner of her eye, Ghislaine noticed the tiniest of movements behind a curtain covering the alcove. For a second she deemed it most odd that whoever was behind there had not emerged before now, but before she could say aught, she realised who it was. Father John! He had been there all along.

A wave of cold fear washed over her. Perhaps the reason why Father John had not identified himself before was because he had heard what was going on. She looked down at the crucifix. Margaret had worn one just like this. Ghislaine closed her eyes, fear seeping through every bone. He had to know the killer. Walter had to know. He had given her a vital piece of evidence to wear around her neck and only she would be able to say who gave it to her. Unless, of course, she were dead.

Her stomach lurched as she took a few steps closer to the curtain. Maybe Father John could help her.

"What am I supposed to tell Sir Arnaud?" she babbled nervously to Walter. "I cannot just leave without a word." Her eyes pleaded with him.

Walter thought for a minute. "Tell him you believe that de Courcy murdered Margaret Staveley and that you can no longer bear living with him. You intend to make the abbey your refuge until the matter is resolved to your satisfaction. With me as an escort and so few men here, Sir Arnaud is not in any position to prevent you."

Ghislaine went quite still. It made sense, and it was well known that they had argued about her going to the convent. Guy had made no secret of it. "You are right, Sir Walter. I doubt if Sir Arnaud will prevent me from leaving. My cloak is in the bedchamber. I will just fetch it."

Somehow she had to let Sir Arnaud know the truth and warn Guy that he may be walking into a trap.

"No." Walter's voice sounded almost irritated. "I will fetch it." This was not an offer, it was a command. Not wishing to make him suspicious nor angry, Ghislaine acceded gracefully.

Sir Walter returned with her cloak within a few minutes, but she could not help but think it odd that he would wish to collect it himself. He had never shown the slightest inclination before to fetch and carry. Perhaps he was already suspicious of her.

The bailey was lit by several torches, but Ghislaine could see how few of Guy's men were left to guard the manor. Were she to cry out now, it would be to no avail. Walter would kill her and escape with little difficulty. Her best ploy would be to try to escape in the dark. Guy's hunting knife lay safely hidden under the folds of her skirt and she would use it if necessary.

"Do you leave too, Lady Ghislaine?" Sir Arnaud's voice sounded harsh and accusing.

Ghislalne turned to face him, the cold night air making her shiver. "Sir Walter has kindly agreed to escort me to the abbey. I have decided I can no longer continue to remain under the same roof as a murderer such as Guy de Courcy."

"I see. You would run like a coward, lady? I had not thought it of you." His contempt for her shone in his eyes.

Ghislaine gritted her teeth. He was not going to make this easy for her. "He would not let me go." Her eyes held his, trying desperately to convey the message. "I really have no choice."

"You do him an injustice, lady. Guy de Courcy is a fair man. I thought you gave him your word you would do nothing in his absence."

"A desperate woman will say or do anything if she has to, Sir Arnaud." She did not move, her whole body trying to tell him of the danger, but his face told her what he thought of her.

"I will have your horse saddled, lady." He whirled round and barked the order.

Surrounded by outlaws and the escort, Ghislaine felt most uncomfortable as the party skirted to the left of the village. Flames still licked at one thatch, and she could hear the shouts of the people as they tried to douse the fire. Walter urged the riders on and they soon left the noise and the acrid smell behind. Sir Arnaud's escort remained at the village boundary without any clear sign of suspicion.

The dark closed in on them as they headed south for the abbey. Strange noises emerged from the unfamiliar world of the night, and Ghislaine gritted her teeth to stop them from chattering in fear.

At one point, Ghislaine was certain she could hear the sound of horses and her heart lifted. There was a slim chance that Guy had turned back and was now on her trail. But it was soon clear that this was a false hope for the sounds died away.

Beyond the meagre light of the torches, she could see very little. It was difficult to tell where they were exactly, for she had been aware for some time that they had been taking odd turns in the road. Walter kept turning to look behind them to see if they had been followed, but so far he had spotted nothing.

"Do you fear attack, Sir Walter?" she asked. His agitation had not lessened.

Walter looked at her and then at Thomas Bollyngton. "There's no telling if his friends will try to rescue him. I doubt that they will have realised yet that he is gone from Chapmonswiche, but with the fire in the village, it is best to be wary."

Ghislaine looked over at the outlaw who was riding just ahead of her. His expression was still calm. It was almost as if he was out on a pleasant ride. His four companions, likewise, did not seem unduly perturbed by their nocturnal exercise. It did seem odd that there were only six men to escort five brutal outlaws.

Her alarm grew as they veered off the track and headed for the edges of the forest.

"Where are we going?" she demanded as Walter picked up her reins.

"We will have better cover in the forest, Lady Ghislaine." His voice was confident.

"But that would be the perfect place for an ambush," she exclaimed nervously. "And we are heading away from the abbey."

Walter did not reply, but kicked his horse on, pulling her behind him. Escape was impossible for she was surrounded by outlaws and escorts, and Walter had a tight grip on her reins. Were she to fall off her horse, she would be trampled underfoot by the others. A deathly fear washed over her. She was going to die.

They had not gone far when Walter drew to a halt in a small clearing. She could hear running water not far away. All around her loomed the tall, black shapes of the forest trees.

"Why have we stopped?" Panic finally hit Ghislaine as Walter strode purposefully towards her. "Is there a problem?" she asked, frantically thinking of anything that could give her a way out.

"No." He held his hands up to her. Wordlessly, she slid into his arms, her heart thundering.

"Will you explain why we are here?" she demanded defiantly. If she was going to die, she was going to do it as a de Launay should. And a de Courcy, she remembered belatedly.

Walter looked at her for a moment. "In good time, Ghislaine." He then turned and indicated that the others should dismount. Nervously Ghislaine glanced at them. The outlaws were rough men who looked as though they had spent a lifetime attacking innocent travellers. As she surveyed the escort they seemed little better.

Her mouth went dry. She had to find out from Walter what was going on. And whatever happened to her in the end, she suddenly found that she did not want Guy de Courcy to think that she had betrayed him. For the moment, silence was probably the best she could do.

Sitting on a fallen log, she was able to watch the others more carefully. Whilst his men were overseeing the outlaws, Walter had walked to the edge of the clearing, distancing himself from everyone else. Sensing the alertness in his still body, Ghislaine held her breath. Was he waiting for someone, or something to happen? After a minute or two, Walter seemed to relax and turned back towards the group. Breathing once more, Ghislaine shivered with the cold and fear. At that moment, she would have given anything to see her scowling husband and his band of marauding oafs. Ruefully reminding herself of the number of times she had wished them to the devil, Ghislaine quickly wiped the brightness from her eyes.

A heavy sigh caused her to look up suddenly. Walter was staring down at her, his face grave.

"You are going to kill me," she stated flatly. It was not really a question.

She could see him debating whether or not to tell her the truth. "Honesty is best," he began quietly. "And I have no wish to insult your intelligence. Believe me when I tell you how sorry I am, Ghislaine."

Ghislaine stared up at him, every bone in her body

shaking with fear. Would he do it right away? "Why? At least tell me why?" Her eyes were round with fear.

Walter turned swiftly to cast a quick glance in the direction of Thomas Bollyngton before carefully arranging his cloak on the soft ground and sitting down.

"I doubt if I should tell you, but in all conscience, I find that I wish to."

"That is most...considerate, Sir Walter."

Her provoking words caused his mouth to twitch in irritation. "It is not necessary," he warned.

"I shall try to curb my tongue henceforth," she replied quietly. "Please explain."

Despite the first spots of rain, Walter did not move. "I am," he announced, "a man of taste. I desire fine clothes, a beautiful home, good food and wine. Such things require a great deal more money than I had, but after a while, I realised that there were other ways of earning the sort of money I needed."

Ghislaine stared at him unblinkingly, desperately trying to keep from throwing up all over him. "Such as?"

"Oh, at first it was only on a small scale. Working for the Earl brought me into contact with a great many undesirable people. I found ways of forcing them into giving me a share of their earnings. It wasn't until later that I realised how much more could be done."

At her questioning look, Walter stared at his hands. "I am not a man who enjoys physical violence, you understand, but I do have my wits. Teaming up with an outlaw, for instance, was the perfect solution." He glanced at Bollyngton, who lounged a little way off.

Ghislaine's mind whirled with this information. He had been very clever. No wonder Bollyngton had survived so long and so well. "What will you do with him now?"

Walter breathed in deeply and shrugged his shoulders. "I have not decided yet," he replied cautiously.

"So," Ghislaine thought aloud. "You visited Chapmonswiche so frequently because it offered you the perfect cover for clandestine meetings in the forest. How foolish and naïve I must have seemed." Ghislaine gave a self-conscious laugh.

"Actually, I quite enjoyed my visits with you. But, as you say, there was a purpose. Indeed, I had considered marriage with you."

"So that was not my imagination?"

"Not until your father became suspicious."

Ghislaine's head snapped up. "It was you!" she accused. "You killed him?"

Walter's face was just a pale blur in the darkness and she could not make out his expression. "He followed me. I was unusually careless, unfortunately, and your father was a quick man. When he saw me with Bollyngton and his men, he drew the correct conclusion. To my immense good luck, he decided to challenge me. That was his mistake."

"And you killed Peter Staveley," she added thoughtfully. Then her blood ran cold. "But Margaret? Why in God's name did you have to kill Margaret too?"

Walter was silent for a moment, considering his words. "She was a rich widow. Like you, she lived close to the forest, but unlike you, sweet Ghislaine, she did not ask so many questions."

"I still do not understand."

"I had not banked on her sense of honour," he

remarked slowly. "Apparently, she was aware that you were expecting an offer from me." He sighed. "There was every chance that she would tell you what had happened. Her death was...unfortunate."

"You are a monster," she whispered. "I trusted you, and you betrayed my trust to your own ends."

"In the beginning," he replied quietly. "But I admit to a fondness for you, Ghislaine. I had hoped that I might have been able to persuade you to help me. Unfortunately, you have a righteous streak like your father. Like him, it will be the cause of your own undoing."

Ghislaine remained paralysed with fear, anger and misery. "You will not escape this," she hissed vehemently.

Walter laughed softly. "Your naïvety astounds me, Ghislaine. The Earl may well have been aware of my...activities for some time. He chose, however, to ignore them. I am sure that he has other plans for me. Those for your husband, however, will be short-lived."

"What have you planned for him?" she asked, her heart thudding loudly.

"The message to go to Chester was false, of course. He will have been ambushed by Henry Dettingham along the way. Any minute now, I expect to have news of his capture."

"He will not be killed?"

Walter shook his head. "I need him to be proven guilty of the crime of murdering Margaret beyond a shadow of a doubt. Your contribution will be invaluable."

Ghislaine looked down at the crucifix. "I could not

live with him for murdering my friend, so I intended to retire to the abbey. Unfortunately, my untimely death on the way prevents me being able to corroborate any defence he may bring.''

The blond curls of her captor nodded. ''More or less. I also took the liberty of placing some of Margaret's jewels and valuables about your bedchamber.''

''And Guy will be unable to refute any of this,'' she added quietly.

''The Earl will not be able to ignore a direct order from the King. Henry Dettingham will bay for justice. I have no doubt that the Court of Eyrie will dispense the correct punishment.''

''And what do you get out of all this?'' she demanded in disgust.

He shrugged his shoulders. ''Dettingham will allow me your manor and a share of your husband's treasure in return for granting him his revenge.'' He smiled bleakly. ''Honest people are so depressingly naïve.''

''You will rot in hell for this, Walter,'' she spat.

At that moment, Walter stood up abruptly. He held his hand up to her, indicating that she should remain silent. Ghislaine could hear nothing odd but sensed, as Walter did, that something had changed.

''De Belleme,'' growled the coarse voice of Thomas Bollyngton. ''Cut me loose.''

Ghislaine swirled round to see the outlaw approach, an angry expression on his ugly face. Walter stared at him silently, weighing up his options. Suddenly, Ghislaine realised what he was planning. If he was expecting reinforcements then he would have no difficulty killing Bollyngton and blaming her death on him. On the other hand, the others had not yet arrived and Walter was simply biding his time. An idea formed from her desperate thoughts.

"Loose?" she repeated with a puzzled expression. "You told me you would kill him!" Ghislaine turned on Walter with an accusing look. "We don't need him now."

The look of shock and then anger on Walter's face would have given her a great deal of satisfaction at any other time, but she was petrified that he would kill her before she had a chance to do anything else.

"Hold your tongue, you lying bitch," he hissed. But the outlaw had clearly been harbouring enough doubts of his own to give her words some credence.

"Then cut me loose now," he demanded angrily.

Realising he was cornered, Walter fought back. "If they send the guards back to check on us, we'll never survive. Think, man. Wait until they arrive."

Bollyngton glared at him, clearly unconvinced by Walter's explanation but unable to do much about it. With a snort of defiance, he slumped down at Ghislaine's side.

Her eyes slid over the surly face of the outlaw and decided he had no real liking for Walter de Belleme. His anger was growing by the minute and Ghislaine could see the tension in his body. Did he hate him enough to kill him?

A steady thud of hoofbeats reached their ears and Walter jumped up. This would be her only chance, she realised. Once Dettingham arrived, she would die.

Whilst Walter was giving orders to the escort, she slid the hunting knife from under her skirts and edged towards Thomas Bollyngton. His face was no more than a pale smudge in the dark, but Ghislaine could see his eyes glittering with comprehension. It was but the work of a few seconds to cut the binding round his wrists, although it had felt like a thousand years. Her hands shook with fear until finally it sliced free. The outlaw's thick fingers curled around the knife.

As the sounds beyond the clearing grew louder, Bollyngton launched himself at Walter with the silent stealth of a practised killer. Her legs would not move as the two men rolled in the mud, fighting for their lives. Suddenly her mind cleared and Ghislaine pulled herself to her feet. She had to get to the shelter of the forest.

A piercing, animal-like scream rent the air. Turning to see what had happened, Ghislaine saw the outlaw fall to his knees, his fists clenched round his stomach. Walter was staggering to his feet, looking wildly for her. Dread surged through her body as she tried to scramble to the safety of the trees. A second more and she would have made it.

As his hands closed around her ankle, Ghislaine fell head first into the mud. Furiously kicking, Ghislaine twisted round and attempted to pull herself to her feet, but he pulled her back down.

"I had meant to do this in your sleep, you stupid wench," he ground out. Transferring her gaze from Walter's angry face to the knife he held at her breast, Ghislaine's hope for a reprieve died.

"Ghislaine!"

Both of them turned at the same time. It was not Dettingham. Walter threw her back to the ground and lurched to his feet, but Ghislaine, realising that he would escape, clung on to his belt.

"Let go of me, you stupid bitch," he shouted frantically. Ghislaine tried to protect herself from his kicks and blows as best she could, pain dulling her senses. Somehow she hung on until she felt the blade in the back of her shoulder. Amid shouts and the grating sounds of swords clashing, Ghislaine slipped into a world of pain and darkness.

Chapter Seventeen

Each time the bells rang her head threatened to explode. When the deep thudding did not abate, Ghislaine attempted to open her eyes. Bright, piercing light flooded her vision, and she blinked hard, raising her hand to allow herself some small respite.

"Ghislaine? Can you hear me?" A low, melodious voice spoke softly near her ear, and she felt a cool, gentle hand on her brow.

"I don't want to hear anything," she croaked crossly. "I want to go to sleep but the bells and my head refuse to allow it."

"Well, I for one am pleased to hear it." The voice sounded amused and Ghislaine forced herself to sit up to try to see more easily. It was, however, a big mistake.

"Am I dead?" she groaned. "I feel as if I am." She was apparently lying in a bed.

"Very nearly," came the more serious reply. "We did not think you would survive at all."

"Survive?" Ghislaine forced her eyes open, but be-

yond the blinding light there were only shadows.
"Where am I?"

"At the abbey."

A cup of cold water was placed at her lips and Ghislaine sipped it warily. It tasted sweet and refreshing.
Moving her hand from her eyes, Ghislaine gingerly
peered at her companion. Gradually, as her eyes ad-
justed to the light, she was able to make out the shape
of a grey-haired woman.

"Helene? I... What are you doing here?" Ghislaine
pushed herself further up the pallet.

"Looking after you," came the reply. "With the
help of Effie and Hulda."

Ghislaine shook her head slightly in confusion. Why
on earth was she lying in a bed in the abbey with Effie,
Hulda and Helene du Beauregard to care for her? None
of this made any sense at all. All she knew was that
her head was throbbing and her body almost unable
to move with exhaustion.

"What did I survive?" She could see the look of
tired concern etched clearly on Helene's beautiful face
as she pulled the sheets into some sort of order.

"Do you remember anything?" Helene reached
over and put her hand on Ghislaine's forehead.

The blank look on Ghislaine's face was answer
enough.

"You were wounded in the shoulder with a knife.
Unfortunately fever set in, and we had a battle to bring
you back. Hulda has created every concoction known
to man. And a few more that aren't," she added in a
wry tone. Helene's deliberately light-hearted chattering slowed into silence as Ghislaine swayed. "I think

it would be best if you tried to sleep a little more. Drink some of this. It will help.''

Ghislaine wanted to refuse it, whatever it was, but the pain and tiredness suddenly overwhelmed her again and it was all she could do to lay her head back on the bolster and drift into oblivion for a while. Strange, half-remembered scenes of forests, knives and tortured screams invaded her memory until a blissful peace slowly billowed through her.

It was the smell of the pottage that woke her. Strong and spicy, the aroma wafted gently in to her room and lingered close to her nose. Unable to resist, Ghislaine forced her eyes to open. Relieved that her sight seemed to have returned without ill effect, Ghislaine hauled herself up a little. The effort caused her to slump back against the wall in exhaustion. Every bone in her body ached and her flesh was bruised and tender.

The room was spotlessly clean and gleamed white from the rays of the midday sun. Her eyes rested on the small window opposite in the bare white-washed wall. The wonderful smell must have come from there.

Casting her eyes about the rest of the room, Ghislaine noticed how oddly comfortable it was. A good fire crackled in the grate on the far side with a small stock of chopped logs piled to the left. Before it stood a comfortable chair covered in a gaily coloured blanket and several plump cushions. Open-mouthed, Ghislaine stared at the tapestry covering the cold floor stones. It hardly resembled the spartan rooms at any abbey she had known.

Running her fingers over the exotic red and gold covering on the bed, Ghislaine wondered why, amid all this finery, she felt so heartsore. Despite the warmth and the colour in the room a bleak sadness drifted around her that seemed inescapable.

The sound of quick footsteps outside her door caused her to look up expectantly.

"My lady!" exclaimed Effie loudly as she hurried to the bed. Her plump face was wreathed in smiles as she felt Ghislaine's forehead. "The fever seems to have gone right enough. I'll go fetch Lady Helene." With a quick reassuring smile back at her charge, Effie bustled out again, leaving Ghislaine bemused.

A few moments later, Helene appeared with a large bowl of steaming pottage in her hands.

"You probably won't feel like eating much," she announced as she sat down on the pallet, "but you need to build up some of your strength."

The smell was even better than she had imagined and Ghislaine's mouth watered. "Is there only one bowl?" she asked as Helene held out a spoonful to her lips.

"My son told me about your love of food," the older woman replied dryly.

"Your son?" questioned Ghislaine as she savoured the wonderful flavour of the pottage.

"Guy," came the reply.

Ghislaine stared at her. "Guy de Courcy is your son?" As Helene merely nodded and held out another spoonful, Ghislaine's mind cranked slowly into thought. "Does he know?"

Helene retracted the uneaten spoonful and looked back at Ghislaine. "He has always known but understandably refuses to admit it," she said simply, and offered the food again.

Ghislaine gulped it down, remembering Sir Arnaud's tale of Guy's parents. "Why did you leave your husband?" she asked, wondering why anyone would leave four sons and a home for a life of exclusion and scorn.

Helene continued to feed pottage to Ghislaine slowly, her mind reliving the scenes and the thoughts that had propelled her into closing the door on her old life. "I was a foolish, young girl who yearned to be loved and needed by a cold, harsh man. My husband viewed me solely as a vessel for more heirs as well as a source of income," she said bitterly. "I was offered the chance of a different life by someone who showed me a world of love and need."

"Was it worth it?" Ghislaine demanded, feeling anger on Guy's behalf. And yet lurking behind the anger, Ghislaine knew that those were the very reasons she had not wanted to stay with Guy.

"I have many regrets of course," she paused. "My lover died and I was forced to survive as best I could. I found protection with a succession of knights, some worse than others. My sons would have suffered far more than I did, had I taken them," she said finally. For a brief moment, Helene's face reflected the pain and the torment she had endured, and then the expression vanished, replaced by the familiar concern she had shown to Ghislaine.

"But God has seen fit to punish me in his own way. There were no more children and I pined for those I had left. Especially Guy." Her fingers traced the intricate pattern on the bedcover. "I have not much time left on this earth and I choose to be near him now. Watching over your manor was but a small thing."

Glancing up at Ghislaine, Helene squeezed her hand gently. "The fact that he came himself to ask me to tend you has given me much joy."

"He did?" Ghislaine was suddenly struck by the importance of those words. "He is alive?"

Helene offered her more pottage. "He brought you here himself."

Despite the warmth of the room, a sudden chill descended on Ghislaine's leaping heart. He had survived the ambush after all, but her gladness was tempered by the fact that the first thing he had done was bring her to the abbey. As he said he always would.

"He was not injured?" she asked, wondering what had happened.

Helene shook her head and pushed the spoon closer to Ghislaine's mouth. "Not physically," she replied absently. "But in the last two weeks, his spirits have been very low. He blames himself for your injuries."

Ghislaine frowned. "I...I don't understand," she began. "How is he responsible? It was Walter..."

Helene eyed her patient with concern. Placing the unwanted pottage on the floor, she turned back to plump up the bolster and make her more comfortable.

"If I have the story right, it would seem that when he received the command from the Earl, Guy suspected that it was a trick. He made a show of leaving in force, but sent your Edwin with some men to hide along the track and return to your manor later. When Walter appeared, demanding the outlaws, Arnaud sent word to Edwin. He trailed Walter and then attacked when he heard screaming. Guy managed to outwit Dettingham and followed Edwin. Unfortunately, they arrived too late to save you from injury."

"I heard the horses coming," Ghislaine remembered.

"Guy blames himself for allowing you to be caught up in the attack. Apparently he did not believe you would go with Walter." Helene watched Ghislaine's stricken expression.

"I wanted to find out what he planned to do with Guy," she whispered. "There was nothing else I could do."

"It would seem that Guy greatly underestimated your courage." Helene smiled at her warmly and squeezed her hand. "If it is any small comfort, he has been greatly distressed by your illness. In fact, when there seemed little hope, I actually saw him pray in the chapel."

Ghislaine stilled at those words, remembering something else. "Father John! He can prove Guy's innocence." She grabbed Helene's sleeve. "You must find Father John."

"Ah, yes. It was Father John who was able to tell Arnaud where Walter was taking you. Fortunately the men I had sent to watch your manor reported the activity and I despatched some soldiers to help. When Dettingham finally realised he had been duped, he came back to the manor in search of Guy. My men persuaded him to wait patiently. Guy's name has been cleared of guilt these past two weeks. Dettingham was allowed his revenge on de Belleme."

Helene's soothing words were intended to calm Ghislaine but they heralded the end of Guy's need of her. He had placed her in the abbey because that was where he wanted her.

"Two weeks?"

"Aye," replied Helene. "You have been very ill and much has happened."

"Has...has my husband been to see me?" she asked wretchedly, knowing the reply, but wanting to hear the words. It would make it easier.

"Every day. I was much struck with the change in him," she added, watching Ghislaine's pale face speculatively.

"Change?" murmured Ghislaine. "What change?"

"He smelled so nice," Helene announced rather proudly. "He was also clean, well fed and handsome."

Ghislaine smiled shakily at that, but, to her horror, tears suddenly began to pour down her cheeks.

"Ghislaine, my dear! Whatever have I said?"

"Nothing. I'm being stupid," she replied tearfully, attempting to wipe them away with the back of her hand.

"Not as stupid as my son, I think," said Helene, handing her a rag.

"What do you mean?" Ghislaine dabbed at the tears.

"I have no idea why you are here and not at home in your own bed. His wits were clearly lacking for he said something about you preferring to be here."

That brought a fresh wave of tears to her eyes and it was several moments before Ghislaine was able to talk again.

"I did say that," she mumbled in between sniffs.

Helene stared at her in astonishment.

"But I didn't really mean it," Ghislaine continued miserably. "I thought it would make him happier."

Understanding suddenly dawned on Helene. "I

think you had better explain," she said kindly. "You may be in need of further maternal advice."

Ghislaine eyed her somewhat warily, but in truth she had sore need of telling someone how miserable she felt. After much prompting, she told Helene as much of the story as she could.

"Well. It seems that the pair of you have been a little foolish, but I am well aware how cold my son can be."

Ghislaine's questioning look prompted Helene to sigh. "He has much of his father in him."

"That is so reassuring," came the muffled reply.

"The difference lies in the way he looks at you," Helene continued. "If my husband had looked at me in the same way, I would not have left."

"What way?" This made no sense.

Helene just laughed. "Rest now, Ghislaine. You are still very weak. Effie will stay with you since I have to leave for a little while." She gave her a reassuring smile. "I want you looking your best for tomorrow, Ghislaine. Promise me?"

Ghislaine nodded wordlessly. She did feel better for talking, but it had not made the problem go away. Helene's suggestion of sleep suddenly seemed very attractive. "I promise," she muttered, closing her eyes, but wondering what was so special about tomorrow.

The next morning, Ghislaine was badgered into breaking her fast with fresh bread and honey by a tyrannical Effie. When she had at last eaten to Effie's satisfaction, she was ordered into a tub of steaming water. Her body was scrubbed clean and her hair washed until Ghislaine wondered if there would be any left.

Sweet-smelling oil was rubbed into her tired and aching limbs and Ghislaine felt a sense of languorous well-being creep through her body. As she sat resting before the fire drying her hair, Effie cleaned and dressed the wound in her shoulder. To complete the transformation, she handed Ghislaine a new night-rail.

Ghislaine stared at the garment in wonder. The linen was the softest she had ever felt, and the sleeves and collar were trimmed with pretty lace and ribbon.

"It's lovely," she breathed, holding it to her. "And it fits!"

"Of course it fits," scoffed Effie. "Your husband had it made for you."

Ghislaine stilled. "He had it made for me," she repeated disbelievingly. "When?"

"Whilst you were ill." Effie smiled. "He was that concerned that you should have lots of gowns and pretty things," she confided. "He had five seam-stresses come from Chester to make up all that cloth Kalim brought. He asked Lady Helene's advice."

Effie crossed the room to the chest at the side of the bed. "Look, my lady. He sent them as soon as they were ready."

Effie was right, realised a dumbfounded Ghislaine. One by one she took out the beautiful gowns, petti-coats, surcoats, cloaks and underwear, taking care to spread them on the bed. The array was breathtaking, it was all so fine. The materials were gorgeous: em-broidered silks, brocaded velvets, finest wools, and some she really had no idea about at all. The instant she saw them, she knew they would suit her colouring:

golds, emerald-greens, peacock-blues, pewter-grey. Ghislaine closed her eyes. He was making it very difficult for her.

"None of this is suitable for the abbey," she said as calmly as she could.

"I don't think so either," replied Effie doubtfully. "But then he was that upset, he wasn't thinking straight," she added quietly.

Ghislaine stared longingly at the gowns. They were beautiful, truly beautiful, and no one had ever given her anything so lovely. But she had no right to any of it.

She sighed heavily and then looked up at Effie who tried hard to quickly mask a very miserable expression. "You never know, Effie. With me in the abbey, you might have more time to persuade Edwin to take pity on you?"

Effie's eyes welled up. "He's gone. Sir Guy asked him what he wanted as a reward for saving you and he took his freedom. Said you didn't need him here any more."

Ghislaine felt numb. Edwin had always been there. "Where has he gone?" Her face was as stricken as Effie's.

"He went in search of his family's killers, he said." Effie subsided into muffled sobbing.

Memories of another lifetime flooded Ghislaine's mind. When they were young, he had always vowed he would search for them and take his revenge. Now Guy had given him that chance.

"He'll be back, Effie," she said quietly. All she could think of was that even Edwin had deserted her.

A knock at the door sent her quickly to her bed whilst Effie went to see who it was.

"Father John!" Ghislaine exclaimed, pleased to see him.

Effie bobbed a curtsey and took the opportunity to escape and find a quiet corner to nurse her sorrows in.

"I hear the fever has passed, Lady Ghislaine," he smiled, sitting at the end of the pallet.

Ghislaine returned his smile. "I believe I have you to thank for the fact that my injuries were as slight as they were."

"You are too kind," he stammered, blushing with pleasure. "I did what I thought was best."

"Aye, you did." Ghislaine's smile faded. "And is your soul at peace now?"

The briefest of smiles touched the friar's lips. "In a way." He lifted his hands in a despairing gesture that she understood. "I think it will take time for me to forgive myself."

"We are often our own harshest critics, Father, but I am most grateful for your intervention." Ghislaine reached out to touch his arm.

The priest placed his long, knotted fingers over hers in an act of friendship. "I am pleased to tell you that your husband has also shown the extent of his generosity."

When Ghislaine raised her eyebrows in enquiry, the friar's face fell. "I hope I have not betrayed a confidence," he frowned.

"Generous?" Ghislaine inclined her head in confusion. "Just how generous has he been?"

"He has donated enough to rebuild the kitchens. It is his belief, apparently, that those spending their lives following the path of goodness deserve a good meal at the end of the day. It was an odd thing to bestow, but we are grateful, of course.''

Ghislaine stared at him wildly for a moment before the amusement bubbled to the surface. ''My husband has a sense of humour, too,'' she laughed.

''Your husband is essentially a good man, Lady Ghislaine. He has, however, found your illness a sore trial, and, I believe, that there will be many at Chapmonswiche who will be singularly grateful for your early return.''

''I... That is, I am sure that my husband expects me to stay at the abbey, Father John.'' Her expression spoke volumes despite her attempted cheerfulness.

''If it helps,'' he began kindly, ''your husband was almost beside himself when he found out you were so badly injured. He insisted on carrying you himself and he spent the first two days here with you. He did not leave your side.''

Father John looked across at her tight-lipped expression speculatively. ''There is something else that I should not in my capacity as a priest divulge. But I am sure that God would perhaps understand. We spoke at length about your desire to go to the abbey. Your husband was under the impression that you wished to go there to escape him and several times stated—most convincingly—that you had no true vocation. He also showed a great interest in when exactly I told you he was not the man who murdered Margaret.''

Ghislaine must have looked perplexed, so he hastened to enlighten her. ''It was not until after...Kalim had left.''

Understanding dawned and Ghislaine blushed.

Whatever she was about to say was interrupted by the arrival of a very flustered Effie.

"It's him!" she shrieked. "He's come for you. The abbey is surrounded."

Closing her eyes, Ghislaine tried to blot out the lurching of her heart and the sudden excitement that was welling within her. She tried to tell herself to be calm, that he was just here to complete their "unfinished business' as he called it. When her eyes opened again, Effie was staring wildly at her, wringing her hands. Father John had rushed to the window and stood on a stool as he looked out.

"It's true," he confirmed quietly. Turning back to look at Ghislaine, he added, "And I think he's come to do more than talk to you."

Despite her outwardly calm appearance, Ghislaine's mind was frantically thinking of what she would say to him if she did see him. She loved him, but she could not stay with him if he did not want her. It would be far better to stay now. Far, far better.

The sound of heavy footsteps thudding along the corridor reminded Ghislaine of a similar occasion, just six weeks earlier. Only this time, she felt very different. Then she had been scared of a monster she did not know, who had been accused of murdering her friend, who had kidnapped her for his own ends and who scowled at the world. This time, she wanted to go with him.

As the wooden door banged open, Guy stormed in, filling the room with his presence.

"Out," he growled. Effie and Father John looked

towards Ghislaine in pity before scuttling from the tiny room.

"Helene du Beauregard said you wished to talk to me." His voice was almost a growl.

Cold blue eyes raked her with deliberate slowness as Ghislaine pulled the sheets closer to her chin. Determined not to show any sign of weakness, she lifted her head in defiance, tossing her hair back over her shoulder. The movement seemed to mesmerise him for a moment.

"Did she?" Ghislaine's voice was almost a whisper. What had the woman done?

"I am pleased to see that you are recovering," he said eventually.

It was hard to tear her eyes from him for he was looking so fine. The unruly, dark hair had been trimmed into order and the dark stubble normally thick on his chin had been barbered very carefully away. Somehow, he did not seem so very threatening.

"No small thanks to you, I believe." She was relieved to hear her voice sound almost cheerful.

Somewhat wrongfooted by the pleasant tone of voice he noted, Guy took a few steps forward. Casting his eyes about the room, his fingers flicked the cushions on the chair. "Have you been comfortable?"

Ghislaine smiled back a little self-consciously. "To be honest I have not really had much time to appreciate it. But I'm sure I will," she added quietly.

At those words, Guy immediately stiffened. "Not as much as you would wish, lady. You return with me this day or I will burn down the abbey."

All her good intentions dissipated at that threat. "You forgot to add that you'll have my people exiled," she railed, the sheet slipping in her anger. "Presumably you've had little opportunity for practising your threats since I've been ill."

His lips tightened to an angry line and his hand raked through his dark hair. "Your stay here has done little to improve your temper," he bit out between his teeth.

"I," she announced with icy superiority, "have been ill. What is your excuse?"

Guy glared at her with narrowed eyes before turning suddenly to stand before the fire. Ghislaine was left to stare at his back. "You betrayed my trust by leaving with Belleme."

"But I did not want to escape with him," she whispered. "He forced me to go and I demanded he take me to the abbey in the hope of finding out what he planned to do with you."

Guy stared at her, a look of disbelief on his face. "Will you return with me of your own free will, then," he asked suspiciously, "or do I drag you back?"

"Why?" she asked quietly. "Why do you want me back? I am pleased to hear that you are now a free man and can return to your old manor. What need have you of me?"

"I have no idea," he said crossly, turning to face her once more. "You eat huge amounts, you drink the cellars dry, you career across the county shooting the Earl's game and you have an abominable temper." He frowned darkly as Ghislaine stared at him, her mouth agape.

"Well, it seems to me that my particular accomplishments do not hold much appeal for you. I see little point in dragging me back for further abuse,'' she snapped.

She sounded so aggrieved by his description of her that Guy could not prevent a smile tugging at the corner of his lips. Walking over towards her, he sat down at her side. The harsh gaze was replaced by a softer, much warmer appraisal.

"Ghislaine, I have no desire to find another wife, I do assure you. My mother has been keen to extol your virtues to me, and in truth her arguments are sound. Nor," he added as an afterthought, "do I think I can persuade Joachim to leave with me. He is under the impression that he is the only one who can control Elfrieda's temper and she is adamant that her place is at Chapmonswiche. They have asked for permission to marry." He shook his head. "I think that finding another wife would be most troublesome to me."

"I thought you did not want a wife at all," she accused. The man was most vexing. "Your old way of life with Arnaud held more attraction. Now that your name is cleared, you are free to return to your old manor."

Guy's head lowered and he rubbed the back of his neck to ease the tension there. "Aye, well, I've become accustomed to you over the weeks," he allowed. He looked up at her. "Besides, my old manor no longer suits my purposes so well."

"It does not?" Ghislaine queried Her husband was a very changeable man.

Guy shook his head. "Dettingham petitioned the King so often that William was forced to make enquiries. Earl Hugh has suddenly shown himself right keen to reduce the number of outlaws in the area and felt I might be of help.'' He smiled briefly at his wife's perplexed expression. ''This will come as a shock to you, but your disreputable husband is now a very respectable shire reeve.''

He reached out and closed her mouth gently. ''Arnaud has gone to take charge of the other manor, and Sir Brian and I have come to a satisfactory working arrangement, but neither of us has proved up to managing the women very well. So you see, I have grave need of a wife.'' Pausing to take her hand, he added softly, ''There are other reasons, of course.''

He was sitting uncomfortably close, and Ghislaine was finding it increasingly difficult to remain calm with her hand in his.

''I know,'' she replied, desperately thinking of these other good reasons. ''You've had all those gowns made up at considerable expense and they are unlikely to suit anyone else.'' Ghislaine found it hard to look into those searching blue eyes.

''No. That's not the reason. Although,'' he added thoughtfully, ''I had not thought of that.''

Ghislaine noticed that his eyes kept straying to the top of her night gown. The sheet had slipped and she had forgotten how transparent her gown was. Glaring at him, she pulled the sheet back up. ''Lust will fade quickly,'' she replied confidently. ''And then you'll be left with a wife you no longer want.''

Guy was speechless for a moment. ''Is that what all this is about?'' he demanded, enlightenment spreading over his face.

Her chest heaving with indignation, Ghislaine turned on him. ''That may be all to you, Guy de

Courcy,'' she fired at him, "but I can assure you it is no small matter to me.''

It took a minute for him to digest that information. "So," he said slowly, "you are confident that your own lust will not fade so quickly?" He raised an eyebrow in question.

Ghislaine blushed furiously at his words. "Nay," she said hoarsely. "I mean…yes… I…''

A finger gently lifted her chin and Ghislaine found herself looking into smiling blue eyes. "Perhaps you would care to tell me how long you think it might last." He was teasing her and she found his humour misplaced.

"I doubt, my lord, that it will last that long," she replied airily. "My duties at Chapmonswiche are so arduous now, with all those oafish men of yours forever creating work, that I am likely to drop dead within the year.''

"Ah! But you are confident your desire will last a lifetime then?''

"Yes!" she snapped back, angry that he had forced such an admission from her. "But I fail…?''

Her words were stopped by Guy pulling her into his arms and kissing her with an intensity that fired her blood. Tearing his lips away, Guy placed his forehead on hers. "I swear to God, Ghislaine, that I never realised how much I loved you until I thought you would die. Marry me.''

Ghislaine disentangled herself from his arms to face him. "You love me?" she whispered in disbelief. "Truly?''

"Aye. But don't ask me why, for it defeats me,''

he said curtly. He looked so disgruntled that she could not repress a chuckle.

"Well?" he prompted. "Will you marry me?"

"We're married already," she said, staring at him in confusion.

"I believe that I was somewhat despotic during the ceremony, and I have to admit thinking that you weren't putting your heart into your vows." The smile he gave her was almost boyish, and very convincing.

"I cannot fault your logic, Sir Guy," she said joyfully, not quite able to believe that this was true. "But I think I will accept your kind offer."

"Think? Perhaps you need some persuasion?" he offered, gathering her into his arms for another heart-warming kiss.

"And the terms of the marriage contract? Are they the usual ones?" Ghislaine turned dark, questioning eyes on him, whilst tracing the outline of his mouth with her fingers.

Guy merely nodded his head, distracted by her finger.

"Then I have an additional stipulation," she announced.

Guy stiffened slightly in her arms. "And what might that be?"

"That you practise your husbandly duties with greater frequency than you did during our last marriage."

Guy's smile was devastating. "You are naught but a saucy wanton sent to try my patience greatly, wench. And if I do not comply?"

"Then I shall have no choice but to send you to the

priory and search for a husband who possesses more natural charm.''

Guy laughed and pulled her back to him, proceeding to demonstrate thoroughly that he was keen to adhere to her demands.

* * * * *

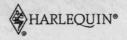

Not The Same Old Story!

 Exciting, glamorous romance stories that take readers around the world.

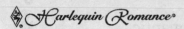 Sparkling, fresh and tender love stories that bring you pure romance.

 Bold and adventurous— Temptation is strong women, bad boys, great sex!

 Provocative and realistic stories that celebrate life and love.

 Contemporary fairy tales—where anything is possible and where dreams come true.

 Heart-stopping, suspenseful adventures that combine the best of romance and mystery.

 Humorous and romantic stories that capture the lighter side of love.

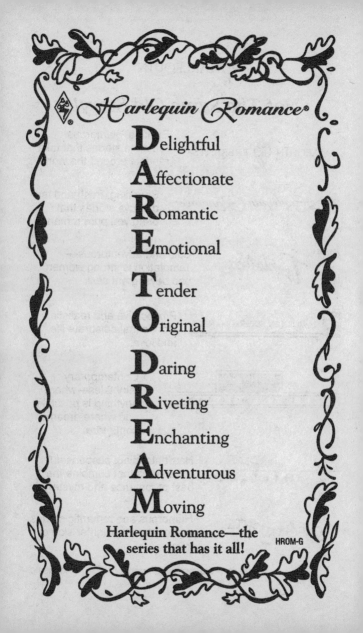

Harlequin Romance®

Delightful

Affectionate

Romantic

Emotional

Tender

Original

Daring

Riveting

Enchanting

Adventurous

Moving

Harlequin Romance—the
series that has it all!

HROM-G

HARLEQUIN PRESENTS®

HARLEQUIN PRESENTS
men you won't be able to resist
falling in love with...

HARLEQUIN PRESENTS
women who have feelings
just like your own...

HARLEQUIN PRESENTS
powerful passion in
exotic international settings...

HARLEQUIN PRESENTS
intense, dramatic stories that will keep you
turning to the very last page...

HARLEQUIN PRESENTS
The world's bestselling romance series!

Harlequin® Historical

From rugged lawmen and
valiant knights to defiant heiresses
and spirited frontierswomen,
Harlequin Historicals will
capture your imagination with
their dramatic scope, passion
and adventure.

Harlequin Historicals...
they're too good to miss!

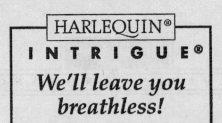

HARLEQUIN®
A M E R I C A N ◆ R O M A N C E®

LOOK FOR OUR FOUR FABULOUS MEN!

Each month some of today's bestselling authors bring
four new fabulous men to Harlequin American Romance.
Whether they're rebel ranchers, millionaire power brokers
or sexy single dads, they're all gallant princes—and
they're all ready to sweep you into lighthearted fantasies
and contemporary fairy tales where anything is possible
and where all your dreams come true!

You don't even have to make a wish…
Harlequin American Romance will grant your every desire!

Look for Harlequin American Romance
wherever Harlequin books are sold!